All he

Paul Bouvet had discovered on his first trip to Rossiter that the café next door to the Delaney mansion functioned as a sort of town club. He'd have to find some way to be—if not accepted—at least tolerated by the locals who ate there regularly. If his mother had come as far as Rossiter before she disappeared, someone might remember seeing her. After all, thirty years ago there couldn't have been too many strangers showing up in Rossiter.

He didn't have a clue how to find out. He didn't dare come straight out and ask. Nobody could know who he was or why he was there. The P.I. his uncle had hired had never been able to trace Michelle Bouvet's movements beyond the bus station in downtown Memphis. The trail had gone cold at that point and had stayed cold until six months ago.

Now—all these years later—Paul finally believed he knew what had happened to his mother. He just had to find the proof.

Dear Reader,

What kind of man abandons his young wife, then kills her when she finds him six years later? What kind of son would that man father?

Those questions have tortured Paul Bouvet his entire life. Now at last he has the means to answer them.

Paul buys the derelict Delaney mansion in the tiny town of Rossiter, Tennessee, and begins to restore it purely to give himself a cover. He wants revenge against his father's family, the wealthy, arrogant Delaney clan.

But he begins to lose his taste for revenge after he meets Ann Corrigan, the art restorer who's bringing his mansion back to life. And teaching Paul what it's like to have love in his life.

But can he abandon the vow he made to his late mother's family? If not, can he endure losing Ann?

To find the answers to these questions, read on. I hope you enjoy the journey.

Carolyn McSparren

Books by Carolyn McSparren

HARLEQUIN SUPERROMANCE

Don't miss any of our special offers. Write to us at the following address for information on our newest releases.

Harlequin Reader Service
U.S.: 3010 Walden Ave., P.O. Box 1325, Buffalo, NY 14269
Canadian: P.O. Box 609, Fort Erie, Ont. L2A 5X3

House of Strangers
Carolyn McSparren

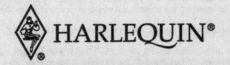

HARLEQUIN®

TORONTO • NEW YORK • LONDON
AMSTERDAM • PARIS • SYDNEY • HAMBURG
STOCKHOLM • ATHENS • TOKYO • MILAN • MADRID
PRAGUE • WARSAW • BUDAPEST • AUCKLAND

ISBN 0-373-71143-3

HOUSE OF STRANGERS

Copyright © 2003 by Carolyn McSparren.

This edition published by arrangement with Harlequin Books S.A.

Visit us at www.eHarlequin.com

Printed in U.S.A.

To Betty Salmon, who gave me permission
to use the name of the Wolf River Café—
it really exists, although the people came out of my head.

To Eve Gaddy, a wonderful writer,
who suggested the idea and graciously let me use it.

DELANEY FAMILY TREE

Delaney house built in 1890

Paul Ezekiel Delaney
b. 1849; d. 1900

m. 1881

Lorece Hutchins
b. 1853; d. 1912

Paul Adam Delaney
b. 1879; d. 1934

m. 1908

Victoria Adams
b. 1878; d. 1930

Paul Barrett Delaney
b. 1897; d. 1948

m. 1917

Patricia Harcourt
b. 1899; d. 1951

Paul Conrad Delaney
b. 1918; d. 1970

m. 1940

Maribelle Norwood
b. 1920; d. 1982

Michelle Bouvet
b. 1949

m. 1967

Paul David Delaney
b. 1941; d. 1977

m. 1968

Karen Bingham
b. 1944

Paul Antoine Bouvet
b. 1968

Paul Edward Delaney
b. 1969

m. 1994

Susan Marshall
b. 1971

Paul Frederick Delaney
b. 1996

Maribelle Delaney
b. 1997

KEY:
b. born
d. died
m. married

CHAPTER ONE

Early March

"I'M SORRY TREY sold the house to a stranger," Ann Corrigan said as she hooked her foot under a rung of her bar stool at the counter of the Wolf River Café. "Not that I really blame him. What else could he do?"

"Two years on the market without a nibble. I guess he could have burned it down and collected the insurance," Bernice Jones answered. She ran a clean rag over the counter. "You want breakfast?"

"Just some iced tea, please. I would have bought the place myself if I had the money and could afford to fix it up."

"What would you do with a big place like that?" Bernice shook her head, picked up a mason jar, filled it with ice and tea, then set it down in front of Ann. "It's about ready to fall down. Trey jumped at that fool's offer, don't you think he didn't."

Ann peered across the counter. "Bernice, don't you have any lemon?"

"If you'll hold your horses, I'll cut you some. The tea's barely had time to steep." Bernice reached for a wicked-looking paring knife, picked up a lemon and began slicing it with speed and accuracy. "Bet you couldn't get iced tea this time of the morning up in Buffalo, could you?"

"Half the time I couldn't get iced tea in the middle of the *day* up there. They have this weird idea that iced tea is for hot weather and never for breakfast. And they never even heard of sweet tea."

"Ought to be glad you finished that job and got yourself back down south. You must be sick of blizzards."

"I spent so much time restoring the proscenium arch in that old theater I didn't much care about the weather outside. I do not want to *see* any more gold leaf for a while."

"Not much of that next door at the old Delaney house." Bernice set a dish of sliced lemons on the counter. "Be better if it collapsed on its own, except it would probably fall on the café and kill us all."

Ann speared two pieces of lemon, squeezed them into her tea, then added a couple of packets of artificial sweetener. "Why are you so down on the place?"

"Everybody who ever lived in that mansion was miserable. Some houses are just unhappy from the get-go. You mark my words. That Frenchman has bought himself a heap of trouble." Bernice looked past Ann's shoulder. "Hold your horses, boys. I'll be there with the coffee in a second." She picked up the big pot and wended her way through the tables occupied nearly every morning by the same group of local farmers indulging in a second breakfast.

When Bernice set the coffeepot back on the warmer, Ann said, "I was happy there. Sometimes after my piano lesson Aunt Addy and I would have lemonade and homemade macaroons in the conservatory. That house is probably the reason I got into the restoration business. Every time I see an old building fallen on hard times, I just ache to make it glow again."

"Huh. That house hasn't done much glowing in my lifetime."

"I hoped if it stayed on the market long enough, maybe Trey would donate it to the town for a museum. Endow it, restore it—something."

"What does an itty-bitty town like Rossiter, Tennessee, need with a museum?" Bernice waved a hand at the walls of the café, which were hung with yellowed newspaper clippings going back nearly a hundred years. "This is as close as Rossiter gets to a museum. It's not like that old house was built before the war."

Ann knew the war in question was the Late Unpleasantness between North and South. Other wars were spoken of as World or Korean or Desert Storm. "I hate to admit this, but I used to swan down that staircase and pretend I was Cinderella. I dreamed about the way it must have looked all lit up for the cotillions and parties."

"At least Trey sold the house to somebody who's got the money to fix it up. And you got you a job close to home into the bargain. You met the new owner yet? That Frenchman?"

"Nope. Daddy's supposed to be meeting him this morning to set up the schedule for the renovations. I might not see him for weeks if he commutes from New Jersey. And Daddy says he's not French."

Bernice leaned her elbow on the counter and rested her cheek on her hand. "What I want to know," she whispered, "is why some bachelor would buy that old house in a little town like this and spend a bunch of money on it."

Ann shrugged. "Daddy says he used to be an airline pilot. He got hurt and can't fly big planes any longer. Maybe he's buddies with some of the pilots who've redone the antebellum houses in LaGrange. He could have heard about the house from them.''

"Those pilots fly out of Memphis, so they have to live close by, and they've got families and more money than sense. He's just some guy who showed up out of the blue, bought the place in five minutes and hired your daddy to fix it." She shook her head. "I'm surprised he didn't try to turn it into apartments or maybe tear it down and build something else—not that the town would let anybody do that to a historic property." She nodded her head sagely. "They say he's *retired*." It sounded like an accusation.

"So?" Ann asked. "Lots of men retire early."

"Not that early. According to Lorene Hoddle, he's no more than thirty-five or -six. I tell you, Ann, there's something strange about it."

"Oh, come on, Bernice. You think he's going to set up a crack house or a high-class bordello?"

"Hush. Anyway, Miss Ann, you and your daddy take care not to do all that work and let him skedaddle without paying you."

"Daddy's checked out his credit references. He's got the money to pay us, and most people don't run out owing the chief of police money." She considered. "Gangsters wouldn't set up drug operations or prostitution in a town of 350 souls, most of whom are kin and all of whom know one another's business. Why drive way out here from Memphis to sin? And with legal gambling just south of the border in Mississippi, he'd hardly be likely to open an illegal casino in west Tennessee."

"Well, just you wait. There's something not right about it." Bernice refilled Ann's glass. "I thought he might be one of those professional decorators—you know, like Patsy's boy Calvin that went away to New Orleans—him not being married and all, but Lorene says he seems real macho. And real handsome. Now, Ann, if you play your cards right..."

Ann laughed into her tea so hard she sputtered. "Bernice, one minute you're convinced he's a drug dealer, the next you're telling me to go after the poor man. No, no and no."

"Why not? You been divorced almost two years. You're too young not to get married again, have some babies."

"Bernice, I love you, but I'm not looking for another handsome man—certainly not one who's retired, as you say, at thirty-five, and definitely not one who bought my family's old homeplace. He'll be my client for as long as it takes to finish the Delaney mansion, then I'm off to restore something else. I've got good reason to know that good-looking men tend to think the rules don't apply to them."

"Then find a man who looks like a boot. But find *somebody* before you get too old for the market. So far you've turned down every man who's even asked you out since you came home."

"I'm not in town often enough these days to date anybody. How can I have a decent relationship when I'm off on a job in Buffalo for three months, and then maybe it'll be Chicago or some railroad town in Iowa that's got an old movie theater they want to restore to its former glory?"

"You're home now."

"This will be the first time I've done a restoration job in Rossiter since I came back with my tail between my legs and started working for Daddy. There aren't that many people around who can afford me or who live in houses old enough to need restoration."

"Well, that one is going to take some time." Bernice

hooked a thumb over her shoulder toward the Delaney house. "Miss Addy didn't do a lick of upkeep on the place in the twenty years she lived there after Miss Maribelle died and left it to her." She leaned closer and whispered, "I swear every field mouse in Rossiter had been living over there, and once Miss Addy died, they all came over here. I had to fumigate twice to get rid of them."

"Not all of them moved. Daddy said they had to have the fumigators twice in January."

From outside the front door came a long, low moan. It grew in intensity and pitch until it sounded as though the town had cranked up its tornado siren.

A grizzled farmer sitting with half-a-dozen friends over the dregs of his coffee sighed and peered over half glasses at Ann. "Fix that. A man's got a right to a quiet breakfast."

"Yes, sir." Ann tossed two one-dollar bills onto the counter and started out.

A second low moan began to escalate. Behind her, Ann heard the assembled farmers snicker. "It's okay, Dante," she called to the giant mournful-looking black hound tied to a rail in front of the café. He shook the heavy folds of skin that hung from his cheeks, but he stopped howling. "Okay, boy, time to go to work."

PAUL BOUVET had discovered on his first visit to Rossiter that the café next door to the Delaney mansion functioned as a sort of town clubhouse. He'd have to find some way to be, if not accepted, at least tolerated by the locals who ate there regularly. If his mother had come as far as Rossiter before she disappeared, someone might remember her. After all, thirty years ago there couldn't have been too many strangers showing up in Rossiter.

He didn't have a clue how to find out. He didn't dare

come out and ask. Nobody could know who he was or why he was here until he'd found out everything he needed to know. The private detective Uncle Charlie had hired never was able to trace his mother's movements beyond the bus station in downtown Memphis. The trail went cold at that point and had stayed cold until six months ago.

All these years later Paul still believed he knew what had happened to her. All he had to do was prove it.

She would have called his father from the bus station. No doubt he jumped at the chance to pick her up there or meet her somewhere he couldn't be identified. Mr. Hotshot Delaney didn't want an inconvenient French peasant girl interfering with his life in Rossiter. She had to disappear.

So he met her, killed her and hid her body so well it had never been found.

What kind of man would do such a thing to a woman who'd loved him so deeply she'd left her own country for him, searched for him for six years and never stopped believing he loved her?

Paul had lived with the specter of his dead mother and her murderer—his father—for most of his life. It wasn't any easier now that the murderer had a name.

The whole sordid story had to come out. His mother's body had to be found and properly buried. Paul wanted the present generation of Delaneys to acknowledge the monstrous thing their father had done.

He wanted them to suffer as he had suffered.

He wanted them to be ashamed.

He slipped into a booth at the café, opened the Memphis newspaper and folded it in fourths as he had learned to do when riding on buses and subways in New York and New Jersey. He was surprised when the owner, a tall, handsome blond woman, set down a steaming mug of coffee in front of him. "Coffee?" she said.

Apparently one didn't ask at this hour of the morning. One simply accepted that coffee was the drink of choice.

"Uh, thank you."

"Cream's on the table. What can I get you?"

"Plain wheat toast and a large orange juice, please."

For a moment she stared down at him. Then she sniffed, went behind the counter at the end of the room and disappeared into the kitchen. He glanced at the group of farmers two tables away.

In a bar in France at this hour of the morning, the farmers would be on their third coffee and brandy. These men, who looked every bit as craggy as French peasants, were mopping up the last bits of egg with their biscuits.

Tante Helaine and Giselle would no doubt have turned up their noses at the food. But after years of grabbing godawful airline meals in flight and even worse in airports, Paul was happy with the menu at the café. These people served actual green vegetables, not simply fried potatoes.

"Wheat toast." His waitress had returned.

"I think we're going to be neighbors," he said.

Instantly her face broke into a smile that lit her hazel eyes. "Wondered if you was him. Hey."

As he was about to get to his feet, she flipped her hand at him. "We don't stand on ceremony. I'm Bernice. Nice to meet you. Thought you was getting together with the chief this morning."

"The chief? Not that I'm aware of."

She laughed. "Buddy Jenkins, chief of police. He's Jenkins Renovation and Restoration."

"Oh, then yes, I am meeting him." He checked his watch. "In about ten minutes."

"You eat up. Buddy's always on time unless there's a law problem he has to handle. We mostly only get speeders out on the highway and drunk drivers." She looked at him hard. "We have some drug problems in the county, but we sure as shootin' don't want any more."

He smiled. "I'm sure you don't. Thank you."

As he bent to read his newspaper, he realized that all conversation had ceased. The farmers at the other table had swiveled in their chairs so that they could watch him. The moment he smiled at them, however, they turned away, hunched over and began to speak softly.

As a stranger moving to a small town, he'd expected to be checked out, but this was ridiculous.

He ate his breakfast, paid his bill, tipped the waitress generously, nodded to the farmers and left.

In Manhattan, piles of dirty snow still lined the streets. Here fifty miles east of the Mississippi River, the March wind was chill, but it smelled of fresh grass and newly turned earth. He'd been warned that west Tennessee summers were brutal, but he was ready to endure almost anything for this gentle early spring. Besides, he planned to install central air-conditioning in his new house.

At some point between the end of the Civil War and prohibition, Rossiter must have been prosperous. The small plaque that leaned against his front steps said that the Delaney house had been built in 1890. A dozen similar mansions along Main Street looked as though they dated from the early 1900s.

The railroad still ran along the far side of the open square that separated the town from the Wolf River bottoms on the north side, but the trains no longer even slowed to acknowledge the existence of the town.

Once there must have been a station. Probably it had stood where the small park with the shiny, ornate Victorian bandstand now perched across the parking lot from the café.

The café stood on one corner of what remained of the town square. About the time the Delaneys decided to build a fine house and move into town from their plantations, the area must have been a crush of mule-drawn wagons piled high with bales of cotton. Probably the café hadn't existed then. He doubted the high-and-mighty Delaneys would have chosen to build their mansion next door to a café.

The pickup trucks and stock trailers parked haphazardly in the area now were not nearly as romantic.

Bank, mom-and-pop grocery, and dingy pool hall sat on the south side across the street from the café. Three handsomely restored row houses formed the west side. The lower floor of the first held his real-estate agent's office and the second a florist shop. On the front porch of the third building, a twelve-foot black wooden grizzly bear advertised something, but Paul couldn't begin to guess what.

Those few small stores constituted the entire business district of Rossiter. The nearest shopping mall was more than twenty miles away, on the road to Memphis.

Paul checked his watch and sauntered along the sidewalk toward his house. *His* house. He still couldn't believe he'd done such an insane thing. He didn't generally operate on impulse.

The sidewalk was dangerously buckled and broken by the roots of several giant oaks and magnolias in his front yard. Didn't the city council, or whatever passed for government in this village, pay attention to things like dangerous walkways? Perhaps nobody in Rossiter actually walked.

When he reached the snaggle-toothed brick path that

led up to his front porch, he simply stood and gloated. His house was younger, smaller and less splendid than Tara, but it must have been imposing in its day.

Unfortunately, at the moment it looked like an aging whore trying to cadge money for her next drink.

"I own your house, Daddy, you bastard," Paul said louder than he'd planned.

Behind him he heard tires squeal. A squad car with the Rossiter seal slid to a stop by the curb. A man climbed out of the driver's seat.

Paul had met Buddy Jenkins only once before, just after his bid to buy the house had been accepted. At the meeting in his real-estate agent's office, Buddy had worn jeans and a University of Tennessee sweatshirt. They'd spoken on the telephone a number of times while Paul was winding up his affairs in New Jersey and storing his few possessions, but Buddy had never mentioned he was the chief of police.

In a town like this, being chief of police probably wasn't a demanding job. No wonder he'd started his renovation company.

At first Paul had been reluctant to give the restoration contract to a local construction firm. How could anybody working out of a town the size of Rossiter be any good?

But when he'd inquired about renovation and restoration experts in the Memphis and west-Tennessee area, Buddy Jenkins's name had come up repeatedly at the top of the list. After Paul checked out the mansions, theaters, government state houses and private homes that Jenkins had restored, he'd decided to hire the man.

"Don't know if you can get him," Mrs. Hoddle, his real-estate agent, had said. "He's usually booked up pretty far in advance. But because the house is in Rossiter, you may be able to convince him to do the job for you."

Buddy's preliminary estimates on doing the job had taken Paul's breath away until he found out what his New York friends were paying to renovate their brownstones.

Paul wanted the job done right. Now that he had committed to this crazy charade, this crazy *crusade*, being able to resell the house for a profit would make his victory even sweeter.

"Hey, Mr. Bouvet," Buddy Jenkins said as he came forward and stuck out his hand. In uniform the man looked even larger. His starched shirt was perfectly pressed and tailored to his barrel chest and broad shoulders. His boots were spit-shined. What little hair he had left was cut in a gray fringe that barely showed against his tanned skin.

Jenkins probably carried 250 pounds or more on his six-three frame. God help the drunk driver who gave this man any lip. At six feet even and 175 pounds, Paul felt almost small by comparison.

"Ready for the bad news?" Jenkins said happily.

"Not really, but there's no sense in putting it off."

"First the good news. In three months or so this old place can look better than it's looked since the day the Delaneys first moved in."

"Three months?"

"Maybe five."

"And the bad news?"

"Come on, I'll walk you through." Buddy reached into his pocket and drew out a key.

"If you don't mind, Buddy, I'd like to use my key."

"Sure." Buddy grinned. "First time you've used it?"

"Since I had the new locks installed." The front door was original, complete with an etched-glass oval in the center. Although the original brass lock remained, the shiny new Yale lock was the one that worked. Paul thought he'd feel a surge of triumph when he stepped into the house again. He felt nothing.

"Let's start in the basement," Buddy said. "We've got a temporary permit for the electricity, so we can see while we replace the wiring."

"All of it?"

"Every whipstitch," Buddy said. "Phone lines, too." The old oak floors echoed their footsteps. "Watch your head."

Over the next hour Paul listened to Buddy's litany of disaster. Maybe the house hadn't been such a bargain, after all.

"Need to jack up at least one corner of the house to replace sills," Buddy said. "Termites."

"The house has stood this long with termite damage. Why disturb it?"

"Because it may decide some night in a storm that it has stood plenty long enough and fall down around your ears. Besides, you won't get any inspector to sign off on the renovations unless we do."

Paul nodded.

"I'll show you when we get to the attic. Needs a new roof and decking, of course."

Another hour of crawling through attics, poking into bathrooms, peering up fireplaces, left Paul even more dispirited.

When at last they moved into the kitchen, Buddy said, "You need new appliances and stuff. I got a kitchen designer working on a plan for a whole new kitchen." Buddy looked at him. "How you holding up?"

"I'll survive. At least I think I will."

"Now we get to the restoration part. Come with me." Buddy shoved the pocket doors aside and ushered Paul into the back parlor. Buddy pointed at the Steinway grand piano in the bay window.

"It's not quite a concert grand," Buddy said, "although Miss Addy used to tell her students it was."

"It's a beauty."

"It's yours."

"I know, but I don't understand why it was built into the house that way."

"The Delaney who built the house in 1890 thought any daughter of his ought to be able to play the piano. He bought this one and literally had the music room—that's what this is officially—built around it."

"But I was under the impression that the man who built this house had only one son." Paul could have bitten off his tongue. At this stage, he wasn't supposed to know anything about the Delaneys except their name.

"Had a daughter died of the yellow fever when she was no more than four or five, so I've heard." Buddy looked at Paul curiously. "How come you know about the son?"

"I, uh…after I bought the house I did a bit of checking with the historical society about it. Just curiosity, you know."

"Uh-huh." The chief seemed satisfied, but Paul knew he'd have to be more careful in the future.

Buddy walked over to the piano and plinked middle C with his index finger. "Needs tuning. Ann thinks she can restore the strings and pads and the ivory on the keys."

"Ann?"

"Ann's the restoration part of Renovation and Restoration. She's the one who's going to strip all that paint off your fireplaces and re-create the old crown molding that's missing. And a bunch of other stuff."

"I see."

"Mostly she redoes the cosmetic stuff. Like that mural in the dining room. It's a fine Chinese rice paper old Mr. Delaney imported. You weren't thinking of stripping it and throwing it away, were you?"

"Not if it can be restored."

"If it's possible, Ann'll do it. It's amazing what she can do. She worked as an art restorer in Washington and New York for a while."

"Then Ann it is." Paul turned to look out the dirty bay window. "What's that old building down there behind the house?"

"Summer kitchen. It may be too far gone to save, but we might be able to salvage enough old wood to rebuild the gazebo so you could use it for a pool house, maybe, if you ever put one in."

"No pool, thank you. Maybe eventually a fountain."

"When you going back to New Jersey?"

"I'm not. I've sublet my apartment."

"You're not expecting to live in the house, are you?" Buddy looked horrified. "Not until it's finished, I mean."

"Actually, I am. I'm used to camping out. If the plumbing works, I can make do with a cot in the back bedroom."

"Son, it still gets very cold at night. The old water heater may hold up until we replace it or it may not. Plus the dust and the noise. You sure you want to stay here?"

"I'll give it a try. If I get uncomfortable, I can always spend a night in a motel."

Buddy scratched his balding head. "Your choice, but I wouldn't advise it. You surely don't plan on cooking, do you?"

Paul laughed. "Not with the café next door."

"Good, 'cause that old stove might blow up the first time you try to light the pilot."

Paul followed Buddy to the front door and opened it for him. He was, after all, the host. Odd feeling. He'd never owned a house or even a condo in his life.

"My crew will be here first thing tomorrow morning," Buddy said. "I got to get back to police work."

"Fine." Paul closed and locked the front door of the house behind the man. He planned to absorb the atmosphere of the place. Maybe meet a ghost. Weren't ghosts supposed to be troubled spirits doomed to walk the earth to pay for their crimes in life?

If that was true, then he knew of at least one ghost who ought to be walking the halls of the Delaney mansion in torment. His father.

CHAPTER TWO

PAUL'S SHOULDER ached. He drove back to his motel using only his left hand. His right arm would never be really strong again. Even with all the physical therapy and the operations he'd endured, he'd been warned the pain might never completely leave him.

The damp chill in the Delaney house wasn't helping. He probably shouldn't have explored the place again after Buddy left. He hadn't uncovered anything worth noting, anyway. The dirt floor in the basement, which hadn't been disturbed since the house was built, was as hard as concrete, and the attic seemed to hold no hidden spaces. He decided he'd explore further when he was rested.

Another night in a good bed was more necessity than indulgence.

Time enough to organize his camping equipment tomorrow. And if he hated staying at the house, he could always check back into the motel.

He shut the door of his room behind him, tossed the key on the dresser and collapsed onto the king-size bed. In his years of flying he'd spent too many nights in anonymous rooms like this. Sometimes when his wake-up call came, he'd have to check the notepad beside the telephone to remember where he was. He never thought he'd miss those days, but now if he had his right arm and shoulder back the way they'd been before the attack, he'd never complain about his crazy flight schedule again.

Not going to happen. But at least he'd managed to pass the physical for a Class III commercial pilot's license. He could still fly his own small plane and would be flying a cropduster for the local fixed-base operation in a few weeks. So in some sense, he still had the sky. Doug Slatterly and Bill McClure would never be able to fly again. Doug still had memory lapses and tremors. Bill had lost the sight in his right eye and along with it, his depth perception.

And all because one of their colleagues had decided to crash the L-10 transport they were flying so that his family could collect double indemnity on his life insurance.

They'd all had military experience, but even so, the attack was so sudden, so unexpected, that they'd all been badly hurt before they'd fought back. It was a miracle Doug had stayed conscious, keeping the man at bay to give Paul a chance to turn the plane and keep it level.

In the end, they'd managed to disarm the man and land the plane safely with no loss of life on the ground, but at a horrific cost to their bodies. Paul smiled ruefully. The lunatic was the only one who got what he wanted. After he'd tried to escape from the plane, a police sniper had shot him, and the insurance company had been forced to pony up the double indemnity.

The three survivors—Bill, the navigator, Doug, the co-pilot, and Paul himself, pilot-in-charge—had been paid off handsomely. The company hadn't wanted any lawsuits with the attendant publicity. They'd settled generously.

But he'd be willing to bet that both Doug and Bill would give back the six million bucks they'd each been awarded if they could still qualify for their old jobs. Paul certainly would.

The last he'd heard, Doug was planning to open a sea-food restaurant in Coral Gables. He didn't know what Bill was doing. Both their marriages had survived, although Bill and Janey had separated for a while.

Maybe Bill and Janey wouldn't have come through if they hadn't actually been legally married with children. Certainly Paul and Tracy hadn't. Tracy had stuck with him in the hospital and for the first month of physical therapy after he came home, but in the end she'd broken their engagement.

He didn't blame her. Tracy had been a flight attendant long enough to have her pick of the prime runs. She'd expected to marry a transport pilot, not a bad-tempered man with a bum arm and no idea what he wanted to do for the rest of his life. *She* wasn't the one who changed. He had.

They'd taken no marriage vows, no "for better or worse." The breakup had been nasty. They'd both said terrible things that could never be unsaid.

Tracy had mailed him an invitation to her wedding a month ago to a pilot for one of the big commercial airlines. He had sent her a very expensive silver tray and toasted her alone in his apartment with too much brandy.

He soaked for an hour in the bath, slept for another and then drove back to the house. He wanted to poke and pry further. Maybe he'd be able to thrash his way through the damp weeds and vines in the garden to the summer kitchen or the garden shack.

Mrs. Hoddle had told him that nothing remained in the house from the Delaney years. The heir had commissioned an estate agent to sell everything he and his wife didn't want. A junk dealer had carted off what remained.

Paul parked in the broken concrete area at the back of the house. No garage, of course. That would have to be built from scratch. He climbed out and stepped into the tall grass that had once been the back lawn. He was surprised to find a herringbone pattern of bricks just visible under the weeds. Must've been some sort of patio. He forced his way through tangled vegetation until he found himself snared by overgrown rosebushes.

Years without pruning should have killed them, but despite the long bracts that snagged his clothing, he could see the beginning of a few green shoots. Maybe they could still be saved.

The door to the summer kitchen had a heavy, rusted padlock on it. Looking around, Paul decided he wouldn't be able to get to the fence at the back of the property without a machete, so he gave up and went back to the house.

Imposing from the front, the house looked much more informal from the rear. He could barely make out the outline of the piano through the filthy bay windows. On his left beyond the music room, the window wall of the conservatory stretched down the entire side of the house. Judging from the layers of grime and the festoons of spiderwebs, no one had washed the outside of those windows in twenty years.

He walked up the two steps to the back door and fitted his new key into its new lock. The door silently opened on oiled hinges. Buddy's doing, no doubt. The broad center hall ran straight through the house. Paul could see shadows of the trees in the front yard through the glass of the front door.

He turned into the kitchen.

An old butcher-block table marred by the nicks of countless knives stood in the center of the room.

He heard the slightly off-key tinkle of the piano.

The hair on his arms stood up. His first ghost?

After a moment he got himself under control and listened. Debussy, maybe, or Ravel. Familiar, although he couldn't identify it. Something soft and sad and French.

When he'd looked through the bay window earlier, he'd seen no silhouette at the piano. There had been no other cars parked either in the driveway or out front on the street, and he'd heard none drive in.

Buddy had the only other key, but Buddy hardly seemed the type to favor Debussy or Ravel.

Paul started to call out, then stopped. He definitely did not believe in ghosts, so there must be ten human fingers on those keys. If the pianist thought he, too, was alone in the house, then hearing Paul's voice might give him or her a heart attack. The sudden sound had definitely accelerated *Paul's* pulse.

The music stopped suddenly.

Paul waited a moment, then crossed the central hall. The music room was partially open. Paul peered in.

No one was at the piano. The room was empty. So was the front parlor, which he could see through the open doors between the two rooms.

He stepped into the music room. Absolutely empty. Had he been hearing things? The piano was open. He remembered Buddy's closing it after showing him how discolored the old ivory keys were.

He touched the bench. Still warm. To the best of his knowledge, ghosts did not have warm bottoms.

Someone was in the house. Heart attack or not, it was time to call out.

He started to open his mouth when a huge black object hurtled through the hall door and hit him full in the chest.

Paul's feet slid out from under him, and he landed flat on his back, barely managing to keep his head from cracking against the bare floor.

He managed a couple of gasps before the black object

reached out a long, maroon tongue and licked him straight across the face.

"Get off me!" Paul didn't think attack dogs were trained to lick their quarry, so he felt relatively safe shoving this one off his chest.

"Dante!"

Footsteps pelted down the back stairs. A moment later he saw a figure silhouetted in the shadowy doorway. "What are you doing here?"

"I might ask you the same thing," he said. "Call off your moose."

"Dante, get off him. Down."

Dante gave Paul one last quick swipe with his tongue, then sank to the floor beside him and stared with beseeching eyes.

"What kind of dog is this, anyway? I've never seen one like it."

"He's a Neopolitan mastiff."

Paul rolled to a sitting position and found himself nose to nose with the mastiff. "He makes bloodhounds look cheerful."

"He's really a happy dog. It's just his woebegone expression and all those wrinkles that make him look miserable. Listen, I'm awfully sorry. He didn't hurt you, did he?"

"Just my dignity, Miss…uh?"

"Ann Corrigan." She offered a hand, and when he took it with his left, she helped him back to his feet.

"Ah—you're the Ann Buddy was talking about."

"You have to be Mr. Bouvet. Do you need to sit down or anything?"

"Not quite that decrepit, thank you."

"I didn't mean…I guess you heard the piano. Buddy swore you wouldn't be back this afternoon, so I borrowed his key to start taking pictures of the inside of the house. When I saw the piano, I couldn't resist."

"You play well."

"No, I don't." Ann laughed. "I play one tempo—slow. And one style—easy with lots of mistakes—although I spent every Tuesday afternoon for years on that piano bench. I took lessons from Miss Addy."

"The lady who owned the house."

"Only for the last few years. It belonged to the Delaneys. When Mrs. Delaney died, she left it to her sister for her lifetime. Miss Addy must have taught most of the kids in the county to play the piano."

"You sounded good."

"I was not one of her star pupils. When I wasn't in school I was either out with the hunt or pitching for the softball team. I hated to practice. Scales, yuck. Now I wish I'd worked harder."

"I attempted to play the tuba in my high-school band. It was a grave error. I lasted less than six weeks. Football was easier, except that I wasn't big enough for a college scholarship."

Dante had not moved from his position but followed the conversation like a tennis spectator, turning his head from one to the other.

Ann lifted her hand, palm up, and Dante hauled himself to his feet and went to stand beside her. He had no tail, so his entire rear end wagged.

"Look, we don't have to stand here in the middle of an empty room," Ann said. "Let's sit on the window seat in the conservatory—if you don't mind getting dirty."

Paul followed her through the archway at the left and into the conservatory. She perched on one of the cushions. "It's pretty dusty."

"I'm already dirty." He sat far enough along the curve

of the windows so that he had a good view of her. "Does Dante always greet people so enthusiastically?" he asked.

"I'm sorry about that. I spend a lot of time in empty, isolated old buildings by myself. When I'm really doing good work, I sometimes keep going all night. There are never any curtains at the windows, so it's like I'm standing on stage under a spotlight while the rest of the world outside is in darkness. I'd feel like a sitting duck without Dante as my early-warning system and my guardian."

On hearing his name, the dog laid his head on Ann's lap. She scratched his small, pointed ears.

"Not much of a guardian, although he looks scary enough," Paul said.

"He'd never bite a living soul, but just having all 180 pounds of him land on you and lick your face would scare most bad guys into cardiac arrest."

"Almost worked with me."

"He doesn't usually go looking for trouble. I guess he decided that since this was an empty house, I must be working. Sometimes he's a bear of very little brain."

"Has he ever had to launch into action before?"

"A couple of times in D.C. he barked and may have scared off the bad guys, but not since I've moved back down here. I didn't even hear you from upstairs. He decided to investigate on his own."

"Buddy says you know this house well."

"I ought to. Miss Addy was not only my piano teacher, she was my great-aunt."

Paul froze. Ann Corrigan was a Delaney? "I thought her sister owned the house and that the other lady only had life tenancy."

"Her older sister, Aunt Maribelle, was the one who married into the Delaneys and inherited the house when her husband died. But Aunt Addy lived with her forever, and Aunt Maribelle didn't want her to have to move.''

"So Mrs. Maribelle Delaney was also your great-aunt?"

Ann nodded. "My grandmother was the youngest of the three girls."

"Is she still—"

"Alive?" Ann grinned. "Is she ever."

"So your father..."

"Gram is my mother's mother."

"So you really are a Delaney?"

"More of a kissing cousin by marriage. Practically everybody in this area is kin to everybody else."

Paul looked at her closely for the first time, trying to discern something in her face that might show her relationship to the Delaneys.

A moment later he decided she was worth exploring for herself. She was of average height, average weight and average coloring. Her medium-brown hair was fairly long and tied back tightly by a red scarf. She had a nicely rounded body with long legs and a generous bosom.

She looked as though she laughed a lot—the sort of girl an earlier generation would have called "a good egg."

Her face was too strong-boned for classic beauty and her mouth a bit too wide. Might be interesting to taste it.

Her eyes were her best feature. They were large, slightly tilted at the corners and the sort of gray-blue that changes color with mood or the color of the background. Although she'd long since chewed off her lipstick—if indeed she wore any—her lips were still the color of a not-quite-ripe pomegranate. Paul could see no resemblance to the Delaney in the only photo he possessed.

She was a far cry from the pencil-thin flight attendants he was used to, but judging from the muscles in her arms, she was in good shape. Probably her job required a certain amount of strength. He felt an immediate attraction.

He had certainly never expected to meet a woman like this in Rossiter.

"If you want to know the history of the house and the family," she said, "check out the library in Somerville and the courthouse records. There's also been a newspaper in Fayette County since before the Civil War. I'm sure they have copies at the morgue."

He stiffened. "Why would I be that interested?"

"I just thought that since you bought—"

"Of course. Now that it's mine, I should find out all I can about its history. I've never owned an old house before."

"I can give you a list of movies to rent that will scare you even more than Buddy did," she said. "*The Money Pit* comes to mind."

"So you think I made a bad bargain?"

She put up her hands. "Oh, no! I think you made a wonderful bargain. It's just that you're going to have to live through three or four months of hell to get to paradise."

"A few months seems a short time to wait for paradise."

"You won't think so a month from now." She stood and Dante walked around to her left side and sat at her heel. "I'm glad to have met you. But I really do have to take some pictures before the rest of the light goes."

"Of course." He stood, as well. "What are you taking pictures of?"

"Details of any architectural detail that may have to be re-created, as well as the pediments and pilasters outside that we may have to rebuild or duplicate. Pictures of the scamoglio on the staircase—"

"Scamoglio?"

"It's a fancy kind of plaster technique that looks like polished marble. You didn't think that staircase wall was real marble, did you?"

"I assumed it was some kind of painted finish."

Ann laughed. "Perish the thought. I've already taken some shots of the overmantel and the fireplaces, but I wanted to take at least a couple more rolls before the crews start cleaning up."

"Buddy says you can salvage the mural in the dining room."

"I'm going to give it my best shot, although it may be too fragile to leave where it is. You can always make a screen out of it."

"You can get it off the wall?"

"We'll see." She stuck out her hand. "Sorry we met under these circumstances, but I'm glad at least we did meet. Next time Dante will know you're a friend. He won't knock you down again."

"Great." He stopped in the front hall. "I didn't see a car out front. How did you come? Did Buddy drop you?"

"Oh, no, I walked. I live in the loft upstairs over the flower shop on the square."

"I assumed the lofts were used for storage. Didn't realize anyone lived there."

"Actually, I have both the end lofts—the one over the real-estate office, as well. I use one for living and one for working."

"What's in the far building, the one with the bear?"

"That? Trey Delaney uses it as a kind of second office when he wants to get away from the farm." She raised her eyebrows. "As well as from his wife Sue-sue and the children. Well, I'm off upstairs."

"And I'm heading back to the motel. See you tomorrow?"

"Maybe." She waved, picked up the digital camera that hung around her neck and trotted up the back stairs. He could hear the click of Dante's nails on the naked risers.

He watched her rear end in the tight jeans. Nice to see a woman who actually looked womanly. The sort a man could enjoy holding in his arms.

He'd be willing to bet that even in jeans, she'd draw the eye of every man in a restaurant. There was an aura of sexuality about her, of passion just beneath the surface. He doubted she was aware of it.

He pulled himself up short. He had not come to Rossiter for female companionship, no matter how appealing. And there were excellent reasons not to become involved with any Delaney kin, even a kissing cousin. *His* kissing cousin actually, although he had no idea how to figure out their relationship. He had a job to do, a promise to fulfill, not only to Tante Helaine, but to his mother.

So Trey Delaney used the office with the bear outside. Paul would have to find out the story behind that bear. Might give him an excuse to start asking questions about Trey at the café. He very much wanted to meet Trey. Always a good thing to know your enemy. And they were, after all, kin.

CHAPTER THREE

BY THE TIME Paul got back to his motel after dinner in a fast-food restaurant, all he wanted was a hot shower and bed. His damn shoulder was no longer just an ache, but a throbbing pain, and he still had his physical-therapy exercises to do. The hit he'd taken from Ann's dog hadn't helped any.

He turned on the television, muted the sound, picked up the telephone and dialed Giselle's number. A moment later a youthful male voice answered.

"Harry, it's Uncle Paul. May I speak to your mother?"

Without replying, the teenager yelled, "Mom, it's Uncle Paul."

He heard the telephone drop with a clunk and his cousin's voice. "Harry, you have the manners of a tarantula! And turn down that music!" Then a moment later, "Paul, why didn't you call last night? I've been so worried."

"Sorry, Giselle. Landed too late to disturb you."

"Was your car waiting for you? No dents?"

Paul laughed. "Yes, Giselle. You can tell Harry that his buddy seems to have driven all the way down from New Jersey without so much as a speeding ticket. He also washed the car, cleaned the inside and left it sitting beside the airstrip with the keys under the fender in the magnetic case."

Giselle gave a sigh of relief. "Thank heaven. I had

visions of Kevin doing a Thelma and Louise somewhere on the Blue Ridge Parkway.''

"He even left me copies of his gas charges on the front seat. Very responsible young man. Tell Harry I'll send both him and Kevin a bonus.''

"Have you decided to give up this madness and come home where I can look after you?''

"You're already looking after two teenage sons and a husband. I'm fine on my own.''

"Humph,'' Giselle said. The sound came out with a Gallic flavor. Giselle spoke both English and French without accent, but her wordless expressions still sounded more French than English. "You don't belong down there. What good is it going to do? You won't find anything. That Paul David Delaney is dead, assuming he is the right Paul David Delaney.''

"Oh, he's the right Delaney—my honorable father, pillar of society, richest man in the county, the man who married and abandoned my mother and then killed her when she found him.''

"I know you and Maman believed that, but you could be wrong. The detective said a serial killer or someone could've picked her up along the way. You don't even know for certain whether she even met your father after she went down to Memphis.''

"Tante Helaine, your mother, never believed that my mother was murdered by a stranger at the precise moment she was due to confront my father, and neither do I. Too big a coincidence. No, he killed her all right. I've always known it in my heart. I had no way to check it out before.''

"No one has ever found her body....''

"That's another thing. I want to find what he did with her, give her a decent burial if that's possible.''

"After thirty years? What would be left to identify? Besides, you can't bring a dead man to justice."

"Well, I want someone to pay. I want to rub the noses of every living Delaney in the muck of what Paul Delaney did. I want them to admit in public that my father was a murderer."

"The present generation had nothing to do with it. Anyone who might have known about it is long dead."

"The present generation benefited from my mother's death. Why should they live out their lives thinking their father was a paragon? I promised Tante Helaine I would expose him, and I will. Let them deal with the truth for a change."

"Then go tell the son what you suspect, who you are. He's your half brother, after all."

"And have the entire clan circle the wagons? No, until I have incontrovertible proof that my father killed my mother, proof that would convince a jury, nobody down here is going to know I have any connection with the Delaneys. Now that I own the family home I have the perfect cover story—it's natural to want to find out the history of an old house. These people will fall over themselves regaling me with anecdotes. The Delaneys were the most important family in the county. Trey Delaney is still one of the richest men. Certainly he owns the most land. I'm really looking forward to meeting him." He tried to keep the sarcasm out of his voice, but Giselle knew him too well.

"You should never have promised Maman you'd avenge Aunt Michelle. You want to destroy the Delaneys for Maman, but in the end, I think you are the one who will suffer. The kind of hate my mother carried around corrodes like acid. It ruined her life, and in the end I think it contributed to her death. I know you're still angry that

you can't fly big jets any longer, but don't transfer your
anger to the Delaneys. That's a whole different issue.''

Paul laughed. "Don't psychoanalyze me, Giselle. I
don't blame the Delaneys for that. Nor for the fact that
Tracy walked out on me because she couldn't take looking after an invalid, nor for the pain in my shoulder. I
blame them because I grew up without either a mother or
a father.''

"Stop it! Maman and Dad loved you like a son.''

"Of course they did. And I loved them both. But having your aunt and uncle take you in isn't quite the same
thing as growing up with the man and woman whose
genes you carry. In my case I didn't even know who'd
donated half of my genes until a few months ago.''

"I have a very bad feeling about this. Not for those
Delaneys, but for you.''

"Who said revenge is a dish best eaten cold? After
thirty years it's damned near frozen.''

"What if you like them? The ones who are left, I
mean?''

"I'll try not to let that happen. If it does, I'll deal with
it.''

"Please call me every night or e-mail me. I want to
know everything that's going on.''

"I promise. I love you, Giselle. Regards to Jerry.''

"Good night, *mon frère*.''

He put the phone back in its cradle and lay back on the
bed.

"Scamoglio," he said, and laughed. "Who knew?''

At least Ann was enthusiastic about something other
than Botox injections in her forehead. He turned the sound
up on the TV, moved to the floor and began the exercises
to stretch and strengthen his right shoulder and arm. He

must be getting better. The tears from the pain didn't begin to run down his cheeks and into his ears for a good five minutes.

"GRAM, WE'RE STARTING the Delaney restoration job tomorrow morning," Ann said as she reached for another ear of sweet corn. "It's going to be fabulous."

"Pass the butter to your daughter, Nancy," Sarah Pulliam said.

"She does not need any more butter," Ann's mother said shortly. But she passed it anyway. "Mother, you are a great cook, but does the word *cholesterol* mean anything to you?"

"Hush. The girl has no meat on her bones as it is." Sarah turned a concerned face to her granddaughter. "I wish they'd tear that old Delaney place down and salt the earth it stands on."

"Whatever for? I *love* that house."

"Ann, honey, I firmly believe that old houses take on the character of the folks who lived in them," her grandmother said, and slid the platter of barbecued pork chops closer to Ann. "Nobody who ever lived there has been happy, starting with the Delaney who built it."

"I know Mr. Delaney lost his only daughter, Gram, but half the people of west Tennessee lost children to the yellow fever. Whole families died sometimes."

"He wanted a houseful of children. Adam was the only child who survived. Delaney's poor wife had half-a-dozen miscarriages trying to get him more. Wore her out and killed her in the end."

"Mother," Nancy said, moving the pork chops away from Ann, "unless you're a whopping lot older than you've been saying all these years, there's no way you could know all that."

"My mother, your grandmother, told me, Miss Nancy.

She wanted to marry Adam's son Barrett for a while. She was glad in the long run she'd missed out on him. A meaner man never lived. During the depression he foreclosed on half the farmers in Fayette County so he could acquire their farms cheap when they were sold on the courthouse steps. One of them tried to shoot him. Missed, unfortunately.''

"But the next generation was happy. Aunt Maribelle and Uncle Conrad doted on each other." Ann said. She started to reach for the chops, but one look from her mother stopped her. "I mean, they seemed to have had a wonderful marriage. Everybody got along, even Aunt Addy.''

"You were much too young to see what was really happening. Two cats in a burlap bag. My sisters barely tolerated each other, and living in the same house didn't help. When Daddy refused to let Addy go to the Conservatory of Music in Philadelphia, I really thought she'd die. She had real talent. She wanted to be a concert pianist. Instead, she wound up an old maid living in her sister's house and teaching piano lessons to children like you. Daddy should have let her go.''

"Why didn't he?''

"He always said that it wasn't seemly for an unmarried woman to live alone in an apartment or a boardinghouse, but the real reason was that Maribelle was engaged to Conrad Delaney and demanded a society wedding. Daddy couldn't afford both.''

"So Aunt Maribelle won?''

"Maribelle always won. Mostly because it never occurred to her she *wouldn't* win. You have no idea how it galled Addy to have to live under her sister's roof all those years. And Maribelle's marriage to Conrad wasn't quite the blissful union she tried to make everybody believe.

Anyway, that has never been a happy house, and it will find some way to make the new owner suffer, too, you mark my words.''

On the drive back to town from her grandmother's farm, Ann absently scratched behind Dante's ears and thought over her grandmother's remarks. Bernice had said more or less the same thing at the café that morning, but Ann hadn't paid much attention. However, she couldn't dismiss her grandmother's concerns as easily. Sarah Pulliam was supposed to be fey. People said she had "the gift.''

As far as Ann could tell, that meant her grandmother could penetrate the facades behind which people tried to hide. Ann had suffered many times as a child because her Gram always knew full well who was responsible for knocking down the rose trellis or forgetting to feed the dogs. It wasn't second sight. It was solid knowledge of the mischief Ann was capable of.

And Gram was the only person who'd warned her she'd be miserable if she married "that Travis Corrigan.'' She'd definitely been right on that score.

CHAPTER FOUR

THE FOLLOWING MORNING, Paul slept later than he'd planned, stood under a hot shower to loosen his shoulder, stowed his bags in his car, grabbed a couple of sweet rolls and a paper cup of hot, bad coffee from the lobby of his motel and drove east toward Rossiter.

He'd planned to arrive before the workmen, assuming they showed up. He'd had enough experience with contractors and their crews when Giselle was remodeling her kitchen. Half the time they simply didn't show—no excuses, not even a telephone call.

Not this morning. Overnight a large blue Dumpster had appeared outside his back door, and half-a-dozen pickup trucks festooned with equipment stood haphazardly on his front lawn. He could hear hammering and shouting before he even got out of his car. He walked up his front steps and through the open door.

A moment later he ducked as a man in overalls carrying a bundle of two-by-fours swung around the corner from the basement steps. He barely glanced at Paul.

"Hey, toss me that hammer, will ya?" a voice called down from the stair landing. "Right there on the toolbox—the claw with the blue handle."

Paul looked around, found the hammer and made the mistake—one he still frequently made—of tossing it with his right hand. The pain made him suck in his breath. The hammer clattered to the staircase several steps down from the man who needed it.

"Sorry," Paul said, and moved to retrieve it.

"Okay, I got it." The man disappeared behind the stair railing. A moment later Paul heard the thud of the hammer against one of his balusters.

"Hey! Should you be taking that thing out? Won't the banister fall off?"

The man reared. He was thin with graying hair and skin like old cypress left too long in the creek. "Yeah, I should be taking it off and no, the banister won't fall down. All right with you?"

Chastened and feeling way out of his element, Paul went in search of Buddy.

He found him and a crew in the basement removing rotten joists and replacing them with good wood. Paul backed out without disturbing them.

At the rate they were going, the structural work could be done in a week. He hadn't even talked to Buddy about any schedule, and he had no idea whether the plumbers came before the electricians or the telephone linemen or the utilities. He had a sudden longing to be sitting in his rented condo in New Jersey. But he'd sublet it.

He could take Giselle up on her offer of a bed.

No way. That house with two teenaged boys was considerably noisier and more confused than this one.

He needed an island of peace and quiet. Simply slipping out and taking up more or less permanent residence at the café next door seemed cowardly. Before the accident he'd have pitched in and at least swung a sledgehammer at the broken concrete of the parking area behind the house. Now he couldn't even do that.

"You look like somebody's poleaxed you."

He heard Ann's voice from behind him with a mixture of relief and happiness that surprised him.

A moment later Dante thrust his slobbery maw into his hand. "Next time you warn me about chaos I'll listen to you." He removed his palm from Dante's jowls and rubbed it dry on the dog's broad head.

Her gray-blue eyes danced and she grinned at him.

"You get off on this, don't you," he said.

"You caught me." She turned away from him, her arms spread wide, embracing the entire house. "I adore helping old buildings spring to life again, and since I love this house, this job is pure joy."

"It's pure madness, is what it is." He had to shout over the sound of at least three power saws and three or four hammers.

"Come on upstairs, it's quieter there." She slipped past him and then hugged the staircase wall to avoid falling through the space left by the missing posts. Dante sighed and trudged up behind her.

She walked into the back bedroom, held the door until Paul and Dante had cleared it, then shut it firmly against the noise. March had turned cool even during the day, and the caulking between the sleeping-porch windows and this bedroom left much to be desired.

"You're going to freeze in that shirt," she said practically, and perched her bottom on the nearest windowsill. "You still planning on staying here at night?"

He ran his hand over his forehead. "At this point, I

have no idea. I've checked out of my motel, but I'm sure they'd take me back.''

''Work quits about five, so if you can stand the chill and the possibility of a cold shower—and if you don't mind the occasional ghost—I don't see why you shouldn't stay here. Just don't try cooking on that stove.''

''Buddy warned me about that.'' He glanced at her. ''What ghosts?''

''All old Southern mansions have ghosts.'' She laughed. ''Let's see.'' She began to tick off on her fingers. ''There's Deirdre Delaney who died in the last really big yellow-fever epidemic. She's supposed to sit on the bottom step and cry.'' She lifted a second finger. ''Then there's Paul Adam—the son of the man who built the house. It's very confusing that every generation names the first son Paul. Fortunately each generation has a middle name starting with the next letter of the alphabet. That's the only way to tell them apart.''

''So Trey's real name is?''

''Paul Edward. He prefers Trey. Anyway, Paul Barrett is supposed to clank chains like Morley because he was such a nasty old miser in life.''

''People have actually seen these ghosts?''

''To hear them tell it.''

''Are those all the ghosts?''

''Not by a long shot. Let's see. Great-uncle Conrad's son David—he was actually Paul David, but nobody ever called him that.'' She must have caught his expression because she said, ''Hey, are you okay? I don't really believe in ghosts, you know.''

''I'm not upset. Tell me about your uncle David.''

''My gram could tell you more. He died when I was

pretty young, so I'm not certain how much I really remember and how much comes from Gram. I *do* remember
that he was the sweetest, gentlest, saddest man I ever
knew, when he was sober, that is. Toward the end of his
life he wasn't sober very often.''

Paul had no desire to hear about what a sweet, gentle
man his father had been. He would have preferred the
kind of ogre he'd dreamed of for years. He fought to keep
his breathing even and his fingers from tightening into
fists.

''So why would he haunt this place?'' *Because he
killed somebody here,* Paul answered his own question
silently.

''He wanted to be a painter and live in Paris, but of
course that wasn't possible.''

''Why not?''

''Because the family needed him,'' Ann said as though
it was the most obvious reason in the world. ''When his
daddy had a heart attack, he called Uncle David home.
He never went back to Paris. I think that's why he was
sad. And probably why he drank like a fish and rode like
a madman.''

''Rode what?''

''Horses, of course. The Delaneys have always been
masters of the local hunt. I can remember my first few
hunts when I was still riding my pony. I was certain the
sweet old uncle David I knew couldn't possibly be the
crazy man in the pink coat flying over the fields screaming
like a banshee. Not that I knew what a banshee was at
the time, of course.''

This was more like it. ''So he liked blood sports,
did he?''

Ann laughed at him. "Foxhunting the way we do it down here is not a blood sport. We never ever kill anything—well, not foxes or coyotes, at any rate. We don't have such a great track record with people."

Paul struggled to remain calm. "What...what do you mean?"

Ann laughed again. "I'm joking."

Paul nodded. "But this Uncle David chased innocent foxes?"

"Sure. But the foxes seem to enjoy it. They actually sit out in the fields and wait for hounds. I swear they can tell when it's Wednesday or Saturday. I've hunted since I was five years old and I have never seen a drop of blood drawn from any animal we chased. When the foxes get tired, they go to ground and leave hounds baying and frustrated. And of course the coyotes can outrun hounds any time they feel like it. It's a big game and an excuse to go yee-hawing over the fields on a horse. Do you ride? You can come along in second field if you'd like."

"What's second field?"

"The old fogeys' field. A nice quiet trail ride with no fences to jump and no pressure. We also have carriages that follow along sometimes. You can ride in one of them if you like. We hunt until the farmers put the crops in."

"I've never been on a horse in my life and don't plan to start now, thank you."

"Suit yourself."

"We've gotten rather far afield from your uncle David."

"I thought we'd finished with him."

"And why he's a ghost."

"He's not, of course. But if there were ghosts, he'd be

a good candidate. So sad in life. As though he searched for something he never found.'' She shook her head. ''Then if you want a tough ghost, there's Aunt Maribelle, his mother. If she turned ghost, you'd know about it for sure. In life, there was never anything shy about Aunt Maribelle. So as a ghost I'm sure if she wanted you out of here, she'd find a way to boot your behind down the front steps.''

''Let's hope she doesn't want me out.''

''Probably happy to have you.'' She checked her watch. ''Oops. Buddy'll kill me if I don't get back to work.''

''What are you doing?''

''I've covered the mural in the dining room so it won't collect any more dust, and I've started stripping the overmantel in the music room. The goo should be just about ready to remove. Want to see what's under the layers?''

''Certainly.''

''Okay. Come on.''

As he followed her down the stairs, he asked, ''Do you know what sort of chandelier hung up there?'' He pointed to the elaborate boss surrounding the hanging lightbulb.

''Sure. A big old brass thing that originally used gas— the first house in Rossiter to have it, by the way.''

''You wouldn't know who bought it, would you?''

''No clue, but if I know Trey Delaney, he's got meticulous records on every purchase from the estate sale, even piddly little stuff like the things I bought.''

Excellent. The perfect entrée to introduce himself to Trey Delaney.

He watched Ann's heavily gloved hands meticulously remove layers of black varnish from the relief on the overmantel. She used what looked like dental instruments to get into the cracks and crevices.

He was definitely in the way.

Even Buddy in his trips from basement to Dumpster hardly did more than nod at him. He finally sat on the fourth step of the staircase and merely watched.

He'd about decided to leave when a tall, slim woman in jeans, cowboy boots and a turtleneck sweater strode in the front door. Her hair was short and snow-white, her face nut-brown with crinkles at the edge of her eyes. One glance at her hands told him she must be in her sixties, but she moved like a teenager.

"Hey," she said as she came forward and extended her hand. "You must be Mr. Bouvet. I'm Sarah Pulliam. I'm a terrible busybody. Couldn't stay away any longer. Had to see what was happening to the old place."

Her handshake was brief but firm.

She glanced around at the organized chaos and then at him. "Welcome to Rossiter, although why in God's green earth you'd want to move to a little town like this is more than I can see." Without waiting for his answer, she strode off through the living room. "You tore down those godawful drapes, thank God. I told Maribelle when she hung them that they were heavy enough to suffocate any small child that got caught up in them. Ugly, to boot. For a woman with strong tastes, Maribelle never did take much to color in her decorating."

He trailed this dynamo without speaking. He had no idea who she was, but she obviously knew the Delaneys well. He had no intention of interrupting the flow of her talk.

"There you are, Ann," she said. "Goodness, I had no idea that was golden oak."

"Neither did anybody else until I started stripping it." Ann smiled at the woman who offered a cheek to be kissed. "I guess you introduced yourself, didn't you?"

"Sure did."

"Did you tell him who you were?"

"Huh?"

"Paul, this is my grandmother, Sarah Pulliam. She and Maribelle and Addy were sisters."

"I was the youngest and the only one who wasn't half-crazy," Sara said with a touch of smugness.

"Crazy how?" Paul asked. Maybe his father's gene pool had been tainted by schizophrenia or manic depression.

"Maribelle had a terrible temper, but she managed to get what she wanted when she wanted it. I suppose that's not really crazy, except that she had tunnel vision about her own needs. And poor Addy probably didn't start out crazy, but she sure wound up that way. Toward the end Esther—the woman who looked after her—said she used to wander around in her nightgown wringing her hands like Lady MacBeth and mumbling stuff that made no sense whatsoever." Sarah shook her head sadly. "She had every reason in this world to hate Maribelle, but they still managed to live in the same house together, God knows how."

"And did you like them?" In New Jersey, Paul would never have considered asking a bald question like that. But these people seemed to delight in a new audience to tell a good story to.

Ann gave him a sharp glance, but if Sarah noticed the rudeness of the question, it certainly didn't bother her.

"Actually, I was devoted to Addy. Only men loved Maribelle. Women saw through her. Men never catch on to that sort of selfishness and greed."

"Sarah, where'd you come from?" Wiping the perspiration from his face with a white towel that said Golf and Country Club on it, Buddy Jenkins walked into the library and came over to kiss Sarah's cheek.

"Had to pick up some laying mash for the chickens, so I thought I'd stop by, maybe take you all to lunch. How about it, Mr. Bouvet? You eaten at the Wolf River Café yet?"

"Indeed I have. Thank you, Mrs. Pulliam, but I wouldn't want to intrude."

"Intrude? Buying this house sort of makes you a member of the Delaney clan—which we sort of are. You look like you could use a good country fried steak."

He allowed himself to be persuaded. This woman was a fount of information. He prayed he could keep her talking.

AT LUNCH Paul couldn't steer the conversation back to Paul Delaney, Sr., without seeming too nosy even for these people. He contented himself with listening to Sarah banter with Buddy and her granddaughter.

He had never been around a family whose generations kidded and laughed together. His *tante* had been a strict disciplinarian who spoke formally always. He'd never seen her smile.

For a man who had done very little since morning, he felt awfully tired. Not physical exhaustion, but the weariness that came from always being on the alert for some tidbit of information about this family of his, about his father.

And from being on guard against revealing that he knew or cared more than he should about the Delaneys. One of his friends from the Air Force Academy, Jack Sabrinski, who had grown up speaking Serbo-Croat and Bulgarian with equal facility in English, had done some spy missions. He told Paul that the two months he spent spying in Bosnia took more out of him than five years of a bad marriage and a nasty divorce.

Paul could believe him. Since meeting Ann last night, another element had been added to the mix. Until yesterday these people had been strangers without faces, without personalities. Faceless entities he felt justified in using.

Now they were real to him. Ann especially. She seemed to be completely vulnerable and open. The perfect mark for a con man, which was what he was.

As he and Buddy stood by the counter waiting to pay their bills—they'd refused to allow Mrs. Pulliam to pick up the check—he heard Sarah's voice behind him.

"Hey, come meet the new owner."

Paul turned as Sarah slipped her arm under that of a man close to Paul's size and weight, but with hazel eyes and a shock of blond hair already bleached nearly white by the sun. He wore immaculate chinos that hadn't come from a discount store, an equally immaculate and expensive plaid shirt, and work boots that were polished to a high shine. Paul glanced at the man's hand as he took it.

Manicured fingernails.

"Trey, honey, this is Mr. Paul Bouvet who is redoing

your grandmother's house. Paul, say hello to Trey Delaney."

"Thought I'd see you when you closed on the house, but I had to be out of town," Trey said. "Glad to meet you at last."

Paul expected to feel a shock of electricity between them when he touched the man's hand. "Nice to meet you." He smiled, but his eyes searched for features he could recognize from the only picture he had of his father. A second later he wondered whether anyone looking at him and Trey could see any resemblance.

"My real name is Paul Edward Delaney, but nobody ever calls me anything but Trey."

The picture of Paul's father had been taken with his mother in Paris when his father was no more than twenty-five. It wasn't a very good one, either, and had begun to fade. Paul was now thirty-five, which made Trey thirty-three.

Trey had their father's eyes and light hair and skin, already roughened by days in the sun.

Paul had inherited his mother's dark eyes and hair, but for anyone who looked closely, the resemblance was noticeable. Paul decided that it would be better if he kept his meetings with Trey as private as possible and away from the knowledgeable eyes of someone like Ann, who must be used to analyzing faces for her restoration work.

Only Paul knew that they were half brothers, one raised as a wealthy planter's son in west Tennessee, one raised by a plumber uncle and a French aunt who baked bread in Queens, New York. He intended to keep it that way for as long as possible.

To everyone around them, it was a casual introduction in a small-town café. Nothing special.

"Glad you're bringing the old place to life," Trey said, "though Lord knows why you'd want to. Sue-sue—she's my wife—and I thought we'd never unload that monstrosity. Oops. Better keep my mouth shut."

"I'm surprised you didn't want to live there yourself."

Sarah laughed. Trey laughed. Ann snickered.

"Aunt Sarah," Trey said, "can't you just see Sue-sue living in a house with itty-bitty closets and no whirlpool? No, Mr. Bouvet. You're welcome to it. Too much ancestor worship around this town, anyway, and a damn sight too much in my family. Doesn't matter who you came from, just what you do on your own, am I right, Annie?"

"It helps if you start by inheriting a bunch of land, a few million dollars and a couple of thousand head of cattle."

"Can't make a dime farming, isn't that right, Aunt Sarah?" Trey turned to Paul. "You ever hear the one about the farmer who won the ten-million-dollar lottery? When they asked him what he was going to do with it, he said, 'I guess I'll just keep farming till it's gone.'" He laughed. A little too loud, a little too long.

Paul smiled back.

"Well, y'all, I got to get my nose back to the grindstone." Trey waved over his shoulder and walked past them out the restaurant toward the square.

Bills paid, the three others went out to where Dante waited patiently with his leash looped around the rail. Paul realized he hadn't asked about the bear in front of Trey's office. He'd make it a point to find out when he spoke to

Trey about the people who'd bought the antiques at Miss Addy's house sale.

"Gotta get back to work," Buddy said. "Ann, you coming?"

"In a minute. Dante needs a walk."

"Okay."

She unhooked Dante's leash and walked off toward the little park beside the railroad track. Dante glanced over his immense shoulder as if to say to Paul, "You coming?"

Paul ambled after the pair.

"I promise I'm not sloughing off," Ann said. "You'll get your money's worth out of me, Mr. Bouvet. I'm planning to work late tonight—unless my being in the house will bother you, assuming you decide to stay there."

"I'm going to give it my best shot. I'm off to stock up on things like an inflatable mattress and some kind of chest of drawers to stow my stuff in. Never did get used to sleeping on a cot even in flight school."

"Flight school? You were in the military?"

"Air Force. Went to the academy, then served out my time before I left to fly transports for a private company."

"So you flew F-15s or whatever number they're up to now?"

"I usually flew C-150s—low and slow. The perfect training to fly civilian package transport."

"Why'd you quit? Uh…retire?"

He grimaced. "Couldn't pass the transport-flight physical any longer. I got hurt in a work-related accident. Left me with a bum shoulder." Technically, the near-crash had been work-related, which was why the payoff had been so large. He was embarrassed that he hadn't prevented the whole incident. His wound and scars embarrassed him further. He talked about the details as seldom as possible.

She must have heard something in his voice, because she dropped the subject. "I think Dante's ready to go back to work. See you tonight, Mr. Bouvet."

"Isn't it about time you dropped the Mr. Bouvet stuff? I've been calling you Ann all morning."

"Sure. Paul. Do *you* have a middle name?"

"I have one, but unlike the Delaneys, no one ever uses it. Actually, my middle name is Antoine. My mother was French."

"You don't look like an Antoine. You need a nickname. How about Top Gun?"

"I was never that. How about One Wing? More appropriate."

They had reached the sidewalk in front of the mansion. She waved goodbye and ran up the walk and the stairs. Her ponytail bounced as the bright red scarf she'd tied around it flew in the breeze. Those jean-clad hips had a great sway to them when she ran.

No way. It wasn't that he was some kind of saint when it came to romancing women, but even he drew the line at seducing a woman merely to gain information. Besides, she was some sort of cousin.

He'd thought he would do anything to find out what happened to his mother. Since meeting Ann and Sarah and Buddy, he knew he had limits. As far as Trey Delaney was concerned, the jury was still out. He seemed pleasant enough, if a little arrogant. No, actually, a lot arrogant. Even Ann picked up on that self-made man crap. Big frog, small pond.

Wonder how Trey would feel if suddenly he was faced with losing it all?

Wills were a matter of record. All he had to do was go to the local county seat and request a copy of Paul Delaney's will from probate court files. He knew that his parents had been married at the time of his birth so no matter how the will was written, he, as the oldest legitimate son, would be entitled to a portion of it. He hoped, however, that he'd find that the oldest son was heir to everything. He could cut Trey out of everything he owned. Not that Paul intended to keep it, of course. What the hell did he know about farming or cows or cotton or soybeans?

But to be able to take it all, if even for a moment, then graciously give it back would be sweet.

Of course, the people in Rossiter would not take kindly to him if he did that. He'd have to sell the house and move away whether he wanted to or not.

But wasn't that what he'd intended from the first? Why should he suddenly feel conflicted?

He looked up at the house from the sidewalk. Not so much an old harridan as a sad, gracious lady fallen on hard times. His gracious lady. She needed him.

The only thing on earth who did. He felt the stab of loneliness that always came when he thought of how isolated he'd allowed himself to become since Tracy had left him. She'd kept the friends they'd made together. He hadn't bothered to make new ones.

After he made his run to the discount store and shoved his air mattress and pump into the back of his car, he decided to drive the thirty-five miles to the county seat.

He arrived at three twenty-five, only to find that the clerk's office closed at three.

On his way out of Somerville, he passed by a rose-brick building with a small sign that said Library in front of it.

Might be as good a time as any to get started on his research.

The man Paul now felt certain had fathered him had died in 1977. He'd discovered that much on an Internet search. Should be some sort of obituary in the country newspaper.

Actually, there were two weeklies. The librarian told him proudly that both had been in operation since Reconstruction. He asked for the microfiche for the time around when his father died and began to reel through.

Maybe he remembered the date incorrectly. There seemed to be nothing in the obituaries about his father. He scrolled back through to rewind the microfiche when suddenly a banner headline on the front page caught his eye.

His father's death had been reported not on the obituary page, but on the front page.

Leading Citizen Killed in Tragic Riding Accident.

Killed? Nobody said he'd been killed. Paul had assumed his father's liver or heart had given out.

Paul Francis Delaney, one of Fayette's leading citizens, was tragically killed in a freak riding accident Sunday morning. Mr. Delaney served as master of foxhounds for the local Cotton Creek hunt. During a

chase last Sunday morning at his farm, Mr. Delaney
was thrown when his horse fell while jumping a
fence. He died before emergency services could
reach him. An autopsy revealed that Mr. Delaney's
neck was broken in the fall.

One of Fayette County's largest landowners, Mr.
Delaney was also known for his charming and sometimes caustic caricatures. Many local citizens frame
these quick sketches and display them prominently.
The local fairs, bake and Christmas bazaars, and
church fetes will sorely miss his talents, as he has
over the course of the years raised considerable
amounts of money both with his artistic skills and
his personal philanthropy.

Mr. Delaney leaves his wife, Karen Bingham Delaney, his young son Paul Delaney III and his
mother, Mrs. Maribelle Delaney, widow of the late
Paul Delaney, Sr. A scholarship fund to send a talented high-school student to the Art Institute each
year for the summer program has been established in
Mr. Delaney's name. The family asks that in lieu of
flowers memorials be sent to this fund. Time and
place of services are pending.

Paul sat back in the hard wooden chair and ran his hand
over his face. A charming caricaturist? Philanthropist?
Sorely missed? He didn't know what he'd expected to
find. How could such a man have deserted and then killed
a wife who loved him?

Paul stared down at the grainy black-and-white newspaper photograph that someone had dredged up from the
files. In what could only be a pink hunting coat, his father

stood with his gloved hand on the reins of a big bay horse. A woman sat on the horse and smiled down. Too old to be this Karen Bingham, his wife. Paul's grandmother Maribelle?

He looked closer. Neither he nor Trey had inherited that aquiline nose, but Paul could certainly see where Trey got his arrogance. This was no knitting, sit-by-the-fire granny. From the casual ease with which she sat on her horse, she was used to command.

"Sorry, sir, we're closing the library," the librarian whispered.

"Oh, sure." He smiled up at her and received a timid smile in return. "I'd like to come back and look some more."

"Certainly. We open at ten o'clock every morning and close at five."

He started to rewind the microfiche.

"I'll be happy to do that, sir."

Paul nodded and walked out, vowing to return as soon as possible to look up obituaries on everyone he could think of in the direct line of Delaneys.

And then there were social events. Didn't hunts have balls and things? Sure the county weeklies would report on them. And graduations. Weddings. There would be names of others who had known his father. He had to discover as much as he could.

He climbed into his car and turned on the air conditioner. It might be March with chilly nights, but the afternoon sun had heated the car beyond his comfort zone. He pulled out and started the drive back to Rossiter.

Weddings. Birth announcements. When had his father married Karen Bingham? Or rather, when had his father committed bigamy with Karen Bingham? He had been, whether he acknowledged it or not, legally married to Paul's mother, Michelle, until she died.

Even longer. He had been legally married to Michelle until seven years after her disappearance when Uncle Charlie had finally convinced Aunt Giselle to declare her sister dead.

He wondered where the Delaneys were buried. Would he feel anything if he stood over his father's grave? Could he curse him then as he had cursed him many times before?

Maybe there was a historical society that kept personal correspondence and histories that were of no interest to anyone except scholars.

Ann's mother would probably be younger than his father would have been, but she must have known him. He needed some excuse to see her again.

And what about Karen Bingham, his father's so-called widow? Was she still alive? How could he wangle an invitation to see her?

By the time he pulled his car into a parking space in the road in front of his house, the workmen had apparently left for the day. There were several lights on both upstairs and down, but no trucks parked on his lawn.

He carried the package containing his air mattress and pump to the front door, then set them down so that he could unlock and open it.

As he stepped in, he called, "Hello! Anybody here?"

He heard the click of Dante's toenails on the wooden floor before the dog skidded around the doorway to the butler's pantry, slid to a stop in front of him and sank onto his haunches, waiting to be petted.

"Good boy. This time you didn't knock me down." He rubbed the dog's wide forehead. "Where's your mistress?"

"In here," came a muffled female voice. He followed Dante through the butler's pantry and into the kitchen. For a moment he didn't see her, then he spotted a pair of jean-clad ankles sticking out of the dumbwaiter. A moment later Ann emerged. Her face was dust-smeared and so was her shirt. She carried a large hand lantern.

"Hi," she said, and wiped her free hand down the front of her jeans. "I figured if we could get this thing to work I could use it to carry supplies to the bedrooms so that I can strip the fireplaces."

"You checked it out by climbing into it?"

"It was a tight fit, but there's plenty of room for paint and stripper and stuff. It's actually in good working order."

"Ever hear of rust? What if those cables had broken? You could be in the basement with a broken back and no one to hear you yell for help."

"I was careful. Besides, for its time, this is a top-of-the-line dumbwaiter. It's got automatic brakes. If the cable breaks, these little feet keep it from going more than one floor down. I don't normally do truly stupid things. I do not like risk. I've had more than my share for one lifetime."

"I doubt if we could replace you easily."

"There are plenty of other people who do what I do. I worked for a really high-class restoration firm in Washington before I came home. I still freelance for them when Buddy doesn't have any work for me. They'd send someone—for a bunch more money than you're paying me."

"I don't know what I'm paying you, but I'll bet it's not chicken feed."

"I'm worth it. Now, I've got to start working that stripper off before it dries too much. Then Dante and I will get out from under your feet until morning."

He followed her to the front hall and started up the staircase. Halfway up he leaned over the banister. "Have you eaten yet?"

"No."

"Then join me for dinner."

"You don't have to—"

"I'm alone. If you're alone, why not be alone together?"

She laughed. "The café?"

"I was thinking about maybe driving into town. Don't you have good barbecue in this area?"

"Oh, for sure. If we do that, I'll have to stop by my place to shower and change. I'm filthy."

"Fine. I prefer to eat late, anyway."

"It'll be midnight if I don't get started."

Upstairs he unloaded his mattress. It took barely ten minutes to turn the lump of plastic into what looked like a comfortable double bed. He'd already hung the few clothes he'd brought with him in the small closet, but he would have to start looking for suitable furniture for this room soon. He had a few decent pieces of furniture from his old apartment, but they were sleek and modern, nothing that would be suitable for this house.

Maybe he could enlist Ann's help. He planned to sell the place furnished. He didn't want any souvenirs of this little venture.

Or did he? He wandered out onto the sleeping porch

that ran across the back of the second floor. With nightfall the air had grown chilly again after the afternoon warmth, but there was no breeze. He felt as though he were in a tree house. Except for the glow from the parking lot next door, he might as well have been in the wilderness.

Someone had left an old folding chair leaning against the wall. He opened it, turned it to face the backyard, sat down and propped his feet on the railing in front of him.

He let the darkness envelop him. Somewhere close by a bird called, and frogs were already making noises. His father should have loved growing up in this house. Why had he run away to Paris?

CHAPTER FIVE

"SORRY. I DIDN'T MEAN to wake you." Ann stood in the doorway to the little porch.

Paul sat up quickly. "I wasn't asleep." He stretched and smiled at Ann. He felt more relaxed than he had in days.

"Sure you weren't. If you'd rather skip that dinner, I've got plenty of stuff at my place. I could at least come up with a decent omelet."

"I couldn't ask you—"

"You're not asking. I am. Actually, I'm being selfish. I'd much rather cook than have to fix myself up and drive into town and back."

"You don't need fixing up."

"Oh, yes, I do." Ann laughed. "So are you game?"

"Yes, and thank you." He pulled himself out of the chair and followed Ann and Dante. His mattress sat in the middle of the bedroom floor. Ann sidestepped it neatly and went ahead down the stairs.

They walked the short distance across the square and around the three row houses to the short alley in back. The alleyway was pitch-dark. The anemic illumination of the wrought-iron streetlights around the square didn't reach over the tops of the buildings, but Ann took a small flashlight from her back pocket and switched it on. Something moved in the bushes on the far side of the alley.

Dante gave a low woof.

"Hush. It's just a cat," she said.

Something, probably the cat, banged against one of the large garbage cans at the far end, then disappeared in a streak of fur. Dante looked up at Ann beseechingly, but she grasped his collar. "No. No chasing cats."

They came to an old wooden staircase at the back of the second building. It looked as though it was ready to collapse into the small parking lot across the alley.

Paul followed Ann up to the little landing at the top and waited while she unlocked and opened her door. She turned on the lights.

Paul was no stranger to lofts. Several of his friends had invested in and restored lofts in lower Manhattan. They usually wound up modern, austere, cold and expensive.

This loft across two of the buildings was still very much a loft. Their footsteps and the click of Dante's toenails echoed on the bare hardwood floors. The doorway opened into the half that Ann used as an apartment.

Beyond it, a broad archway led into the workshop half. Since the lights came on in both at the same time, Paul could see a large worktable in the center and cabinets along the back wall.

There was also a table saw, router table, a lathe, industrial shelving with molds, brushes and all sorts of equipment Paul couldn't identify.

To the left of the door they'd come in was a galley kitchen, separated from the rest of the room by a high breakfast bar with stools. A harvest table and two benches constituted the dining room, and a heavily carved Victorian credenza served as a room divider from the living area, which was delineated with a soft, worn Oriental rug. To the right white duck curtains obviously divided the public space from bedroom and bath. The walls were the

original rose brick, and overhead naked trusses held up
the roof.

"Take a seat." Ann pointed to one of the steel stools
in front of the counter. She rummaged in a stainless-steel
refrigerator and came out with bacon, green onions, sweet
bell peppers and a carton of eggs.

"May I help?"

"Nope. I'm used to juggling stuff." She set everything
on the counter. "Would you like something to drink?
Beer? Wine?"

"White wine if you have it."

"Sure." She reached into the refrigerator, brought out
a bottle and poured them each a glass. *"Salut."*

He looked up into those wonderful gray-blue eyes of
hers. Their glances locked and held for too long. He felt
his body tighten and knew that she felt the same pull he
did.

He should never have come up here, never have allowed himself to see her in her own habitat. Not if he
intended to keep his promise to keep her at arm's length.

She broke eye contact first with a tiny gasp. The tips
of her ears were red, and she sounded brusque. "Okay,
now, you can help me chop the bell pepper." She seemed
to skitter away from him. The reluctant female, aware of
him but not certain she wanted to go any further.

Nor was he.

His gaze lighted on a pencil drawing in a simple
black frame hanging on the wall beside the refrigerator.
He was instantly certain it must be one of the caricatures his father was noted for. He wanted to leap over
the counter, rip it down and stare at it for any revelation
of the hand behind it. Instead, he said casually, "The
drawing. Is that Buddy?"

She laughed. "Look closely." She reached up, took it down and handed it to him.

He'd have known Buddy anywhere. The big bullet head with only a fuzz of hair, the black sunglasses. He wore his police uniform, but instead of a Sam Browne belt, he wore a tool belt, and instead of aiming a revolver, he pointed an electric drill. His fierce expression said he was definitely going to "drill" somebody.

In spite of himself, Paul laughed. "I'd know him anywhere. It's really good."

"Kinder than a lot of Uncle David's sketches. If he didn't like somebody or thought they needed taking down a peg, he could be really wicked. I like that one. It's Buddy to a T."

"I guess he didn't want it hanging in the police station."

"Actually, I had to beg him for it. He gave it to me for Christmas a few years ago. He couldn't very well refuse his own kid, now could he?"

Paul turned slowly toward her. "His kid?"

"Yeah. Buddy's my father. Didn't you know?"

"I had no idea. How come you call him Buddy?"

"I started when I was a teenager because I knew it got his goat. Then when we started working together, it seemed an easier way to maintain a professional relationship and reassure the clients. It's better for me to yell 'Hey, Buddy,' than 'Hey, Daddy.' Would you trust a contractor who hired his own daughter to restore your woodwork?"

"I would if the contractor were Buddy. But I understand clients might feel uncomfortable, especially if they had a complaint about your work."

"Never happens. I'm too good."

"Do you work with your father—Buddy—exclusively?"

"I try to give him first dibs, is all." She began to break eggs into a glass bowl with one-handed expertise. "He has to bid for me just like everybody else. I've just gotten back from three months in Buffalo restoring the proscenium arch of an old movie theater that's being converted into a community theater. Before that I spent a couple of months in Colorado Springs redoing woodwork for a prairie mansion that's being restored. This is actually the first job I've had this close to home since I moved back to Rossiter."

All the time she talked, she was constructing the omelet. He was impressed. He knew the way good cooks maneuvered in the kitchen.

"There are some fresh bagels in the bread box. Split us a couple, would you, and stick them in the toaster."

Paul did as she asked, then returned to his place at the counter.

He enjoyed watching her. She worked efficiently, and before long was ready to pour the omelet mixture into a hot frying pan.

"Okay. While I'm doing this, you can set the table," she said. "Place mats and silverware are in the top drawer of the Welsh dresser. I'll bring the rest. Honey all right for your bagel?"

Ten minutes later he sat down to an omelet, green salad and hot buttered bagels. He was growing mellow from his second glass of wine.

His small sojourn on his porch had begun the job of relaxing him. Sitting opposite Ann in this pleasant place completed the job. Even the ache in his shoulder had subsided. He felt Dante's heavy head against his ankle and looked down to see hungry eyes.

She noticed and said, "Don't you dare. Dante doesn't eat at the table. He'd be impossible if he ever started."

"The omelet is as good as I've ever eaten. Thanks for taking me in tonight. I promise you dinner in return." He wasn't flattering her. He hadn't realized how hungry he was until his first bite. After a moment he said, "Tell me about the artist who did that caricature."

"Uncle David tossed off those little sketches. He sold them at charity functions."

"And gave the money away?"

"He certainly didn't need it himself."

"Did he do other things—portraits, landscapes, still lifes?"

"A few portraits. He never sold anything, never had an art gallery to represent him or did a show that I'm aware of. His studio was in the old summer kitchen behind your house."

Paul caught his breath. "I haven't even tried to get into it. I assumed it was derelict. Buddy said it would probably have to come down to make way for the new garage."

"You didn't go in when you were looking at the house before you bought it?"

"It was padlocked, and Mrs. Hoddle didn't have the key. I've tried to see in the windows a couple of times, but they're filthy. The door may be old, but it's solid, and the padlock is one of those that can't be broken open even with a pistol shot."

"Don't need a pistol. Just need a good strong pair of bolt cutters. I can get you in there tomorrow morning if you like."

"Do you think there might be other drawings left after all these years?"

"Possibly. More likely the rats and mice have shredded them for nests."

"Wouldn't Trey have included any sketches he found in the estate sale?"

"Somebody else handled the details of the sale. Besides, Trey always thought his father's artist thing was a pose. He hated it. Trey and Sue-sue came by two days after Miss Addy's funeral and took what they wanted. Then the estate people moved in, set up the sale and ran it. They probably didn't even attempt to get into that summer kitchen. Must have thought it was empty the way you did. Besides, work by an unknown artist wouldn't be worth much, and most of the stuff at that sale was going for premium prices. I could barely afford the button box."

"I beg your pardon?"

"Miss Addy's button box. Come on, I'll show you. It's in the workroom."

He followed her to a shadowy corner of the workroom where a small table stood. Fitted neatly within a rim on top was a tole box less than two feet long, a foot or so wide and perhaps five inches deep. It was formed and painted to look like an old leather-bound book.

"She had the table built specially to hold it. She used to tat and sew while her students played their pieces. I was always dying to look into it, but I never did until after I bought it and brought it home."

"The title on the cover reads *Romeo and Juliet* by William Shakespeare. Interesting choice for a woman who never married."

"She didn't have it painted, silly. She bought it that way."

"So what treasure does it conceal? Or was it empty?"

"No, it was just the way she left it." Ann raised the lid. Inside lay a jumble of different colors of embroidery thread, a pair of elaborately carved silver sewing scissors, several hand-painted thimbles and forty or fifty small packets, some in yellowing envelopes, others in small plastic bags.

"Buttons," Ann said. "When women buy a new dress or blouse, usually the manufacturer includes a couple of extra buttons in case one falls off. The average woman takes the dress home, removes the little envelope with the buttons, stuffs it in a drawer, forgets where she put it and can't ever find it again when she needs it."

"Miss Addy was organized."

"She sure was. She must have inherited some of these buttons." Ann picked up one of the envelopes and opened it so that Paul could look inside. "See—these are real ivory. They're not made any longer." She put back that envelope and chose another. "And these are hand-painted cloisonné. Very old and very fine." She chose a third envelope. "These are hematite—that's a kind of jet Victorian ladies liked to use on their dresses. Some of them are museum quality. I really lucked out. I wouldn't sell this for a million dollars."

"So there actually might be something worth having in the old studio?"

"It's possible, I suppose, although I doubt it."

"I *would* like to get in there."

"Not a problem. How about another bagel?"

"No, thank you. I'm stuffed. Much better than any restaurant we could have gone to."

"I like to cook." She gestured at herself. "Like to eat, too. Honestly, I have no idea how those skinny models do it."

"They've inherited high metabolism and they starve. I know from firsthand experience."

"With stewardesses?"

"Not stewardesses any longer. Flight attendants. My fiancée was a flight attendant." He'd barely spoken of

Tracy to anyone, not even Giselle, since they'd broken up. Somehow the pain he'd been expecting at the mention of her desertion hadn't come. He felt relief, instead.

"I didn't know you were engaged."

"I'm not. She left me and married another guy."

"Oh, I'm sorry."

"Don't be. Better this way. It was my fault. After I got hurt I turned really nasty while I was recuperating. Tracy stood it as long as she could, then she left. She was right. I was impossible."

"You seem so even-tempered."

He laughed. "I was a monster."

"So you had to retire? No wonder you were a monster."

"Yeah. Look, can we change the subject?"

"Of course. Sorry."

"Tell me more about the Delaneys. Every day I'm in that house I get more curious about them." He ignored the small voice in his head that reminded him of his intention not to use Ann for information.

"Let's see, you know about the first Paul Delaney, who bought a lot of land, married a rich wife and built your house for a bunch of children he never had."

"And I know about his son Adam. And his son Barrett, the forecloser."

"Right. Barrett's son, my uncle Conrad, married my aunt Maribelle."

Paul raised his eyebrows. "Am I detecting a pattern here?"

"So tacky!" Ann laughed. "But disgustingly Southern. The Paul Delaney who built the house had some sort of weird biblical middle name like Hezekiah or Elijah. He named his son Paul Adam. Then came Paul Barrett and Paul Conrad."

"Then Paul David?" Paul asked.

"Right. And Trey's real name is Paul Edward. His son is Paul Frederick. I pray Freddie doesn't name the next generation something like Paul Gormless."

"If he does, he'd better teach the kid to fight."

"Gram says the only good thing about this stupid name business is that by the time they get past Zebediah and have to start over with Aaron and Billy Bob, we'll all be dead and gone."

Paul thought about his own middle name—Antoine. Did that perhaps signify the start of a new dynasty?

"Uncle Conrad was sweet as pie so long as he got exactly what he wanted when he wanted it. The only person he could never bully was my aunt Maribelle. *Nobody* could bully her."

Paul wanted to tell Ann about the news photo he'd seen, but couldn't think of a safe way to introduce the subject.

"Gram says he and Aunt Maribelle had the fanciest wedding since the depression began. Twelve bridesmaids and people arriving from as far away as St. Louis. Then they went to Hawaii for their honeymoon. Back in those days you had to take a ship from San Francisco. So romantic. Gram says by the time they got back they were so bored with each other she thought they'd get a divorce."

"But they didn't."

"Nope. Aunt Maribelle was pregnant with the next Delaney, and once they both got back to doing some real work, they got along fine. Too much togetherness will kill any relationship." She glanced away quickly.

Paul had an idea she wasn't talking about her great-aunt and uncle. Ann's last name was Corrigan—another reason he hadn't twigged to her relationship to Buddy.

There was apparently no husband in the picture, so she must either be divorced or widowed. She wore no wedding ring—no jewelry of any kind. Of course that could be because the chemicals she worked with would damage her jewelry.

"I assume Conrad ran the farms."

"By that time it was agribusiness—another word for a hell of a lot of land, crops and money."

"What kind of work did your aunt Maribelle do?"

"She made a career out of driving everybody nuts."

"I beg your pardon?"

"Aunt Maribelle not only had an opinion about everything, she expected that opinion to take precedence over anybody else's. One time my mother bought a sofa—a big expenditure on a policeman's salary. Aunt Maribelle took one look at it and said the color was only appropriate if we expected the dog to throw up on it nightly. I thought Gram would kill her."

She stood and began picking up the dishes. He rose to help, but she pushed him down again. "Nope. It's a one-person kitchen with a dishwasher. Want some decaf?"

"No, thanks." He really should get up, thank her for dinner and leave. "Do the Delaneys always give the oldest son the first name of Paul?"

"Actually, since the first Paul, the one that built the house, there's only been one son per generation, and he's always Paul the-next-letter-of-the-alphabet." She placed the dishes into the dishwasher, then leaned on the counter. "Suppose they'd called them the way the English did? Adam the Inheritor, Barrett the Forecloser, Conrad the Roarer…"

"What would my…Trey's father be known as?"

She thought a moment. "David the Artist? David the Drunk? Not quite right. I think he'd be David the Sad."

Paul caught his breath. So maybe his father hadn't quite gotten away with what he'd done. Maybe he had had a conscience. If so, it apparently hadn't stung him hard enough to make him confess.

Ann began to knead her left shoulder. Despite his resolution, he'd taken advantage of her. She had worked long and hard today even if he hadn't. He didn't want to leave the comfort of this room, the pleasure of her company. When he wasn't forcing himself to probe for facts, he found he was enjoying himself in a way he hadn't since long before the accident.

In the end, she solved his problem. "Go home," she said, but with a smile. "You're tired, I'm tired, and we both need to get to bed."

"You're right," he said, and stood. She followed him to the back door and flicked a switch that turned on a light above the outside landing. "Wait a minute. You'll need a flashlight or you'll break your neck on the garbage cans."

He stood with one hand on the doorknob. "The dinner was wonderful. Good night." He started to leave, then turned back to her. "Will I screw up the employer-employee relationship if I kiss you?"

Her eyes widened. "Uh—"

"Damned if I care." He slid his good arm around her waist and pulled her toward him.

She came readily into his arms, dropped the flashlight onto the floor with a clatter they both ignored and wrapped her arms around him.

God, she felt so soft. Her mouth, still sweet from the wine, opened to him. He pressed her hips against him, knew that he was already too aroused for a single kiss and didn't let her go.

She shoved him away. "I don't think this is such a good idea."

"I think it's a great idea."

"Go home. Please. Just go home." She turned away.

He caught Dante's curious eye, but the big dog made no move toward him.

"All right." He wrapped his fingers gently around her ponytail. "I still think it's a great idea. Thanks again for dinner. I owe you one."

He shut the door quietly behind him.

Halfway down the stairs to the alley he stopped. A great idea? It had been a great kiss, but a lousy idea. Hadn't he been telling himself that over and over again? Somehow whenever Ann was close to him, all his good intentions evaporated, and pure animal lust—or something—took over.

ANN HEARD his footsteps on the stairs. She wrapped her arms around herself. "No, no, no. This will not happen. He's everything I do not want in a man ever again. You hear that, Dante? No more good-looking, sweet-talking, mystery men. No more risky relationships. No more getting myself in over my head because of my heart, not to mention other parts of my body." She turned to the kitchen and began to polish the slate countertops viciously. "It's been so damn long since I went to bed with anybody, Dante. I thought maybe I was past all the sex stuff. Hah! He even asked if he could kiss me. Is that a ploy or what?" She scrubbed and dried the frying pan and hung it back on the pot rack.

Then she picked up the telephone and dialed a New York number.

"Hey, Marti, it's me."

"Good evening, Ann. If I sound cool, it's because I

am. I have not had so much as an e-mail from you for a month. Where are you? Still in Buffalo?''

"Sorry," Ann said softly. "I'm back home doing the Delaney job I told you about. I truly have been busy. And I haven't had one interesting thing to say. Boring, boring, boring."

"So now you do have something to say?"

"I need some advice. Who else would I call except my dearest girlfriend?"

"Oh, God, can it. I would like to make you grovel some more, but I'd prefer to hear about the advice thing. Advice graciously given 24/7. What have you done now?"

"Kissed a client."

"God forbid. Twenty lashes. Wait a minute. This calls for a glass of wine and a cigarette."

"Marti! I thought you'd quit."

"Yeah, yeah, yeah. I'm down to six a day. This will be the seventh, but what the hey, it's a special occasion. So what's wrong with kissing a client?"

"He is gorgeous, well-off, smart and funny, and he's restoring my favorite house in the world."

"So that's bad? What's wrong with him?"

"He's gorgeous, well-off, smart and funny, and he's restoring my favorite house in the world."

"This does not compute."

"Damn right it doesn't. I keep asking myself why, why, why? What's his agenda?"

"Why does he have to have an agenda?"

"Because men do, as you very well know."

"I know that the agenda of most of the men I meet is simply to get into my knickers," Marti responded. "Then to get out of my knickers and walk away. Do you think that's your client's agenda?"

"His ex-fiancée was a flight attendant, for God's sake!

Somebody asked one of those big rock stars—I can't remember which one—why he only dated beautiful women. Know what he said? 'Because I can.' Trust me, this guy can, too. I'm not about to be a stopgap because Rossiter is a small town with a limited pool of available flight attendants and models. I'm available, he's horny and too lazy to go cruising for somebody better.''

"Who said there was anybody better?"

"Want a list? Starting with Travis?"

"Your ex-husband never believed there was anybody *better*. He just wanted *more* women, not better ones. You were the one who wanted the divorce."

"He wanted me as a meal ticket while he pursued his career. The point is, I never figured it out. I thought we were totally in sync, saw the world the same way, saw our whole lives together the same way, were there for each other. It took me forever to get it through my head we weren't."

"Yeah. You were there, and he was in somebody else's bed."

"It hurt, dammit, Marti! Every time I caught him in another affair and bought into his promises that it would be the last time, a little bit more of my self-esteem vanished, along with a little bit more of my love for him. Finally there wasn't much left of either. I'm just starting to feel that I'm not such a loser, but I'm not ready to put my ego to another test. Certainly not against flight attendants and models."

"So, if he's Mr. Wrong, who's Mr. Right?" Marti coughed. "That's it. I quit smoking completely as of right this minute. Better I should breathe."

"Good thinking. Mr. Right is some nice, middle-aged farmer or an accountant or somebody safe with a nine-to-five job, decent prospects and the desire to settle down and raise a family."

"With a wife like you who spends nine months of the year restoring stuff all over the country?"

"I'd cut back on my job for a husband and babies, but I want somebody who would be there for *me* for a change. Somebody who was content with me and only me."

"This guy isn't?"

"How could he be? Except as an interim measure? I don't want to find out I'm being used again."

"When was the last time you went to bed with somebody?"

"You don't even want to know."

"That long? Okay, here's the deal. You don't have to be head over heels in love with a guy to have great sex with him. If it gets that far and you want to try it, then try it. If it's great, then enjoy it without getting emotionally involved."

"Oh, sure, like that's going to happen."

"If it's lousy, kiss him goodbye and go find your farmer. Lust in the dust. God, I love it."

"Marti, I wish I'd never called you."

"Other than taking another job out of town and dropping this one, I don't have any other suggestions. Unless, of course, you want to fall in love and take your chances."

"No way! For once in my life, I intend to listen to my head and not my heart." Ann hit the counter with the flat of her hand. "Ow, that hurt."

"An affair isn't so bad," Marti said. "I prefer affairs. They leave me more closet space."

"I don't think I can do affairs."

"Big surprise. I would never have guessed. Then start hunting for your farmer or your accountant and drop your— What did he retire from?"

"He was a transport pilot. He's going to be a crop duster down here."

"A pilot?" Marti groaned. "You can definitely pick 'em. Good luck, sweetie, and keep me posted. By the way, have you heard from Travis lately?"

"What makes you think I might have?"

"He called and tried to find out where you were working."

"Did you tell him?" Ann yelled into the phone so loudly that Dante jumped up in alarm.

"Of course not."

"Well, somehow he got my number in Buffalo and called me. Would you believe he wanted me to send him some money so he could get the brakes fixed on his car? 'You can't live in Los Angeles without a car, babe.'"

"I can just hear him. You sent it, didn't you, you idiot."

"Yes, all right. I sent it, but it's supposed to be a loan, not a gift."

"You should have told him to get it from whatever woman he's sleeping with at the moment."

"Marti, it's only money. That's the one thing I've got enough of at the moment."

"Well, did the bells still ring when you heard his voice?"

"I didn't even *recognize* his voice. I used to think I couldn't live if I weren't married to him. Now I just wish he could get a decent job."

"I wish he'd get boiled in oil."

"At least I've got a grip on reality finally. I don't want to lose it."

"Good luck with your gorgeous guy. Better check him out before you fall too far and too hard."

They talked for twenty minutes longer, but only in generalities. Finally Ann hung up, flung herself down on her bed, laid her head on Dante's dark flank and decided to stop worrying about the state of her heart. She'd concentrate, instead, on her libido. At least that she could control.

As she slipped into sleep, she thought, *I wonder what we'll find when we open Uncle David's studio?*

CHAPTER SIX

"ONLY A MAN would have bought a house without looking into this old place," Ann said. She peered at the padlock on the old summerhouse in Paul's backyard, then offered him the bolt cutters. Behind them, Dante was investigating some newly turned earth that was probably a molehill.

Paul reached for the cutters, then dropped his arm. This was one of the things he most despised about his injury. "Better get one of the workmen. I doubt if I can put enough pressure on them."

"It's okay. I can do it." She slipped the hasp of the lock into the jaws of the cutter, gave a couple of grunts and bore down. Paul stood by helplessly.

"There," she said as the hasp gave a satisfying snap. "Want to do the honors?"

But he was in no mood to accept her salve to his ego. "You broke it, you get to take it off."

She slipped the padlock off the hasp. "First time anybody's been in here since Uncle David died, I guess. He always kept it locked when he wasn't working and sometimes when he was. Gram said Maribelle pocketed his key to the padlock at the funeral home when they brought his body in. Watch out for snakes."

"Snakes?"

"Sure. Bound to be holes in the floor and cabinets. Toasty place for a snake to spend the winter. They haven't warmed up enough yet to run away from you. At least you should open the door. It's your building.''

Suddenly Paul felt nauseated. He did not want to touch that knob. ''You do it.''

''Okay.'' No hesitation there. Ann was unlikely to hesitate. And if there were ghosts or snakes, he couldn't think of anyone he'd rather have with him when he encountered them. The door creaked on its hinges like a bad melodrama and scraped along the floorboards as it opened. ''Shove, for Pete's sake,'' she said. ''It's stuck.''

Paul braced himself against the door and pushed. It squealed, but gave. A breath of stale air slipped past him.

Ann found the light switch beside the door and flipped it on. Nothing happened. ''Not surprising the light's blown after all these years.'' She picked up her flashlight from the doorstep and shone the beam around the space. A single bulb hung down on a black cord above their heads.

''Yuck. Watch out for black widows and brown recluse spiders. Talk about spiderwebs! Dracula's castle had nothing on this.'' She used the light to brush away the cobwebs in front of them.

Paul heard the scuttling. Mice.

Dante let out a healthy bark.

''Hush, you can't get to them, Dante,'' Ann said, then turned to Paul. ''If you'd had a lick of sense, you'd have had Daddy break that padlock, then fumigate and bait this place when he did the rest of the house.''

''I didn't think of it, and he didn't mention it.''

''Men.''

Overhead he heard a rhythmic scratching sound. At some point the room might have had a ceiling, but it had been removed so that the rafters were exposed. A large skylight not visible from outside covered nearly the entire north slope of the roof. It was so dirty that it let in almost no light, but through the gloom, Paul could see the long fingers of branches scrabbling against it like talons.

"Go away, snake!" Ann said, and stamped her feet.

Paul caught his breath.

"Just a precaution," she said. "But don't open any cabinets casually. Look, I'm going back to the house for a broom, some cleaning cloths and a couple of work lamps. You want to stay here or come with me?"

"I'll stay."

"Back in a minute."

As his eyes adjusted to the gloom, he saw several ghostly shapes. Walking carefully in case the floorboards were rotten, he inched toward a tall, sheet-covered rectangle. An easel. With a canvas on it. He pulled out his handkerchief, wrapped it around his hand and lifted the edge of the sheet, then flipped it back so that it landed on the floor.

The dust storm made him cough and started his eyes watering. "I should have waited for Ann," he said, then looked up at the canvas.

White. A big canvas with an initial coat of white sizing. His father had not began even to sketch out the picture he planned to paint.

Paul felt a stir of disappointment. A second, smaller easel sat at right angles to the first. He covered his mouth and nose with his other hand and flicked off that sheet, as well. Another blank canvas. Had his father used this room, his painting, simply as a ruse to have a private place to get stinking drunk and sleep off his stupor in privacy? Across the far wall lay another sheet on what must be a sofa of some sort. It looked like a corpse laid out for burial.

"Hey."

Paul started as Ann came in. He took the lamps from her.

"There's a plug in that overhead light fixture," she said. "Can you reach it?"

He stretched up and plugged the heavy orange cord into the plug on top of the naked bulb, then waited while Ann flipped the switch on the lamp.

"Great," she said. "Now all we have to do is to find someplace to hang it. I brought a new bulb." She reached up and hooked the light over the top of the door.

He unscrewed the broken bulb, taking care not to break it. He could see that it was rusted, but he managed to ease it out, then insert the fresh bulb. Miraculously the fixture still worked. The light chased the shadows to the far side of the room. "He was a painter. Even with the light that should be coming through that skylight, he had to have needed more light than this."

Ann pointed the flashlight toward the roof beams. "There's a couple of fluorescent lights up there. Unless they've gotten wet, they might still work. Now, how do you turn them on?"

She began to amble around the room. He watched her. There was no reason she should feel anything about this room. To Ann it was simply an interesting curiosity to be explored.

"Here we go," she said, and flicked a switch on the side of one of the waist-high cabinets that were built against three of the walls. Three of the fluorescents flickered, then lit. For the first time Paul could take a good look at the room.

He saw evidence that it had once done duty as a kitchen. In the corner by the door was a heavy double sink with old-fashioned brass faucets. Farther along the eastern wall a break in the cabinets indicated a stove must have stood there. An aged and possibly deadly portable electric heater now occupied the space. The stove pipe that would have vented the stove outside had been left attached to the wall with only a cap at the lower end to keep any vermin out.

Ann walked over to the couch and tossed back the sheet that covered it.

"Wow," she said, and coughed, "Look at this."

It was a Victorian recamier elaborately carved to resemble a swan. The back of the recamier was a lifted wing, the couch itself nestled where the swan's body would have been. Since his father's death it had obviously become not only a home but a source of building materials for the mice that had moved in when the place was padlocked.

"Real horsehair," Ann said, "or what remains of it. Ever sit on horsehair? It's slick as glass and not nearly as comfortable." A couple of aged pillows and a filthy patchwork quilt were laid neatly on the end of the sofa. The down from the pillows lay around the floor by the sofa like snow. He thought he could see holes in the patchwork. "This is wonderful. You'll have to have it reupholstered after I restore it—you do want it in the house, don't you?"

He wasn't sure he did, but she seemed so eager he didn't have the heart to disappoint her. "Of course. If you make it decent again."

"I know just where to put it." She began to wander again. "Wonder where he kept his liquor?" She spotted the two white canvases. "Maybe he didn't even try to paint, just came out here to get sozzled."

On one of the counters sat a dusty portable record player with a few records in their sleeves beside it. Ann picked one up and blew a cloud of dust off it. "Edith

Piaf. Great singer, but she could drive even a *happy* man to suicide.''

Paul watched her move around the room. Let her do the exploring. He found he didn't want to touch this stuff. It gave him the creeps to see the sad remnants of his father's life. How could a man who had done that perceptive sketch of Buddy sink so far into alcoholism and despair that he simply sized canvases on which he couldn't lay down even a single stroke?

''You said Maribelle wouldn't let anyone in here after he died?'' he asked.

''She must have come in at least once. I doubt that Uncle David draped that couch or those canvases as an ordinary thing. That must have been done after he was dead. Maribelle always said he had left strict instructions with her that this place was not to be disturbed if something happened to him.'' She shrugged. ''But according to my grandmother, Aunt Maribelle would say anything if it got her what she wanted. I can't see her simply tossing sheets on stuff and walking out without at least peeking into the cupboards, can you? I sure couldn't.''

''I don't think I could, either. But she was grief-stricken, remember. She'd lost her husband...''

''Then she saw her son die.''

He gaped at her. ''She saw it?''

''She was riding right behind him. She was a whip.''

''And that is?''

''A whipper-in. There are usually two or three on every hunt. They're in charge of keeping the hounds in order. She was one of the first to reach him.''

''She must have been—what?—in her sixties at the time?''

''So?''

He remembered that picture of mother and son in hunting gear. He'd assumed it had been taken years before his father's accident. "She was still riding horses over fences?"

"I certainly expect to be riding over fences when I'm ninety."

Paul shook his head. "I keep thinking of her as a Southern lady wearing white gloves and a hat." Despite the picture, he still thought of her that way. A formidable lady, maybe, but still a lady.

"Hah. I don't think she put on a hat except for church on Sunday. Your views of little old Southern ladies are about three generations out of date. Aunt Maribelle drove tractors and cotton pickers and exercised horses and drove her pickup truck like a maniac almost up to the day she died. Now, if you want a little old Southern lady, Aunt Addy played the part to a T, but in her way she was stronger and tougher than Maribelle."

"How so?"

"Can't have been easy being the poor relation living with your rich sister and teaching piano lessons out of the music room. Addy must have bitten her tongue so often it's a miracle she still had one."

As she talked, Ann had been wandering around the room with her broom brushing cobwebs off countertops and ceiling beams. She wasn't following any particular pattern or showing any urgency. Now she stopped in front of the cabinet beside the sink and hunkered down.

"Watch it," he said. "Snakes, remember?"

"No self-respecting snake would stick around with all the noise we've been making," Ann said. "At least I hope not." She pulled a pair of heavy work gloves out of the waistband of her jeans, slipped them on and gingerly opened one of the cabinet doors.

She picked up her flashlight and pointed it inside.

"Aha! The stash." She reached in, pulled out a liquor bottle and blew a cloud of dust off it. "Uncle David did himself proud, I'll say that for him. Napoleon brandy— very old, very fine." She set the bottle on the counter and pulled out another. "Jack Daniel's Black Label. Tons of it. His drink of choice." She pulled out a heavy crystal glass. It was filthy, but obviously fine.

Ann set it on the counter. "Okay. Now assuming you were a painter and were actually painting, what would you need?"

"Paints, brushes, palettes, turpentine, charcoal pencils canvas, paper—I'm no artist."

"Good start. He was always fastidious, but my grand-mother said that was just because he was always drunk. He had that squeaky-clean look that so many real alcoholics get. He always smelled of aftershave and pepper-mint."

Ann began opening the rest of the cupboards and re-citing her inventory. He knew he should help, but he sim-ply could not bear to touch the things that his father must have touched, possibly might have loved.

"Here we go—the oil paint in the tubes is still squishy. Pencils, sketch pads…"

"Anything on them?"

"Blank." She held out a block of sketch paper to him, then set it on top of the counter. "Blank, blank, blank. Poor guy. Looks as if his muse abandoned him."

"Probably chased off by Bacchus."

She looked up at him. "That bothers you, doesn't it? The whole alcohol thing, I mean."

"Yes, it bothers me." He hoped his tone would cut off any discussion. "Alcohol has never been my drug of choice."

"What is?" She looked up at him curiously.

"Flying."

"Oh." She gave a small nod and moved to the next cabinet. In twenty minutes all the tools of an artist were spread on the tops of the cabinets.

"He must have done some work sometime," Paul said. "More than the quick caricatures, I mean. If he never sold or showed anything, he had to have done something with his finished canvases."

"Maybe he destroyed them. More likely, Aunt Maribelle destroyed everything she found distasteful. His paintings might have been as wicked as his caricatures."

"Would she destroy his things?"

Ann chewed on her bottom lip. "I can't see it, personally. In Aunt Maribelle's eyes, Uncle David could do no wrong. She must have thought his work was genius. That was all of him that was left. Why would she destroy it?"

"So maybe he didn't want anybody to see what he was working on." He moved around the room. "Why hide anything? The place was padlocked. He had the only key."

Ann laughed. "You can bet Maribelle had a duplicate key long before she snatched up the one he had with him when he died. Maybe she didn't use it very often, but it wouldn't surprise me if she snuck in here to check up on him when he wasn't around. Besides, what if he passed out in here or the place caught fire after he'd locked himself in? I certainly would want to be able to get in fast if my son were drinking and playing with turpentine in a room with an open wall heater."

"Maybe there wasn't anything to destroy."

"I don't believe that," Ann said. "Gram says he always had little bits of paint under his fingernails even after he scrubbed himself raw." She peered around the room. "Either Maribelle took everything with her when she closed the place up, in which case it should have been among her things after she died, or Uncle David took the stuff somewhere else, which I doubt, or he hid it.''

''Why hide it?''

''If I guessed that Aunt Maribelle would sneak in, you can bet he knew, or at least suspected. He may have left one of those James Bond traps for her—you know, the matchstick in the doorjamb.''

''Wouldn't he have confronted her after the first time he caught her?''

''You're joking, or you come from a whole lot more functional family than most. I'll bet it became a cat-and-mouse game with them. Both of them knew, and neither of them said anything. But he would have grown more and more secretive.''

''She wouldn't have been able to actually search, would she?'' Paul said. ''Not until after his death.''

''Wouldn't think so. One invasion she could blame on Esther's wanting to clean up in here. Once he'd told her that he didn't want anyone to clean up after him, she wouldn't be able to get away with that.''

''And Esther was?''

''Housekeeper, cook, maid. After Aunt Maribelle died she moved in to look after Aunt Addy. Stayed with her until the end.''

''Is she still alive?''

''Lives on a pension about four houses down the street from your house.''

''Do you think she'd like visitors?''

Ann laughed. ''Esther? She'd love to meet you. Probably sit you down with a glass of sweet tea and a plate of cookies and talk your ears off about the glory days.''

Perfect. Paul suspected that Esther knew a great deal more about the Delaneys than they knew about her. He made a mental note to take her some flowers and some candy and pay a neighborly call. He realized Ann had said something. "What? Sorry, I was thinking about something else."

"I said that somewhere there should be finished paintings."

"Maybe he kept them in the house he built for his family."

"I doubt it. If so, they may well be gone. His wife, my aunt Karen, hated the time he spent painting. Gram says she treated his painting like a mistress."

"I can understand that if he refused to share what he was doing with her." He grinned at Ann. "Women hate that."

"Oh, we do, do we?" Ann turned around. "His work wouldn't be worth anything, you know," Ann said. "He was just an amateur. Nobody outside of Rossiter ever heard of him."

"They'd have sentimental value, perhaps, to the family—his son, say, or even your grandmother. The rest of the family apparently did not resent the time he spent painting."

"The rest of the family sure would like to have them. Gram's got a sketch he did of her framed on the wall of her bedroom. Not a caricature—a real portrait. She loved his stuff."

"Then if we start with the assumption that he left at least a few things here, where do we look?"

"Not the floor. There's nothing under the floor but dirt." Ann looked up. "Not the rafters, either. Too hard to get up and down and there's no ladder in here. Baseboards maybe, or false backs to the cabinets." She wandered over to stand in front of the two blank canvases. "What would you do if you didn't want to throw something away, but you didn't much want anybody looking at it, either?''

"Disguise it some way," Paul said.

"Mm-hmm." She picked up a broad paintbrush from the cabinet nearest to the white canvases. "This brush is stiff as concrete. See all the white paint in the bristles?"

"He used it to size the canvases."

"Or somebody did." She picked up the can of white sizing paint. The lid was slightly askew. The contents had long since solidified with a skim of pure oil on top. "This is a pretty neat room for an artist's studio, wouldn't you say?"

"You said he was a neat freak."

"Wash those boar's-hair brushes of his out in a little warm water and soap, they'd be as good today as they ever were. He cleaned them and stored them properly. Same thing with his oil paints and even his charcoal and pencils. Amazing when he must have been falling-down drunk half the time he was in here. I can tell you the twist tops of my paints are never that clean. Neither is the top of my toothpaste tube. But those tops are pristine. No oozing paint at all. Arranged by color. Even his palettes are orderly."

"But well used. So he must have actually painted at some point. There should be finished paintings here, or at least color sketches."

"Either he had a premonition of his death, or some-one—most likely Maribelle—could have painted over those two canvases at the same time she sheeted the furniture."

"Why?"

"Maybe they were still wet. She may have thought that painting over them would destroy them. A lot of people think that."

"And it's not true?"

"Not usually. Not unless the paint was really runny. If we had an X-ray machine, we could see whether there was anything under that white layer."

"But we don't."

She grinned at him. "There's an easier way, if you're willing to trust me."

"You want a shot at cleaning them? Can you do that? Without ruining what's underneath, I mean?"

"Easy. It's not like this is Michelangelo's stuff with four hundred years of grime embedded in the varnish. This is almost like whitewash. I can go at it with a towel and some alcohol. Should come right off. Do you want to see what's under there?"

"If anything."

"Sure, if anything. I'm dying to see, but they're technically your property."

"Have at it. Should I stay?"

She shook her head. "I'll go after the little one first. Why don't you run next door and get us a couple of burgers and some tea at the Wolf River? This is pretty boring stuff."

"Right." One part of him wanted to run from the little house and never return. The other part wanted to watch every flake of white paint come off that canvas. He didn't dare let Ann see how passionately interested he was. He went to get lunch.

With the crowd already standing in line for tables at the café, it took him more than twenty minutes to get his take-out order. He'd found the gap in the overgrown hedge that allowed him access to his own backyard without going along the street, and he used it now to slip back into his own yard. He nodded to several workmen as he passed, but didn't stop to speak.

He could see the light through the open door of the studio and heard Ann whistling what sounded like an Irish jig. Since his hands were full, he kicked the open door to let her know he was back.

"Hey!" she said happily. "No wonder Maribelle covered this up."

He set the food on the nearest counter. Dante sat down at his feet and stared up at him balefully.

"Not for you, boy," Ann said. "Wait a second before you look. I'm not through with the background, but I've got the center cleaned off. Maribelle would have definitely hated this." She dropped her hand. "Okay, come look."

His father had been a superb portraitist. The picture had the same insight he'd seen in Buddy's caricature. This, however, was serious. Ann had managed to clean the figure completely. Some of the background had been brought to light, as well. He caught snatches of what must be cotton fields.

"Who is she?" he whispered.

"Maribelle."

He'd seen a picture of her only in that grainy old newspaper print, but in another minute he'd have recognized her, although this showed a much different woman.

He'd seen the last series of portraits Rubens had done of Catherine de Medici. She must have hated them. In each one she grew older, fatter and meaner-looking. This woman was leaner than Catherine, almost masculine, with muscular arms ropey with age. She stood leaning on a saddle that sat on a rack beside her. Much of the saddle was still covered by the white paint, but enough was visible to discern what it was. She wore a short-sleeved red polo shirt open at the neck. The artist hadn't backed away from the liver spots on her hands or the sun-damaged ostrichlike skin revealed at the neck of her shirt. Her brown hair was pulled back tight and tied with a scarf. A theatrically placed streak of white arched from her left temple to disappear behind her head.

Paul could see that she must have been a great beauty as a young woman. In some ways she still was. Bones that perfect, a face that oval, eyes that wide would not fail her if she lived to be two hundred years old. Her eagle's nose gave character to a face that might otherwise have been bland.

No—never bland. Abraham Lincoln once said any man over forty is responsible for his face. If the same held true for women, then this was the most formidable woman he had ever seen—she made Catherine de Medici look like Mary Poppins.

If Paul had been able to put words into her mouth, he thought they would be something like "I am entitled." No hint of insecurity, of compassion, of empathy in those eyes and that full mouth. A woman capable of great passion, certainly, but love? Paul wasn't so sure about that.

She would have acquired what she wanted and devil take the hindmost. His father had caught that quality in this portrait. He had painted her with vision, with talent, but without much love. He had seen her much too clearly for a loving son.

Wasn't there a poem somewhere that said something like "look on me and be afraid?"

"Man." Ann whispered. "Can you see Aunt Maribelle hanging that over the living-room fireplace?"

"Not if it's a true likeness."

"Too damned true. I'd love to have Gram take a look at this. Would you mind? After I've finished cleaning it, that is?"

"Not if I can be with you when you show it to her."

"Sure. She loved talking to you at lunch the other day.

Get her started and she'll regale you with tales of Rossiter for hours.''

He dragged his gaze from the face in the portrait. His grandmother. Maybe it was best his mother had never met her. He didn't think Michelle Bouvet Delaney from Paris, France, would have been happily accepted by this Delaney doyenne. He turned to the larger canvas. ''What about the other one?''

''Hey, give me time. Besides, I'm hungry.''

They sat on the steps of the little house and ate their burgers while Dante lay at their feet and sighed deeply every few minutes.

Even in its tangled state the garden was being forced into life by the coming of spring. Paul didn't want to lose the wild spirit the garden had developed on its own. He didn't think it should be straitjacketed into something formal, but it might be teased into something lovely.

After lunch, Ann picked up the trash, saw nothing to use as a garbage can and set the box in which their things had come on the counter. ''We'll take this stuff with us when we leave. No sense in leaving more goodies for the mice.''

Paul was champing at the bit to see what lay under the paint on the other canvas, but he couldn't let his impatience show.

Ann stood in the center of the room with her hands on her hips and turned around in a slow circle. ''There's got to be more stuff here somewhere,'' she said. ''I can almost taste it.'' She grinned at him. ''It's not psychic ability, although I wish to God I had some. Sometimes I just get a sense about bits and pieces hidden in old places.''

''You said maybe baseboards. Should we try to loosen them? Or tap the backs of the cupboards?''

''Guess we'll have to. You don't have to stick around

if you've got stuff to do and if you'll give me leave to do things on my own. I may have to be destructive.''

"I'll stay," Paul said. As if he could have been driven away by a tank. "Shall I go get us a couple of crowbars?''

"In a minute. Buddy says this place will probably have to come down, but I'd rather not start destroying it right now if we can help it." Ann folded her arms across her chest and frowned at the room. "I know where people hide stuff. I've done this for years. I ought to be able to figure it out."

She hopped up on one of the counters that was free of painting gear. He leaned against the wall beside the door and simply watched her.

He enjoyed watching her under any circumstances. This, however, was different. It was like watching a football coach plan a touchdown drive, or a pilot plot crosswinds so that he didn't land in the sea, instead of on the deck of his carrier. Paul knew better than to break her concentration.

She sat back against the wall and closed her eyes. She wrapped her arms around herself and began to swing her legs.

Suddenly she straightened and opened her eyes. "Oh, my."

"What?"

"Look, I may be wrong. He would have wanted easy access, right? He needed to stash stuff where he could take it out again. He was probably too drunk half the time to unscrew baseboards or build hidey-holes in the backs of his cupboards. Even his sketch pads are fairly large and unwieldy." She wiggled her eyebrows at him. "I've a good mind to tell you to go outside while I look so I can say 'ta-da' like a magician if I'm right and not get your hopes up if I'm wrong."

"Not a chance."

"Okay." She hopped off the counter. "Hand me that palette knife, will you?"

He did.

She moved to the space heater, raised her hand and whacked the stove pipe. Instead of the metallic ring that should have come from the pipe, Paul heard only a thunk.

Ann turned around and bowed. "Ta-da. There *is* something in there. It may be rotten, it may have disintegrated, it may be the carcass of a possum long deceased, but something is definitely there." She began to scrape the rust around the end cap with her palette knife. "Don't get your hopes up."

He moved her out of the way, wrapped his handkerchief around the metal cap, put both hands around it and twisted. He felt a tiny movement and heard an even tinier metallic squeal.

"Come on," Ann said. She sounded excited.

He planted his feet and twisted harder, ignoring the pain in his shoulder. He felt the cap give a centimeter or two, then without warning, it simply twisted loose. He wasn't expecting it and nearly fell over the space heater. She grabbed his arm.

Nothing had fallen out except a shower of soot. His lungs deflated.

The stove pipe was broader than the diameter of a hand—six or seven inches—and ran straight up the wall for a good four feet before it made a right-angle turn to cut through the wall.

Ann gave the pipe a couple of hard whacks with the palette knife. "Get rid of any varmints," she said. Then she stuck her gloved hand up the pipe. "Damn!"

"Nothing?"

"No, there's something. I can't quite reach it."

"My arm's longer than yours. Let me try."

She stepped aside.

This time he managed to grasp the edge of whatever it was. At first he thought he wouldn't be able to budge it, but it began to slide and suddenly fell to the floor at his feet.

It was some sort of plastic mailing tube nearly as big as the pipe and almost as long. It was filthy and covered with cobwebs, but as far as he could see, it had escaped the teeth of rats and mice.

Ann picked it up and took it to the counter under the skylight. A plastic cap had been plugged into the end of it. She grasped it with her fingernails, pulled it out and upended the tube. The tiniest edge of white paper showed. She grasped it carefully and began to pull. "I can feel sketch paper and what feels like watercolor paper. Maybe there are some canvases rolled up inside," she said. "It seems perfectly preserved. Hand me a couple of those cans of turpentine. I need something heavy to set on the edges while we unroll it."

Paul leaned over her and held down one side as Ann gently rolled the paper out. The sheets inside were of differing textures and sizes. The one on the top was a charcoal drawing of a street scene in the rain. He recognized the Champs Elysées and the Arc de Triomphe. A standard subject for an art student in Paris.

"Lovely," breathed Ann. "Leave it flat. We shouldn't roll it back up again. Don't want to break any more fibers if we can help it."

Paul gently moved the single sheet of paper to one of the countertops and used another pair of cans to hold down the edges.

"Oh, look at this one!"

Paul peered over her shoulder. It was a pastel portrait

of a boy about two years old. The blue eyes were mischievous, and a shock of unruly blond hair fell across the forehead. Paul had seen that shock of hair. The blue eyes were still mischievous, although there were fine lines around them. Trey Delaney. Couldn't be anyone else.

"It's charming. Why would he hide this?" Ann asked.

"No idea. It's really good." He thought for a moment. "Do you think your aunt Karen might want it?"

"You know she would! I don't think she has any of Uncle David's work." She grasped his arm. "Would you give it to her?"

"Of course. But I'd like to present it in person."

"Sure. When?"

"As soon as possible, don't you think? Where does she live?"

"In town. She remarried not long after Uncle David was killed. Trey has a half brother and half sister. They're much younger. I don't think they communicate much—at least I didn't see them at the Fourth of July barbecue. Any mother would love to have a picture like this. He's captured that catch-me-if-you-can look Trey still has."

"Would you call her for me? Maybe come along to introduce me?"

"Perfect. I'm dying to see her face when you give her this." She sounded excited. "How about I find out if she's free tomorrow afternoon? Assuming you are."

"Where else would I be? It's too early to start crop dusting. Yeah. Tomorrow afternoon would be fine." He kept his tone even although his heart was in his mouth at the prospect of interviewing the woman who'd taken his mother's husband from her. He laid the pastel carefully on top of the Paris scene and moved the cans to keep it flat.

"Whew!" Ann said from behind him.

He turned back and his breath caught.

The girl his father had sketched looked back over her shoulder, laughing. Her long dark hair blew in the wind. For a moment he didn't recognize this laughing innocent, so full of life, so joyous. In the only photo he had of her, she looked as though she'd been through a war—tired, much too thin, older than her years, unsmiling, and that wonderful hair dragged back into a tight chignon at the back of her neck.

"She's lovely," Ann said. "I wonder who she was."

He nearly said, *My mother*. He stopped himself just in time.

"Let's see if he did any more like that."

As each sheet peeled away, they saw pose after pose of the same girl, joyful, in the rain, in the sun, laughing up at the snow, eating an ice-cream cone, licking the stuff off her nose. Some were fast charcoal sketches, but many were watercolors. In all of them only the figure of the girl was finished.

"He put the landscape on top so that if anybody found them, they might not look any further," Ann said. "Poor guy. I don't know who she was, but he was obviously nuts about her."

Maybe in the first flush of their relationship he *had* loved her. That made his betrayal even more hateful. How could he have drawn her like this with something akin to worship and yet have run away to hide in America only a few months after they'd married?

They were down to the last four of five sheets. Paul didn't think he could endure even one more sketch of that laughing girl. He had never heard her laugh. Not once in the six years she'd been with him.

"Here we go," Ann said as she used her hands to spread the picture. "I was wondering why they were all

just head-and-shoulder portraits. These make Wyeth's
Helga portraits look chaste.''

The watercolor took his breath away. The girl was no
longer a girl. She was a woman, beautiful, passionate,
sated with love, naked on her lover's bed, open, vulnerable. Her hair lay tossed against the pillows, her lips were
swollen, her eyes drowsy.

''Roll it up,'' Paul said. He turned away quickly.

''I never pictured you as a prude,'' Ann said. ''This is
lovely.''

''It's intrusive.''

''It certainly is. There was nobody else in that room
except the woman and the painter. Obviously she was
Uncle David's mistress.''

Paul wanted to scream, *She was his wife!* Instead, he
gritted his teeth and kept his mouth shut.

''Okay,'' Ann said. ''I've rolled it back up. Be careful.
It's beautiful and possibly valuable.''

He turned away after a single glance at the next picture.
How could his father have seen this woman's love for
him so clearly, put it down on paper so perfectly, and
then left her? His love for her was in every brushstroke.
How could he have deceived her so viciously? Destroyed
her? Because that was what he'd done. The woman in
these pictures had truly died in spirit long before her son
had been born, when she realized she'd been abandoned.
She might have breathed afterward, but there was no real
life in her.

Ann unrolled the last watercolor. He heard her breath
catch. ''Okay, this one you can look at.''

He glanced at it, then moved closer. Her head drooped
forward. Her long hair curtained and concealed most of
her face. The picture spoke of sorrow and loss.

He caught his breath. Could his father have drawn this

from memory? Could he have sketched it just before he left her in Paris to come home?

Or did he sketch her from life just before he killed her?

PAUL SPENT the afternoon flying his Cessna. He hadn't done much flying since he'd flown his plane down, and he needed to clear his head. He'd wanted to find his father, learn what made the man tick. Now Paul had to accept the evidence of his own eyes, even if it didn't jibe with what he wanted to believe. Maybe a couple of hours in the clouds would help him focus.

He definitely needed to avoid becoming too involved with Ann. Not only for his sake, but for hers. At the end of this quest, he, too, would have to walk away as his father had done. He must not leave a brokenhearted woman behind.

Not that avoiding a relationship with Ann would be easy. The more he knew her, the more comfortable he became with her, the more he wondered whether, if there was a woman in the world for him. Ann was that woman.

The question was, should he give up his desire to punish his father and find his mother's grave to pursue Ann on the off chance they could be happy together?

No. This mission had been the driving force in his life for too long. In school, in the academy, afterward in the air he'd tried to let it go. Sometimes he wouldn't think about his mother's death for weeks at a time, then something would trigger his anger. He'd see Tante Helaine's face begging him to avenge his mother's death, to give her a decent burial in consecrated ground.

His anger had been less than useless until he'd seen the evidence Tante Helaine had kept hidden all those years, but now, he had a real goal in life for the first time. Not revenge, but justice.

Justice? For whom? His mother? She was beyond caring. His family? Tante Helaine was also beyond caring. Giselle wasn't interested in revenge. And as for Trey, Paul didn't truly believe the sins of the father should be taken out on the sons.

But wasn't that what had happened to him all his life? His father's sins had shaped him, walled him off from any real intimacy.

He wanted the whole affair over. Maybe then he'd be able to find some peace.

Without Ann? Without Rossiter? Without these people who were, whether they knew it or not, his family?

The only alternative was to drop the whole thing now, sell the house and find himself a desert island somewhere.

Not good enough.

He'd bull his way through and hope to God there would be some forgiveness for him in the Rossiter hearts. In Ann's heart. But he didn't think there would be.

When he got back to the house, the workmen were packing up for the day. Buddy met him in the front hall. He was wearing his police uniform. "I'm about to go on patrol. all the chimneys are in good shape, apparently," Buddy said cheerfully. "They need cleaning, of course, but the tuck pointing's fine. I've got the plans for your new kitchen and some sample cabinets and countertops. They're in the kitchen. Look them over tonight, why don't you. Then tomorrow we can make any changes and start tearing out the wall between the kitchen and the butler's pantry."

"Sounds good."

"And I've got Jim Bob, the landscaper, coming at eight in the morning. He's going to look over the garden and design a plan. Time to start clearing and planting."

"Fine."

"Wiring's just about done. Heating and air-conditioning should be installed by the end of the week."

"Telephone lines?"

"That's going to take some time," Buddy said apologetically. "Have to work by their schedule, and sometimes they're slow as molasses in January."

"What about the work on the house itself?"

"Termite inspection was this afternoon while you were gone. It's not nearly as bad as I thought. Probably take us a couple of weeks to get all the bad wood replaced."

"Plumbing?"

"You did say you wanted to keep the bathrooms as close to the period as you could, right?"

Paul nodded.

"That means replacing the broken tile, one toilet and matching a couple of pedestal sinks. When we open the wall we can create a dressing room, as well as a closet for the master bedroom."

"Frankly I'm overwhelmed. In any case it sounds as though you have everything in hand. How's Ann doing?"

"I haven't seen her all day. I think she's been out there in that summer kitchen."

The pager on Buddy's belt buzzed. He clicked it on and read the message. "Damn! Some idiot just drove off the road east of town. I've got to go."

Paul walked through the back hall, out the back door and onto the brick patio. He could see a faint shimmer of light coming through the dirty skylight and the grimy side window of the studio. He picked his way to the door and knocked on the frame. "Just me."

"Great," Ann called.

He walked in.

The windows weren't the only grimy thing in the studio. Ann's jeans and shirt were covered in splotches of white paint. Her face and hair were smudged, too. The dirt from the room seemed to have gravitated to her. He thought he saw a cobweb hanging from the bedraggled scarf she'd used to tie back her hair.

The face she turned to him, however, was radiant. So radiant he felt a jolt when he looked at her. She shared none of his ambivalence. She knew nothing of the quandary he was in. She was simply delighted with a good job.

"It's the other canvas—the big one," Ann said. "It wasn't completely set when it was painted over, so I had to be very careful not to smear the paint underneath. I think you ought to see it."

Paul wasn't certain he wanted to, but couldn't think of an excuse to avoid it. He moved slowly to Ann's end of the room. What he really wanted was to bury his face in her hair, wrap his arms around her and walk away from this whole thing. He couldn't do that, either.

"Look at the picture," Ann said quietly.

He blew out a breath and walked around the canvas. He felt his stomach lurch. It was a self-portrait that might have come out of Dorian Gray's attic. The only photo he had of his father showed a young man full of energy and drive. And love.

This was the portrait of a man in mortal agony.

His mouth was open and slack. His left hand reached forward as though to save himself from falling. Paul didn't recognize the woman he reached out to. She was turned away, unseeing of his gesture.

"Who is she?" he asked.

"That's Aunt Karen, his wife. They seem cut off from one another. It's so sad."

His father had barely begun to sketch in another figure behind him, reaching out to him. The figure was still without a face, but Paul felt certain it was to have been his mother. The man in the portrait was turned away from her and toward Karen. He didn't know that she was there.

Had his grief over the murder he'd committed driven him to paint this picture? The man in the painting was in pain, but he was also guilty. Paul looked away, unable to bear the suffering in the figure's face. How could he hate a man who'd been in such pain?

Easy. Paul's father might have suffered, but he suffered in luxury surrounded by wealth, privilege, approbation.

While Paul's mother lay in an unmarked grave.

While her sister died, still mourning her.

While her son grew up with people who were not his parents.

No. Even from beyond the grave, his father had to pay for what he had done.

CHAPTER SEVEN

"YOU SURE YOU DON'T WANT to bring these sketches and paintings to your house?" Ann asked. She was folding up the dingy sheets that had covered the pictures.

"They've been safe in the studio all these years. They should be safe another couple of nights."

"From mice? I don't think so. Not any longer."

He sighed. "All right. We'll move them into the house."

"They'll get filthy with all the work going on. How about I take them to my place? I've got closed cupboards in the workroom where they'll be safe. I can flatten the sketches out properly and keep the paintings out of direct light. I don't have mice. Dante and the local cat see to that."

"If you think that's best."

"I do. I don't want anything to happen to them. How about I bring my truck around here, we load up the portraits and the drawings, and move them right this minute?"

"They'll fit in the back of my car."

"Yeah, but Dante won't." She touched his arm. "Be right back. Come on, Dante, you can run better than that, you old fat thing."

He considered going back in and staring at the portraits, but decided he'd had enough revelations for one day. Nothing seemed to add up about his father. If he'd loved his mother once, when had he stopped? He'd *married* her, for God's sake. Tante Helaine said he married her because he couldn't entice her into his bed any other way. That might be partly true. Still, his mother had told him his father had planned to live in Paris the rest of his life.

Lieutenant Pinkerton had married Madame Butterfly and abandoned her. Had his father wanted to marry an *American* girl? Had he felt that marriage to a *French* girl in France did not bind him?

Paul had news for him. If there was one thing the French were good at, it was legalities. David Delaney had used his address in Paris on the marriage license, and the marriage banns had been posted in his *arondissement* rather than in Michelle's neighborhood where her parents might spot the announcement. That made no difference. The marriage was legal in France, and by extension, the whole world.

It was sheer luck that they had managed to pull it off. Banns stayed posted for three weeks. Any time during that period a friend or neighbor of the Bouvets might have happened upon the names of Michelle Bouvet and Paul David Delaney on the banns and queried the Bouvets.

Maybe David Delaney had counted on just that. If he'd offered to marry Michelle and been thwarted, she might have turned to him in disappointment and come to his bed, anyway.

But in the end the marriage had taken place. Paul hadn't inherited much from his mother, but he did have her *livret de famille*—the little red book that constituted a decree of marriage in France. His name was entered on the first page devoted to children of the union. There he was listed as Paul Antoine Bouvet Delaney. When they came to the States to live with Tante Helaine and Uncle Charlie, his mother had decided he should use her parents' name, Bouvet. Tante Helaine said she'd rather not have to explain the circumstances of being Delaney.

Paul thought Michelle must have been embarrassed, as well as angry and sad at her husband's duplicity. Tante Helaine had berated her again and again about allowing her husband to spin falsehood after falsehood about who he was and where he came from.

After his mother disappeared to look for his father, when Tante Helaine was filling his ears for the umpteenth time with the story, she'd always tell him, "I could not believe she had married the man without once looking at his passport. She didn't copy down the number or the information." Helaine would throw up her hands. "If I had still been in France, I would not have allowed her to be so naive."

He knew from Helaine that Michelle's parents had been furious when her pregnancy had forced her to tell them about her marriage. They'd threatened to throw their younger daughter out on the streets until Helaine called them from Queens and convinced them to forgive her.

It had been bad enough when Helaine had married her GI, Charlie, and moved to the States. In New York their elder daughter was as good as lost to them. They never saw their grandchildren. They didn't particularly like Americans. Everyone knew they were crude and loud and had no idea how to hold their cutlery.

Michelle was supposed to marry a hardworking provider who could take over the business when her parents retired, give them grandchildren to spoil and help support them in their old age.

Suddenly she'd betrayed them by marrying in secret— and another American at that. Then she allowed him to desert her and leave her *enceinte*—with a baby on the way. Another mouth to feed. Not a child they would enjoy spoiling, but a burden.

And Michelle was no longer a marketable commodity. She refused even to consider requesting an annulment, though they argued and threatened and begged her to try for their sakes, as well as her own.

Michelle swore that her David had not deserted her, that he would be back to claim her and live with her in Paris as a good French father should. Even after the letters she sent to him were returned ''address unknown,'' even after she faced a blank wall when neither the American military nor the American embassy would help her find him, she still swore that he loved her and would come back for her.

But he never knew about the baby she was expecting. They'd agreed not to have children until his career as an artist was well under way.

Tante Helaine had told him that David's mother had continued to send him money in Paris secretly until he'd returned to the States. His father cut him off after he chose to leave the army in Europe, rather than return to the States. Conrad must have felt that if he deprived David of money, sooner or later he'd get sick of poverty and come home.

Even with the money his mother sent, David was still poor. Michelle lived at home after their marriage. Their only moments as husband and wife had been stolen on afternoons when she told her parents she was studying or nights when she swore she was staying over with a girl-friend.

Years after his mother disappeared and Tante Helaine knew she, too, was dying, she'd finally told him how his mother came to get pregnant so soon after the marriage. Helaine had met and fallen for Corporal Charles Parker in France and had married him five years before Michelle met David Delaney. Despite her parents' disapproval of the union to an American, she'd had a decent wedding in a church before she moved to the States.

She'd had sense enough to start a baby right away, Helaine said, whatever she and Charlie had agreed on. As a good Catholic, she wasn't supposed to use birth control, anyway, but Charlie insisted.

"But one has ways," Helaine said. By the time Paul's conversation with his aunt took place, Uncle Charlie was dead of lung cancer and Tante Helaine was failing. "I wrote your mother and told her how to do it," she said with satisfaction. "The American GIs all bought their *capots*—their condoms—in the PX, and her David still had a large supply after he left the army to move to Paris. They come in these small square foil packets."

As if Paul hadn't known since he was thirteen what condoms looked like.

"They are very good, very safe. The Americans depended on them. But even the safest birth control can fail." The old lady had grinned like a child who has discovered a way to steal candy without being caught.

"I wrote Michelle from America and told her that she must become pregnant at once. Otherwise it would be too easy for her David to leave her. It is only a matter of heating a needle very hot and piercing through the foil and into the little condom rolled up beneath. Very simple."

"But the hole would be tiny. Surely it wouldn't work."

Tante Helaine laughed. "Michelle was eighteen and a virgin when she married. Even one small hole would be enough if the time of the month were right. She took all the condoms from David's bedside table while he was out painting in the gardens of the Louvre, she used her needle, and poof, she was pregnant.''

At that point Tante Helaine had become sad. ''If I had known that he would abandon her, I would never have taught her my little trick.''

At that point she'd stroked his cheek. ''But you were a blessing, *cher* Paul. God took my sister, but He gave you to me because I could not give Charlie any sons.''

He'd had to leave her then because she was on the verge of falling asleep in her chair. He tucked her frail hand under the woolen rug that covered her knees and slipped out of the room. His cousin, Giselle, had been waiting at the door. She tugged at his sleeve, drew him into the kitchen and out of earshot, then said, ''Well, would you believe that? If I'd ever tried that on Harry and been caught, he'd have killed me. Great way to start a marriage, right? Lie to your parents, lie to your friends and then, by God, lie to each other.'' She shook her head. ''Aunt Michelle must have been out of her mind to try something like that.''

''Some part of her subconscious must not have trusted him even then. It was a terrible thing to do, and God knows she paid for it with me, but I can understand why she did it.''

''I suppose you're right,'' Giselle said, leaning her hip against her mother's kitchen counter. ''I've read magazine articles about all those trophy wives that say the first thing a woman should do after she marries her aging multimillionaire is to have a baby. That way she'll be a wife and not just a mistress with a piece of paper in her hand.''

Paul laughed. ''Don't forget the French are the most practical people in the world about marriage. It does not always go hand in hand with love. The French understand that marriage is about property and children, period. Mistresses and lovers are for romance.''

"Huh. Not in my family. If my Harry ever took a mistress, I'd poison his brioche.''

ANN LEANED on the doorjamb of the studio. Paul sat on the bottom step with his head bent forward on his folded arms. If he wasn't asleep he was pretty close to it.

She wondered how much the pain of his injury took out of him during any given day. His body was muscular—wonderfully muscular, if the way his jeans fit was any indication. She longed to caress that wounded shoulder, to take away whatever pain he felt, to hold him in her arms and let him sleep until he wasn't tired any longer.

And then what? *Do not go there,* she told herself. *The more exhausted he is, the safer I am from my own libido.*

He lifted his head and sighed deeply.

"Hey, every time I leave you for five minutes, you fall asleep,'' Ann said.

Paul stood up and stretched. "Not asleep. Thinking deep thoughts.''

"I'll just bet you were. Okay, help me get this stuff into the truck.''

"You'll never be able to get those paintings up your stairs alone.''

"I wasn't planning to.'' She smiled at him. "You're helping. It's your stuff.''

"I intended to help, but I didn't want to intrude again without being asked,'' Paul said.

They wrapped the paintings in one of the sheets from the studio, taking care to put the clean side toward the paint. They laid them carefully in the bed of Ann's small truck, then carried the pastels and sketches out.

"Get in," Ann said. "I'll lay them in your lap."

Dante climbed carefully into the rear of the crew cab and lay down behind Paul's seat.

They made the short trip to the alley in less than two minutes. It took much longer to get the paintings and sketches up without damaging them.

Inside, Ann laid the sketches flat on her worktable. The pastel of Trey Delaney gazed up at them.

Ann pulled sash weights from a drawer under one of her cupboards and began to lay them carefully on sheets of wax paper at the edges of the stack of prints. "While I was over here picking up the truck, I called Aunt Karen," she said as she set the last of the weights carefully across the upper end of the stack. "She said she'd love to meet you and tomorrow at four will be fine."

"Should I bring flowers? Wine?"

"Good Lord, no." Ann pointed to the pastel. "Bring this. That's enough."

"If you say so." He started toward the door. "Are you up for that dinner I promised you yesterday?"

Her breath caught, but she managed to keep her smile bright. She wanted very much to have dinner with him, to find out more about him. Not a good idea. "Thank you, but I think I'll have an early night. Some other time."

After she closed the door behind him, she leaned against it and listened to his footsteps descend her stairs. "Close one, eh, Dante?"

"Is DANTE GOING with us?" Paul asked the following afternoon when he arrived to pick her up. The dog sat at the door of the loft with an expectant look on his face.

"Not this time. Sorry, Dante. Stay."

The dog gave Ann a look of reproach, sighed deeply and dropped to the floor.

"We'll be back before too long," Ann told him, and preceded Paul down the stairs, carrying the pastel of young Trey. She'd placed it on a sheet of poster board, covered it with plastic, and wrapped the whole thing in brown paper.

He drove out onto the highway and turned toward Memphis. "Tell me about your aunt Karen. You said she'd remarried. What's her name now?"

"She married Marshall Lowrance a few years after Uncle David died. She has two children by him, a boy and a girl. I think they're both away at college."

"You don't know?"

"I told you, the children don't usually come to the family picnics and holiday celebrations. Not surprising. They're city kids and almost a generation separated from Trey. I don't think they like Trey much, although I've never heard anybody actually say that. Truth be told, they're probably jealous. Trey is still his mama's fair-haired boy."

"And your uncle Marshall?"

"I think of him as Aunt Karen's husband, not as my uncle, though I suppose he is. He's a partner in a big law firm in town. I don't imagine they're hurting for money."

Thirty minutes later Paul pulled into the circular drive-way in front of the Lowrance house.

"You were right about the money," Paul said. "This place reeks of it."

They barely got out of the car before the front door opened. "Ann Corrigan, come in this house! I haven't seen you in a coon's age."

A moment later Karen Bingham Delaney Lowrance turned the full wattage of her smile on Paul. "You, too, Mr. Bouvet. Welcome." She extended a long, fine and beautifully manicured hand. As Paul moved to take it,

Karen blinked hard and seemed to tighten every muscle, but a moment later she relaxed once more into the gracious hostess.

Had Paul imagined that moment of unease? He couldn't be certain.

Karen led them into a small library with comfortable leather chairs and hunting prints on the walls. ''I've always loved this rug,'' Ann said. ''Makes me want to sit on the floor and stroke it.''

''That's what the Bedouins must have done with it originally,'' Karen said.

This library looked the way a real room for books should. No yards of fancy leather-bound editions here. Paul observed that the books all looked as though they had been read. Their covers were modern and bright and seemed to be shoved into the shelves in no particular order.

He waited for Karen to seat herself on the sofa across a heavily laden tea table, then for Ann to sit, and he finally took the wing chair opposite her.

''Now I know I told Ann tea, but if you'd rather have a real drink, I can certainly manage that.''

''Nothing for me, thanks,'' Paul said.

''Really? Nothing at all?''

''I'm afraid I've overdosed on tea since I got down here.''

''Then how about a soft drink? Or some wine?''

''I'm really fine. I just wanted to meet you and bring you this.''

''Well, all right. Ann?''

''I can't overdose on tea, thank you, Aunt Karen.''

''Well, *I'd* much rather have a drink.'' Karen stood, and Paul started to rise, but she stopped him. ''Stay where you are. Bar's right over here.'' When she came back she held a glass full of ice and what looked like straight bourbon all the way to the brim. "There. It's too early for gin and tonic. Sure you won't have one?"

He smiled and shook his head.

"Ann?"

"Not for me, thanks."

"Well, if you're sure." She went about the business of filling a crystal glass with ice and tea from the heavy crystal pitcher and handed around fancy square tea cakes which Paul also refused.

"Now. Let me see what you've brought." She wiggled her fingers for the package Paul held. She reached for it and opened it.

For a few moments she said nothing, then laid it on the sofa beside her. "It *is* Trey." Her fingers caressed the young face gently. When she looked up at Paul her eyes were swimming with tears that had begun to spill over. She ran her fingers expertly along the skin beneath her eyes and sniffed. "There. Can't have my mascara running down my face. Where on earth did you find this?"

"It was…put away in Uncle David's studio," Ann answered.

"I had no idea he'd ever used Trey as a model. Was there anything else?" She turned quickly to Paul. "Not that I'm laying claim to any of it. If David had a Rembrandt hidden in that studio, it belongs to you. I'm just curious."

"A few other sketches," Paul said. "Some landscapes." He ignored Ann's raised eyebrows.

"Any of his famous caricatures? He occasionally showed me some that were too scandalous to circulate. I'd hate to have the people he drew see them. They'd be mortified."

"Nothing like that," Ann said, obviously picking up that Paul didn't want Karen to know about the paintings.

"Since seeing his sketches, Mrs. Lowrance, I must admit I'm becoming really interested in your husband as an artist. Why didn't he ever show? Ever sell anything?"

She brushed away the thought. "Van Gogh never sold anything."

"He certainly tried."

"Well, David didn't." Her voice had developed an edge. "His family would have disliked the idea of having his work hanging out there for the world to see and critique. They put up with the caricatures because people loved them and they made money for charity. He could hardly have set himself up as a portrait painter. He had enough to do running the farm and the cattle operation. Besides," she added, "most of the time he was too drunk to pick up a brush."

Paul was stunned at the baldness of her statement and the depth of anger and pain revealed by the words.

Ann started to respond, but Karen held up a hand. "It's true. Everybody knows it. If Buddy hadn't made him promise not to drive drunk, he'd probably have been killed sooner and taken a few other people with him."

She smiled at Paul as though they'd been talking about the weather. "You've heard of the unhappy artist? Well, my husband must certainly have been an artist because he was definitely unhappy." She looked down at the portrait of her son. "And he made everyone around him miserable, as well." She looked up and laughed. "Not what you expected to hear, is it? If you want to keep any illusions about my husband's talent, I suggest you stop poking into his life."

"Ann says he studied in Paris."

Karen sighed. "Yes. His father couldn't keep him from

being drafted into the army the minute he got out of college, but Conrad had sufficient political clout to keep him out of Vietnam. He was assigned to a small post outside Paris. He refused to come home after he finished his service. He took his pay and moved to Paris to become an artist." Karen rolled her eyes. "An *artist*. He knew he had responsibilities at home. Conrad was furious. Refused to send him a dime, but of course Maribelle sent him money every chance she got. He was her precious boy, after all."

"If he planned to stay in France, why did he get discouraged and come home?"

Karen laughed. "Get discouraged? Not David. He'd already had a couple of portrait commissions. He wasn't part of the Paris avant-garde movement that made paintings out of garbage and sculpture out of empty soup cans. He liked painting people who were recognizable."

"I saw that in the sketch of Ann's father. It was funny, but I never had any doubt who it was. Why did he come home, then?"

"When his daddy had his heart attack and we all thought he was going to die, Maribelle sent David a first-class ticket. So of course he came. Once he was here, he was trapped. He couldn't just walk out while his father was sick. There's only one Delaney heir per generation and he was it."

"He didn't try to go back?"

"Of course he did. He fought like a tiger, but he knew from the start it was a losing battle. So he gave up, married me and settled down to the job he was bred for."

"Maybe you should have let him go," Ann said quietly.

Karen took a deep breath. "Maybe we should have. He'd have come home on his own after a while, I'm certain of it. He really wore his life here like a comfortable shoe, even if he tried to pretend he didn't. I think when Conrad finally persuaded him to stay, David was actually grateful to have the decision taken out of his hands. Ann, you go back and forth to Europe all the time. You know how exhausting living in a foreign country and speaking a foreign language gets to be.'' She shrugged. ''Or maybe you don't, but David was never any good at languages in school. Barely passed his two years of Spanish in high school.'' She turned to Paul and laughed. ''Maribelle couldn't get him to eat anything except cheeseburgers and chocolate milk shakes at the café for a whole week after he came home.''

''But Conrad Delaney didn't die until later, did he?''

''No, he didn't. But he was never right afterward. His mind started to fail quickly. They doctors said it was from lack of oxygen during his attack. He lost his short-term memory. He could remember what happened in 1939, but not five minutes ago. Between them, Maribelle and my David ran the business. And, of course, I got pregnant with Trey almost at once. That really nailed David's traveling foot to the floor.''

The conversation became more general. Karen expressed a desire to come look at Paul's house when it was finished. ''I never wanted to live there,'' Karen said. ''The house isn't that large, and I hated being under my mother-in-law's watchful eye.''

Eventually they said their goodbyes and drove away while Karen stood on the porch of her elegant mansion and waved.

THE MOMENT Paul Bouvet's car disappeared up the street, Karen Lowrance ran to the library and phoned her son. ''Sue-sue, I need to speak to Trey.''

"Trey's out on the terrace with the kids," Sue-sue said. "He's trying to get the cover off the pool. Can I give him a message?"

"Now, Sue-sue. Right now."

"Well, all right. Just a minute."

A moment later Trey drawled, "Hey, Mama, what's up? How come you snapped at Sue-sue?"

"The hell with Sue-sue. Get your tail over here this minute."

"Are you all right? You haven't fallen or anything?"

"For heaven's sake, Trey, I am not a decrepit old crone. Now do as I say. We'll talk when you get there. And not a word to Sue-sue." She hung up before he could refuse.

By the time her son skidded into the library, Karen was on her third bourbon-and-bourbon, but she was cold sober.

"Mama?" Trey said, and started to kiss her. She shoved him away.

"Sit down."

"Yes, ma'am."

She couldn't sit. She prowled the room with her drink in her hand. "What do you know about that Bouvet person?"

Trey shrugged. "Not a whole lot. He paid cash for the house. No need to check up on him. And he's spending money like water fixing it up."

"Why?"

"I guess he likes it."

"Guesses won't do. Who is he?"

"Some sort of pilot, from what Bernice at the café said. Had an accident and can't fly big planes any longer, so he's looking for a project to keep himself busy. What's all this about?"

"Don't ask questions. Do as I say. I mean that. I want you to find out everything you can about this Paul Bouvet.

Who he is, who his people are—his whole family history. Then I want you to bring me his iced-tea glass from the café.''

"Mama, have you gone crazy?"

"He may be dangerous."

"Some sort of serial killer?"

"Dangerous to this *family*, Trey. I don't give a damn about the rest of the world. Let the serial killers have them, for all I care. But nothing is going to happen to this family. Not to me, not to you and certainly not to Paul Frederick and little Maribelle.''

"How could this guy possibly be dangerous to us?"

"I said don't ask questions. If I'm right, and God knows I pray I'm not, then we will have to do something to make certain Mr. Paul Bouvet leaves Rossiter with his tail between his legs. And soon."

"Bernice'll kill me if I walk out with a mason jar from the café.''

The whine in Trey's voice infuriated his mother. "Cultivate the man. Let him ask his damn questions. Take him to lunch somewhere other than the café.''

"Mama, I'm starting to think you may have had a teensy little stroke or something."

"My brain is functioning perfectly, thank you." She sat up and grabbed at Trey's hand. "It would be natural for you to want to see the progress on the restoration. Stands to reason you'd be interested in your grandmother's house." She set her glass down on the side table so hard it splashed. "Go through his things if you can. His toothbrush! Steal his toothbrush. And some hairs from his comb. That'll be perfect.''

"How many of those glasses of bourbon you had this afternoon?"

"That's none of your business. Unlike your father, I

am not an alcoholic. I can quit any time I choose. In this case, however, a little alcohol is good to clear the brain.''

''Uh-huh.''

''Oh, get out.''

''I can't go through this guy's stuff, Mama. What if I get caught?''

Karen gave an exasperated sigh. ''Then hire a private detective. A good one.''

''Great. I'll ask Marshall who he uses.''

''No!'' Karen shouted, then continued more quietly, ''Someone with no connections to us. Someone good who keeps his clients' secrets.''

''How do I find him?''

She shoved him toward the door. ''For God's sake, Trey, look in the Yellow Pages.'' As he started down the hall, she said, ''And bring that detective's report straight to me without opening it. You hear?''

''Yes, ma'am.'' Trey walked out, shaking his head.

After Trey left in his fancy pickup truck, Karen went back into the library. Marshall probably wouldn't be home for a couple of hours yet. Suddenly every bit of adrenaline that had kept the liquor in her system at bay drained out. She sank onto the sofa, leaned back and closed her eyes against the throb in her temples. She loved Trey dearly, but knew that her son was no genius. He'd always need supervision and guidance. She only hoped that Sue-sue would be up to the task when Karen was no longer around.

WHEN DAVID had stopped writing her from France, when he'd stopped asking about her in his calls to his mother, Karen Bingham knew he'd found someone else. She came close to saying the hell with it and marrying one of her other suitors. There were plenty of them. Marshall Low-rance had been among them.

But there had never been anyone for her but Paul David Delaney. Not since he'd knocked her down and broken her elbow in the first grade. He'd been so sorry and so sweet. They'd grown up together, learned to ride together, hunted their first ponies together, taken their first communion together, played their first game of Doctor, Doctor together, gone to the movies and the dances and the junior and senior prom together. Attended Ole Miss together, pledged sister and brother sorority and fraternity. Lost their virginity together.

At college they broke up a time or two, dated other people, but they always made up. How could they not? They were different halves of the same soul.

Or at least Karen had always thought they were.

David asked her to wait for him the two years he'd be away with the army, and he gave her an engagement ring that same night.

Both the Delaneys and Karen's mother wanted them to go ahead and get married when David came home on his first leave after basic training and before he went off to Europe. Unfortunately they'd agreed to wait.

She and David had talked about moving to Europe so he could become an artist. For Karen it had been one of those dreams she'd never considered a real possibility.

He must have fallen for the woman after he'd left the army, because Karen had visited him in France six months before he was due to be let out, or whatever it was they did to drafted soldiers. They'd had a marvelous time making love in little inns hanging off the sides of mountains in Alsace and picnicking beside chateaux in the Loire Valley. They'd even spent a weekend seeing the museums in Paris. David was his old self. Then he told her that when he got out of the service, he was staying in France.

That gave her some worry, but she figured he'd work it out of his system and come home in six months.

When he begged her to leave Rossiter, come to France and marry him, she should have jumped at the chance. Instead, she let her mother and Maribelle Delaney talk her into a big wedding at home.

So he must have met the woman in Paris. He didn't have money enough to leave the city. Karen had never known who the woman was, but the moment David stepped off the airplane in Memphis on his way to see his sick father, the moment she threw her arms around him and felt his shoulders stiffen, she knew he'd fallen in love with someone else.

Maribelle had known, too. Karen would never forget that interminable drive with Maribelle from Rossiter to pick up David at the airport. She remembered every word, every nuance, every gesture of Maribelle's.

"Do you still want to marry him?" Maribelle had asked.

"Of course I do. Why wouldn't I?"

"He's in love with somebody else. Somebody he met in Paris."

Karen flinched. The words, so baldly stated, had a chilling effect.

"I read between the lines of his letters and I heard it in his voice. I know the signs. I've recognized them often enough in the men in my life."

That startled Karen even more. The only man she was aware of in Maribelle's life was her husband, Conrad. She'd never seen any evidence that he strayed. Maribelle would have flayed him alive if she'd caught him with another woman. Yet apparently he had been unfaithful and lived to tell the tale.

"So do you still want to marry him?" Maribelle asked.

"I want him to be happy."

"He will be, once he gets this infatuation out of his system. He's always loved you. The two of you belong together."

"David may not agree."

"I doubt he does, at least at the moment. It's up to you to convince him he wants you more than some little French trollop who probably only got her hooks into him because he's a ticket to a cushy life in America."

Karen felt that Maribelle was probably right. She doubted that nice French girls were allowed to run around with ex-GIs who'd turned into starving artists.

"How am I supposed to convince him to stay?" Karen asked.

"He's going to stay here if I have to chain him to the wall. But I want him to embrace his chains. Like you, I want him to be happy."

Karen thought, but only the way *you* want him to be happy. Screw what he wants.

"So you have to make him happy. What does he like to do in bed?"

If Karen had been driving, she'd have crashed the car. "I beg your pardon?"

"You won't shock me, dear. Adam and Eve invented most of the sexual permutations known to man. The rest of us have merely been embellishing their basic construct. So what does he like?"

"Maribelle, I can't talk about this to you."

"Whatever it is, do it. Quickly and often. A man sated by a woman is much more likely to think he's in love with that woman than one who is keeping a friendly arm's length away.''

''What if he doesn't want to...you know?''

''David is twenty-five years old. Trust me. Get him in the right setting, he'll want to. The rest is up to you.''

So she had. She'd gone carefully to work seducing him, though he obviously hadn't wanted to make love to her. Maribelle and Karen's mother threw them together in ways he could not avoid, and finally, after a romantic movie, she'd persuaded him to park in their old lovers' lane ''just to talk.''

She went home with her underpants in her purse and a pleasurable ache between her legs that she hadn't experienced in far too long.

Their marriage hadn't all been her doing, of course. She had no idea what his father had said to David in those long talks on the sleeping porch of the Delaney house, nor what layers of guilt Maribelle had covered him with when she was with him. He'd fought his parents—and Karen—for almost a month.

At one point she'd even offered to grab her passport and go back to France with him.

He'd simply shaken his head.

As the weeks dragged by, he took over more and more of the family business.

He was good with the men. Better than his father ever had been. He obviously enjoyed the life of Southern planter into which he'd been born. The mantle of power settled on his shoulders easily. He might have shrugged a few times, but as the days passed, he talked less and less about Paris and his art, and more and more about the extra cattle they could run once the Delaney ranch merged with the acreage Karen's mother had inherited from her husband.

Maribelle and Karen's mother had covertly resurrected the wedding plans, but had scaled them down. Just a small wedding. Even Maribelle didn't think David would hold still for a twelve-bridesmaid affair. And her husband's health couldn't tolerate the strain of a big wedding.

The day David and Karen bought their marriage license in Somerville, he'd practically shoved her out of his convertible at her front door and laid rubber getting away from her. She didn't see him for two days.

She found out later that he'd spent most of those two days closeted with his father and riding his hunter across the fields like a madman.

Not quite the reaction she'd hoped for.

Maribelle said it was only premarital jitters.

Karen wasn't sure he'd be able to go through with the wedding, but when the morning dawned, he was there waiting for her at the altar of the small Episcopal church. He looked green, and when he kissed her she smelled alcohol on his breath. But he was there. She was now Karen Bingham Delaney. She had her dream.

She couldn't have guessed how quickly it would turn into a nightmare....

It wasn't until after his death that she'd climbed out of that nightmare and found peace with an indulgent new husband and a couple of children who would probably do well in the world.

Then Paul Bouvet got out of his car and walked into her house.

One look was all it took.

For years she'd dreaded that the woman David had had an affair with in France would show up. Worse, that they had produced a child.

But as the years passed her fears had seemed more and more groundless. She began to relax. When no one appeared to claim a portion of David's estate after his death, she felt certain she and Trey had escaped, that the woman had been childless. The woman had probably married someone in France and might have grandchildren of her own by now.

Now Paul Bouvet was here and her world collapsed.

David's eyes had been blue like Trey's, but much darker. This man had dark eyes, but they were set like David's. David's hair had been much darker than Trey's. Actually, this man looked much more like David than Trey did. He had David's fine bone structure. He moved with the same athletic ease. He even had the tiny hitch in his walk. Despite his Yankee accent, he spoke to her in David's voice, used his hands like David.

She could barely look at those long, fine hands—so like her husband's. Hands that had caressed and wounded her.

Maybe someone who hadn't known David so intimately wouldn't have seen the resemblance, but she knew. She would have guessed this man was Paul David Delaney's son if she'd met him walking down Fifth Avenue. Even the name Paul was no coincidence. She wondered if he, too, had a middle name.

She prayed she was wrong about his background. She'd have to find out from her doctor how to get a DNA test done secretly. She must not frighten Trey until she was certain.

If the DNA results proved Paul Bouvet was a Delaney, she'd have to sit down with Marshall and Trey to decide how best to proceed to save both the family honor and the family fortune.

Until then, she didn't dare let the possibility that he might have a bastard half brother occur to Trey. He might very well want to throw his arms open and welcome the man. That would be just like Trey. He wouldn't realize until later that Paul Bouvet could be legally entitled to a hefty portion of the money Trey and Sue-sue spent so cavalierly. He might also realize that he would become a laughingstock, having a father who'd dishonored him.

Dammit, her husband had dishonored *her,* never mind Trey.

If she was right about Bouvet, he must be stopped before he could damage Trey or her grandchildren. He must be stopped before the revelation of her husband's affair could destroy *her.*

He must be sent politely away.

And if not sent, then driven away before he could open his foul French mouth.

CHAPTER EIGHT

"ARE YOU COMING to dinner Sunday?" Nancy Jenkins asked her daughter when she called that evening.

"At Gram's or at home?"

Nancy sniffed. "You act like I can't cook. Your grandmother has kindly invited everyone after church."

"Then sure, but I don't think I'll go to church. I'm behind on refinishing the trim on those bookcases at the mansion."

"I have an idea. Why don't you bring that nice young man with you? He's all alone and the café is closed Sundays. I'm sure he'd appreciate a home-cooked meal."

"I've barely seen him to speak to in more than a week," Ann told her mother. "He's either flying that plane of his or off doing research of some kind."

"Really? What? Why?"

"How would I know?"

"Your grandmother says he's nice as pie. And a hunk."

"My grandmother is a lecherous old biddy, and you can tell her I said so."

"You tell her yourself. Is he a hunk?"

"I suppose so."

"Buddy likes him, too. Bring him to dinner Sunday so I can check him out."

"Mother, I'm not interested in another relationship. Certainly not with a hunk. I *had* a hunk. They make lousy husbands."

"Not all of them do. Just because you had a bad experience—"

"Mother, stop it. I didn't have a bad experience. I had a six-year train wreck of a marriage."

"This man apparently has money. He's not going to ask you to support him the way Travis did."

"He is definitely not going to because I'm not going to marry him. Or anybody else. Not for a long, long time."

"I want grandchildren."

"Then adopt."

"Ann, sometimes I could throttle you."

"Then we're even. Bye, Mother dear."

"Wait. What about Sunday dinner?"

"Oh, Lord. All right."

"Fix yourself up a little. You might even consider wearing a dress. The last time I checked, you had legs, but it's been so long since I've seen them I'm really not sure. You haven't developed thick ankles, have you?"

Ann took a deep breath. "My ankles are fine, Mother, thank you for asking. I don't think I own a dress, but if you promise never to mention the subject again, I will dig out a skirt. And if I see Paul, I'll invite him."

"Good, because if you don't, I'll have Buddy do it."

With that parting shot, her mother hung up.

In the minds of most of the women of Rossiter, a woman needed a husband even if she had a career of her own. Almost any husband was better than none. Ann's mother and grandmother had changed their minds on that score after Ann eloped with Travis Corrigan and moved to Washington so that he could become a theater director.

Ann's master's degree in art history wasn't enough to get her an assistant-assistant-curator position at any of the myriad museums and galleries. But her schooling in art restoration got her a job cleaning and restoring paintings and art objects for a chic gallery in Foggy Bottom. The work was tedious and painstaking. But she didn't mind devoting herself to a six-inch square at the corner of some giant sixteenth-century landscape. The painter might be unknown, but he deserved as much care as she'd take with a Rembrandt.

She occasionally made a major discovery when the layers of grime came off. The gallery owner paid her a handsome commission for uncovering a missing hand that had been painted over in a seventeenth-century Spanish madonna.

She spent most of her nights helping to build sets and create furnishings and props for her husband's theater. She'd fall into bed at night completely exhausted, but happy.

Until she discovered Travis's first infidelity. Travis denied anything was going on at first. Then he said that he'd gone hunting for another source of sex because his wife was never home, always working, and when had she gotten a new hairstyle or put on eye shadow lately, anyway?

He was right, of course. She hadn't been seductive enough or inventive enough in bed. She and Travis both ended up in tears, protestations of love and bed in that order. The greatest sex they'd ever had.

Each time it happened, Ann withdrew into herself a little further, became a little quieter, buried herself even more in her work.

After he was fired for messing around with the producer's wife, Ann missed the theater. It didn't seem fair that she should be kicked out when she was the best set painter and designer they had.

Then one day he met her at the door, waltzed her into their galley kitchen and kissed her fiercely. "We've moving to New York!'' he said gaily. ''We'll sublet this apartment, get a place in the Village or Soho or somewhere. I'll get a job as a stage manager on Broadway and do some directing off-off Broadway.''

She was too stunned to answer.

''I thought I'd take some acting lessons. At the Actors' Studio or somewhere. I've got the face for it, you have to admit, and I was great in *Hedda Gabler* in college.''

She started to tell him that the male roles in *Hedda Gabler* weren't exactly showcases.

''It'll be great, babe! Just like honeymooners!'' He grabbed her around the waist and danced her around the tiny living room.

When she finally managed to free herself, she asked, ''What about me?''

''You can do what you do anywhere. With the references they'll give you, you can probably go to work restoring stuff for the Frick Gallery or someplace.''

''So I quit my job—which is paying the bills, by the way—pack up and move to New York with no prospects for either of us?''

He frowned down at her from his six foot three. ''All right, so you're paying the bills right now. Throw that in my face, why don't you?'' He whipped away from her, his hands in the air. ''God, I thought you'd be thrilled! Talk about your selfish...''

She fell in love with New York just as she'd fallen in love with Washington. She found a job quickly with a big firm that did full restorations—furniture, houses, sculpture—anything that was broken or needed attention. She spent six months learning more techniques. She became the most expert restorer the company had. She did jobs in the Hamptons, Vermont, Philadelphia and country houses in between. Clients began asking specifically for her.

With Travis usually either rehearsing or playing in some avant-garde thing in some church basement, she was on her own most nights. And, if the truth be known, she enjoyed having the apartment to herself.

When she felt like some company, she sought out her four co-workers. They made a team that was unbeatable. Marti, two hundred pounds of wild Barnard graduate who did kick-ass wood carving, became the sister Ann had never had. Marti's mother even taught Ann to make liver knishes and gefilte fish.

Then there was Zabo, a transplant from Benin, who knew how to work metal with as much skill and art as his sixteenth-century ancestors. Next came Sebastian, tall, thin, gay, with eloquent hands. He knew everything there was to know about period architecture.

The last of the group, Tonio, was whipcord thin with flashing dark eyes and a smile that melted female (and male) hearts in every direction when he turned it on. He was the marble expert, having been born and raised in Carrara.

Zabo taught Ann to use a lathe to re-create missing wood pieces. Marti taught her to carve. Sebastian taught her the wonders of plaster, and Tonio tried to take her to bed.

She and Travis lived like roommates.

Then one afternoon Travis burst into the apartment with a bottle of champagne in one hand and a bouquet of roses in the other.

"Babe! Pack your bags! We're off to L.A.!"

Half-asleep over a new detective story, Ann jerked awake. "Huh? What?"

"The big H., babe! Holl-y-wooood."

"What're you talking about?"

"It's the promised land, babe. I got the face for it, I got the body for it, I got the star quality for it."

What could she say to that?

"I'm flying to the Coast—God, how great that sounds—on the red-eye tomorrow night. Sid's got me two auditions and one commercial already." He turned to her with a puzzled expression on his face. "Hey, babe, what's the matter? This is what we've been working for. Two years and we'll be living in a mansion in Malibu."

"No." She was as stunned as Travis when the word came out of her mouth.

"What?"

"I'm not going."

"Sure, not right away. I got to find us a decent place to live first, get a few residual checks under my belt."

"I don't want to leave my job."

"What job? That glorified carpentry work you do down in Soho? This is what we've always wanted."

"Not what I wanted, and until a year ago, it wasn't what you wanted, either."

"I always wanted to be in theater."

"Not as an actor."

He dropped the roses on the battered coffee table. "You've always resented my aspirations. You're the one who's been holding me back."

She sat down so hard she felt the broken spring in the sofa poke her rear end. "I'm responsible for the women, too, am I?"

"The truth is I've outgrown you. I understand why all those guys in Hollywood dump their wives when they get to be stars. You think I'd want to be seen walking down the red carpet with you on my arm?"

"You're right. You've outgrown me." She began to

giggle. "How about we crack the champagne and drink to our pending divorce?"

"What?" He looked stunned. He'd obviously not expected things to go this far. He would need the money from her paycheck for acting classes and a new portfolio and a pleasant apartment. "One remark and you want a divorce?"

"You're much better off divorcing me in New York before you get rich, you know. California is a community-property state. Once you establish residency there and make your first million, I can really take you to the cleaners with alimony."

"Don't joke."

"I'm not joking."

"You're angry."

"I'll call Marti tomorrow morning and get the name of a cheap divorce lawyer. We can split the CDs. You can have the furniture. Thank God we sold the car when we moved up here. We can pay the lawyer and split what's left, I suppose. Is that agreeable to you?"

Travis really didn't want a divorce. Did he feel safer not being able to continue an affair for very long because he had a wife?

"Come on, babe, let's go to bed." He held out his hand. She took it and let him lead her to the bedroom.

The next day he left for L.A., and she convened a meeting of her colleagues at her apartment to tell them what had happened.

The consensus was that it had taken her long enough to kick the bastard out.

Ann realized she wanted to go home.

They were all horrified when she told them. They didn't want to lose her friendship. "And we damned well don't want to lose your skill at crown molding," said Sebastian.

"Maybe we won't have to," Marti said.

When Ann talked to her boss about moving home and taking commissions from him and any other restoration jobs as a freelancer, he hated the idea. Two days later he agreed. "But only if I get first crack at you," he said.

She hugged him.

When she called her parents to say she wanted to come home to work for her father on restoration, her mother merely said, "It's about time," and burst into tears.

So here she was divorced from a man who so far hadn't shown up in any major motion pictures, living in a pair of lofts, spending half her time in hotel rooms while she worked on jobs out of town and sharing her life with a big dog who, unlike her ex-husband, was loyal.

PAUL CLIMBED OUT of the Stearman biplane with a real sense of accomplishment. He'd forgotten how touchy the old tail-dragger could get in a crosswind. His Cessna practically flew itself. A very forgiving aircraft but not nearly as much fun to fly.

"You better not try them barrel rolls with weed killer in the tanks, son."

Paul looked up from his logbook and grinned at Hack Morrison, the man who owned the Stearman, the man who'd be employing him part-time as a crop duster. Hack also owned a pair of Air Tractors and the local airfield.

"You're the one who took me up and damn near made me toss my cookies," Paul said.

He'd been horrified by Hack's appearance the first time he'd met him. Hack walked with a slight limp he said he'd gotten from a piece of shrapnel in 1944. He wore filthy coveralls over a ragged white undershirt that exposed ropy sunburned arms and a barrel chest.

His disreputable cap featured the logo of one of the

high-priced cotton fertilizers. Oil and grime were deeply imbedded in his hands.

He wore boots that had been brown once, but were now permanently dirt-colored and would never take a shine. He lived in an aging trailer behind the first of six hangars where owners kept their private planes. To top off this country-bumpkin act, he always had the stub of an unlit cigar in his mouth.

After he and Hack landed from Paul's ride in the Stearman, Paul turned to him. "You're an old fraud, Hack Morrison. What'd you do? See an old geezer in some World War Two movie and decide you could out-character him?"

"I got no idea what you're talking about."

"I checked up on you before I parked my plane here. You graduated from West Point, you retired a bird colonel, and if I had as many hours in the air as you do, I could probably fly without a plane."

"Now you listen, son. Don't you go talking. I don't want another soul in on the facts."

"Sure, but why?"

Hack sighed. "I had twenty-five years of spit and polish. I got sick of it. After my wife died I decided I'd spend my declining years as an eccentric." He grinned at Paul. "Most of the time it works."

"Your secret is safe with me."

"Good. Keep it that way. Now, we're gonna start pre-emerge spraying in two weeks. You gotta be able to stroke that Stearman like a beautiful woman, or you're gonna wind up wearing a couple of utility wires. When you gonna come do some more flying?"

"Do I have to take you with me?"

"Not necessarily. You're a pretty fair pilot all told. The

Stearman's a hell of a lot of fun to fly. Bring your girl-friend. Pay for the gas is all.''

"I don't have a girlfriend."

"Then get one." Hack walked off with his dirty hands in his dirty pockets.

Paul knew he'd been dismissed.

CHAPTER NINE

THE DAY HE STARTED dusting crops for Hack Morrison,
Paul lost all contact with the work at his house. He came
home only to shower, sleep, shave and change clothes.
Hack flew with him the first couple of days before turning
him loose with his precious Stearman.

What was supposed to be a part-time job quickly turned
into dawn till dusk seven days a week. If Paul had missed
flying, he was certainly making up for it now.

"Won't last long," Hack assured him. "Once they start
plantin', we'll have six weeks before we start spraying for
insects."

One late afternoon as he climbed down from the Stearman so tired his legs were shaky, he finally asked Hank,
"When are you going to come up and join me in one of
your Air Tractors?"

Hack hemmed and hawed and dug his hands deeper
into the pockets of his dirty coveralls. "Well, see, it's like
this. Reflexes aren't what they were. Eyes, either, although I can still pass a flight physical. Since you're a
young pup and you need the experience, I thought I'd just
let you handle it."

"I see. You conned me."

"Maybe. I've sort of been looking for somebody to
take over the business. It makes good money, and I'd stay
as a pilot as long as I could, plus keep the place up, but
I'm really sick of being tied down so much. I'd like to

revisit a few of the places Virginia and I lived in before I die.''

"Oh, no, you don't, you old devil. I am not buying a crop-dusting business, and I'm certainly not buying a private airport.''

Hack's face was open and guileless. His blue eyes, however, were shrewd. "Never asked you, did I?''

"I'm not even certain I approve of the effect all the dusting has on the environment.''

"You'd rather starve, I suppose.''

"I don't eat cotton.''

"Lot of folks wouldn't eat *without* it. Besides, the EPA's put so many restrictions on us it's a miracle we can even lift off. They've tested the stuff we use six ways to Sunday. Won't affect anything but the weeds and the boll weevils. Can't fly when there's even a hint of breeze, can't allow spillover into adjacent fields. Never mind that a man could stall out and kill himself trying to bank too sharp.''

"Frankly, Hack, I'm tired. I could use a day off.''

"Then pray for rain. Can't spray in the rain, either.''

HE AWOKE next morning to the swish of the trees against the screens on the porch and the patter of heavy rain on his new roof. "Thank God,'' he said, and rolled out of bed.

The work on the house seemed to go on and on with no discernible progress. He now had heating and air-conditioning and plenty of hot water. He was grateful for all three, but they didn't show. The house still looked as though it were caught in a time warp, not certain whether to allow itself to be resurrected or simply give up and fall down.

This morning he sought Buddy out for a progress report.

"The kitchen, Buddy? When can I start cooking?"

"You cook?"

"Would I have bought that steel restaurant stove otherwise?"

"Guess not. Since you picked a standard cabinet for the base cabinets and the island, they could be delivered as soon as ten days from now. We install 'em, cut and install the granite countertops, hang the light fixtures, get your other appliances delivered and hooked up, and you ought to have a kitchen. Not much left to be done."

Paul looked for the joke, but Buddy seemed perfectly serious.

"We've already sent that old beat-up gas stove to the dump and capped the gas line into the kitchen until the new stove goes in. Gas is turned off outside, but if somebody was to hit it a good lick with a ladder passing by, then the cap came off that gas line in the kitchen, might be enough gas seep in to blow us all to kingdom come. I've put a sign on it inside and out. Don't you go messing around with it."

"I wouldn't dream of it."

"Good. When you gonna let me tear down that old studio so I can start building you a garage?"

Paul hadn't decided whether he wanted the studio demolished. His father had spent so much time there that it seemed to be imbued with the best part of his spirit. Maybe he should restore it and move it to the corner of the property to be refitted as a guest house. He'd have to ask Ann her opinion on whether it could be saved.

He'd had only fleeting encounters with her for more than a week. Every time he found her, she pleaded work and sent him away. He wasn't certain what he'd done wrong, but obviously something had put her off.

He even stopped going to the café for lunch. He still had breakfast there every morning and was finally giving and receiving nods of recognition from the regulars. A couple of the old farmers even gave him a grudging "'mornin'" when they passed. Bernice stuck a newspaper in his hand the minute he sat down. She knew how he liked his coffee. It wasn't exactly acceptance, but it was a start.

This morning as he finished his second cup of coffee, a shadow cut across his paper. He looked up to see Trey Delaney standing over him, hand outstretched, broad grin on his face. "Hey, man. How you doin'?"

Paul half rose and shook Trey's hand. "Please, join me," he said. Always be cordial to one's enemy—especially when you want information from him.

"Sure. Hey, Bernice, I need some coffee and a big ol' o.j." He turned guileless blue eyes to Paul. "Been meanin' to see how y'all are doing over at the house. Suesue wants to see it, too."

"Certainly. Anytime. The workmen are there all day, and I'm usually home from the time they leave."

"Got a telephone yet?"

"Still using my cell phone. Actually, I'm glad you're here," Paul said. "I've been planning to come over to your office. I'd like to track down some of the original light fixtures from the house, especially the big chandelier that used to hang in the front hall. If I can find out who bought them—and if I can afford to—I'd like to try to buy them back."

"Sure. I got the records in my office." Bernice set his coffee and orange juice in front of him. "Thanks, darlin'," Trey said with easy familiarity. The sort of familiarity Paul would never attain if he lived in Rossiter forty years.

Not that he planned to. These people were charming and friendly, but he'd heard enough *Y'all come see us now*s to recognize an empty invitation when he heard one. Tante Helaine and Uncle Charlie had very rarely invited anyone to their apartment, but when they had, they'd meant it.

"When may I come see the list?"

"Shoot, how about soon as I have my coffee? I'm headed over that way, anyhow." Trey tossed back his orange juice and swilled coffee that would have taken the roof of Paul's mouth off.

Over Trey's protestations, Paul paid both their checks and followed him across the square, past the bear chained to the column and into Trey's office. It held two beat-up old wooden desks, four beat-up chairs, a bank of file cabinets, a pair of enormous computers, a large laser printer, a fax machine-copier, a telephone and a small refrigerator. Except for the equipment, the place looked as though nothing had changed since the first Paul Delaney had used it. "Got that list somewhere," Trey said. "Sit down. Want a drink?"

Since it was barely nine o'clock in the morning, Paul decided Trey wasn't offering him liquor. "No, thank you."

"Come on, it's hot. Have a cola. I'm having one." Even as he asked, Trey reached into the top drawer of one of the file cabinets, pulled out a couple of glasses, filled them with ice from the small refrigerator, poured soda into both and handed one to Paul. "Here's to you and your house." He drained half his drink, set it down on top of the second cabinet and began to rummage.

Paul did not want a soft drink this early, either, but

knew it was impolite to turn it down. He took a sip and set the glass on the scarred desk. His wouldn't be the first ring from a wet glass. The desktop was covered with dark circles and cigar burns.

"Shoot," Trey said. "Probably misfiled the darned thing. Tell you what. I'll crank up the old computer, run you out another list and bring it over to the house sometime today. How's that?"

"I hate to put you to that trouble. It's not urgent."

"No trouble. Been planning to visit, anyway. See how my little kissin' cousin's doing on that old woodwork."

"Kissing cousin?"

"Ann Corrigan. She's my second cousin. That's more than far enough away to kiss." He laughed. "Glad that little lady's come home. She had a real bad marriage." His face turned serious. "Wouldn't want to see her hurt again."

A warning. Definitely a warning. Paul nodded, said his goodbyes and started to leave when he stopped and turned back. "This may be rude, but I have to ask. What's with the bear?"

"What? Oh, ol' Smokey Joe? Long story. You come on out to the house one night next week and I'll tell you all about it."

A real invitation or one of those *Y'all come* things?

"How's Wednesday night sound? Unless Sue-sue's promised to be somewhere else, we'd love to have you come for dinner. Bring Ann, why don't you? Sue-sue hasn't seen nearly enough of her since she's been home."

"I'll ask her."

"You can let me know when I bring that printout."

This time Paul went out and closed the door behind him.

So he *was* invited to dinner. And with Ann. He wasn't certain how he felt about dining at his half brother's table.

HE FOUND ANN coming out of the living room. The newly stripped and refinished pocket doors to the music room beyond were shut. He'd never seen them shut. The walnut and golden oak gleamed in the morning sunshine pouring through the curtainless front windows.

"Good, I was hoping you'd show up," Ann said. She sounded serious.

"Is there a problem?"

"Not exactly. Close your eyes and give me your hand."

Her hand felt small and warm nestled in his. That warmth traveled up his body as she led him toward the salon doors. Even with his eyes closed he knew that was where they were going.

"Don't look," she said, and let go of his hand. He heard the doors slide back almost noiselessly, then her hand slipped back into his. "This way." She led him forward a few steps, then turned him. "Okay. Open your eyes."

She'd finished restoring the overmantel. The golden oak figures now stood out as fresh as the day they were carved. Riders and horses galloped, hounds bayed, stags bolted, and all through fields of grain and under trees tossed by the wind.

She was staring at him with a broad grin on her face. "Well?" she said.

"It's incredible. How did you know that under all that paint and varnish you'd find this?"

"I knew it was good. I had no idea *how* good. There were so many coats of old varnish and dirt embedded in it that it might as well have been flat carving." She reached out and caressed one of the stags. "When I find something like this…God, I love my job."

"Is this where I acknowledge you're a genius?"

"You bet."

"You're a genius. You deserve a reward." He swept her into his arms and off her feet. He kissed her hard and pressed her against his body. For an instant she struggled, then she coiled her arms around his neck, fitted herself against him and kissed him back.

It was some kiss, at least from his standpoint. She did things with her tongue that left him breathless. The kiss deepened until he didn't think it could go any deeper. He was hard as a rock against her and could feel her nipples under the thin T-shirt. If he'd been upstairs and close to his bed, he'd have tumbled them both into it without breaking the contact between them. She tasted sweet and as wild as blackberries in summertime.

"Oops. Sorry." Paul heard the pocket doors sliding closed.

Ann broke the kiss. "Oh, Lord, I hope that wasn't Buddy."

He held on to her. "You're a grown woman."

"Tell that to my father." She pushed away from him and smoothed her shirt down. "He knows I was married for six years. He just doesn't want to consider what that means."

"Six years?"

"I'm not a fast learner. And I prefer the devil I know to the devil I don't know. I warned you I don't take risks."

Ouch. He looked back at the overmantel. "You may not be a fast learner, but I'd say you're a good one, at least where your craft is concerned."

"What craft would that be?" She grinned at him. "Oh, you mean the carving."

He arched an eyebrow at her. "Right. The carving. Although you do show some promise in that other craft. With practice you might turn into a real expert. I'd be happy to tutor you privately."

"Thanks, but I prefer to pick the professors I study under—uh... Back to our previous conversation, please. The man who carved that mantelpiece was a genius. I'm just the cleanup crew."

"Any idea who he was?"

"None. I know the Delaney who built the house imported some things from Germany, and this looks like German carving. Beyond that, *nada.*"

He looked over her shoulder. "And the bookshelves. How the hell did you get all this done so quickly?"

"I word hard."

"Yes, you do, and you deserve a treat. How about I drive you into town, we have lunch and then I take you flying? The weather's starting to clear."

"That means Hack will have you up in the air dusting."

"Not today he won't. So you'll come flying with me?"

"No way."

"Why not?"

"I hate flying. It's risky and it scares me. I prefer two-dimensional traveling—back and forth and sideways. I don't do up and down."

"You won't be scared with me. I'm an ace."

"You're an unknown quantity. You know about white-knuckle flyers? I am more of the white-elbow variety."

"Then at least have lunch with me. I still owe you a meal, remember. Give Dante an afternoon of sleeping on your sofa and come with me."

"Sorry. Give me a rain check."

"If it's raining we can't go flying."

She said over her shoulder, "My point exactly."

ACROSS THE STREET Trey called his mother. "Mama? I got a glass he's been drinking out of. Really good set of fingerprints on it. That's why you want it, isn't it? Who is he?"

"Excellent. Put it very carefully into a brown-paper envelope without smearing his prints. Use a paper towel. Then bring it to me."

"Does this mean I don't have to steal his toothbrush?"

"Steal it, Trey. Just in case this isn't enough."

"Mama, I feel like a total idiot doing this stuff."

"It may save us all in the long run. Now bring me that glass."

AT LUNCH Trey checked the parking lot behind the mansion. Paul's car wasn't there. Good. After he ate he strolled over to the house. Ann volunteered to take him around.

He had to admit he was impressed. He'd never seen the house in its glory days, but he felt some strong pangs of jealousy that this stranger, this outsider, should be the one to resurrect his family's home.

Sue-sue wouldn't like it one bit. She'd turned the house down flat after Aunt Addy died and had made Trey put it on the market immediately. But Sue-sue tended to want what other people had. When Sue-sue was angry, she made Trey's life hell. He could deal with the no-sex part, but having to keep her from yelling at the kids wore him out.

He was afraid he wouldn't be able to ditch Ann long enough to go upstairs to steal Paul's toothbrush, but just as they started up the front staircase, Buddy called her from the kitchen.

"I know my way around," Trey said. "You go on. You don't have to play tour guide."

"Okay, but watch your step."

He ran up the stairs. He didn't know which bathroom Paul was using. The master bathroom was a mess. Unusable. The middle bathroom hadn't been touched, but showed no signs it had been used, either.

He opened the door to the back bathroom. Jackpot. Paul's toothbrush hung on an antique rack beside the equally antique medicine chest. He checked for Ann or workmen, then wrapped a paper towel around his hand, snatched the damp toothbrush and stuck it in his pocket.

He opened the door to the back bedroom. The suitcase beside the bed showed just how primitively Paul was camping out. He might be able to search Paul's luggage, after all, but as he started across the room, he heard voices coming up the stairwell. He barely had time to back out, shut the door and meet Ann and one of the crew coming up the stairs.

"You see everything?" she asked.

He knew his face looked guilty. "Wonderful, wonderful. Can't wait to see it all done. Well, gotta go." He pushed past her and raced out of the house and to his truck in the square. He called his mother from his cell phone. "Got it, Mama. I'll bring it to you right this minute."

SINCE THE RAIN had changed its mind again and decided to continue, and since he couldn't persuade Ann to come with him to lunch in town, Paul spent the afternoon in the library morgue. He found the story about his father's wedding to Karen Bingham. He looked further back without finding an announcement of their engagement. In a socially prominent family like the Delaneys, he would have expected a story on an engagement party and a formal photo of the bride-to-be.

Four bridesmaids and a champagne brunch at the Delaney mansion didn't exactly constitute a shotgun wedding, but it wasn't the big shindig he'd have expected of the Delaneys. He noted that Karen Bingham had been given away by her grandfather, because Mrs. Bingham was widowed. At the end of the story the reporter slipped in a statement that the combination of the Bingham and Delaney holdings would eventually make the young Delaneys the largest landowners in the county.

He checked the byline at the head of the story. Wilda Mae Hepworth had written it. He remembered seeing the name somewhere recently. He went to the desk and asked the librarian, Vivian, if he could look at her copy of the county paper.

He was right. The byline was still at the head of the society news column. Either Wilda Mae had started reporting when she was in diapers or she was still writing in her dotage.

"Vivian," he asked, "do you know this Wilda Mae Hepworth?"

Vivian giggled. She was given to giggling and turning bright red every time he spoke to her. "Know her? She's my great-aunt on my daddy's side. I've known her all my life."

"And she's still writing this column?"

"Yessir."

"Do you think I could talk to her, off the record, that is?"

"I don't see why not. Aunt Wilda Mae loves to talk.

There's precious little about this county she doesn't know.''

"Would you mind calling her for me?"

"When would you like to see her?"

"Does she live in Somerville?"

"About four miles out toward the interstate."

"Then how about now?" He looked at his watch. It was four o'clock.

"Okay." Vivian's pointed little face was avidly curious, but she didn't ask questions. She went into her small office and came out smiling a few minutes later. "She says come ahead. She'll brew some fresh sweet tea. Let me give you directions."

Twenty minutes later Paul pulled into the gravel driveway of a white cottage that had been well maintained and probably predated his house by fifty years. The garden would be a riot of color in a month or so. At the moment there were butter pats of jonquils everywhere and a carpet of purple hyacinths.

He'd expected a fragile little lady in a lace collar. Wilda Mae, however, outweighed him by at least fifty pounds, was nearly as tall as he and had apparently put on eye shadow and lipstick just before he arrived. Her white hair was short and crinkly and he could see pink scalp beneath. She leaned slightly on a twisted blackthorn cane with a silver fox head as big as his fist.

After he had introduced himself and gone through all the formalities and given the information he knew would be required of him, his hostess, who sat stiffly in a large Victorian velvet armchair, asked, "So why do you want the dirt on the Delaneys?"

He blinked. She had a voice as big as the rest of her. He hoped there was no one else in the house.

"Don't worry. I live by myself. Put three husbands in

the ground and don't plan to follow them in any time soon." She paused. "Drink your tea."

"Yes, ma'am."

"I asked you a question."

"Can this be off the record?" he said.

"Unless you're planning to commit a crime, then I have to report it. Otherwise, I never tell anybody anything."

"I don't exactly want the dirt on the Delaneys, but I would like some information."

"Which generation?"

"How about starting with Trey Delaney's father?"

She shook her head and sighed so deeply her bosom rose and lowered like a drawbridge. "Sad story. I wouldn't have expected the rest of them to stand up for him, but Adelina Norwood should have. She'd been through the same thing."

"Adelina Norwood?" This was a new name.

"Miss Addy. You bought the house from her estate."

"Oh. I didn't know her name."

"There were three sisters. Maribelle, the oldest, was wild as a March hare from the time she hit this earth. Addy was the quiet one, but she fought hard for herself. Pity she lost. She had the talent to become a concert pianist, I do believe."

"I've heard. I have her piano."

"Oh, good." Wilda Mae slapped her hand against the velvet. Paul saw that the fingers were twisted with arthritis. He wondered how she managed to write her column.

She noticed his glance. He decided there wasn't much she didn't notice. "I've got a big computer on the dining-room table. I write from here, then modem my copy to the paper."

"I see."

"Got to go with the times, I say. Now, where were we?

Oh, Addy was the middle daughter. Sarah was the youngest and the only one still living. She had the good sense to marry Harris Pulliam and get away from her sisters. You met Ann yet?"

"She's helping to restore my house." He realized that at some point the Delaney mansion had become "my house." He couldn't remember exactly when he'd begun to call it that, but it surprised him.

"Darling girl, that Ann. Talented, too. Should never have married that Corrigan boy. He bled her dry and ran around on her all the time, is what I heard. She deserves a decent man who loves her and will give her a big family." She peered at him with the unspoken question—Are you that man?

Suddenly he didn't know the answer. Could he be that man? The prospect was becoming more and more appealing every time he looked at Ann.

He said nothing.

"Conrad—David's father and Trey's grandfather—had a coronary and was never right in the head afterward. His death nearly killed Maribelle. She did love the man, God knows why. You seen Burl Ives do 'Big Daddy'? Well, that was Conrad. Thought his word was law. It wasn't, of course, Maribelle's was, but Conrad never saw that. He decided it was time for David to come home, take over the business and marry the girl he'd been engaged to for three years. Between them, he and Maribelle and Karen's momma drove that poor boy until he didn't have any choice but to do what they wanted." She shook her head. "Killed him in the end."

"Killed him? I thought he died in a hunting accident."

"Oh, he did. But he'd never have been riding that crazy horse with a fifth of bourbon in him if he hadn't been the unhappiest man ever walked this earth. I got one of his caricatures. Want to see?'' She started to heave her bulk up, but he stopped her.

''Later, before I go.''

''It's a real killer. I look like a blimp with an attitude.'' She roared with laughter, then turned sober instantly. ''There was some legal shenanigans went on about then, but I never found out what.''

Paul's ears pricked up. ''What sort?''

''Conrad called in his lawyer and Judge Dalkins, his pal on the bench. They had a couple of secret confabs. I suspect they were working a deal about Mrs. Bingham's land. I heard tell it was something about the marriage.'' She shook her head. ''I hate not knowing.''

Paul just bet she did. Something about the marriage. Had his father gotten a quiet divorce from his mother, or even an annulment? He'd have to check the county records.

Wilda Mae's next words, however, startled him even more. ''Whatever they were up to, they never got it done. Judge Dalkins hit a deer driving home from court two days later and was killed. I kept an eye on court records for a time, but nothing came up with the Delaney name on it. Then Conrad had that stroke a week before the wedding. He couldn't even go to the ceremony. I doubt if he remembered what he'd been trying to do.''

Had David told his father about his French marriage? ''What about the lawyer?''

''Long dead. If it was something illegal, and knowing Conrad it could well have been, he'd never have put anything down on paper, anyway.''

''Tell me about the wedding.''

''Not much to tell.'' Wilda Mae shrugged. ''Little Episcopal church looked pretty enough as I recall, and I imagine Karen looked radiant—all brides do. It was a real small affair. I had to pull strings to get invited myself. The one thing I do remember is that the bridegroom looked like he was about to throw up. Maribelle said he had a touch of food poisoning.'' She snorted. ''Food poisoning, my foot.''

''He looked scared?''

''Miserable is more like it. Everybody assumed Karen was already pregnant, but she didn't have Trey for a full eleven months.'' She grinned that malicious grin. ''You have no idea how many ten-pound, seven-month babies we have around here.'' Wilda downed the remains of her tea. ''Young man, this has been delightful, but I got a deadline at six o'clock and I haven't written the first word. You come back and I'll dish some more dirt for you. For instance, about Addy and Conrad.''

''I beg your pardon?''

''They were lovers for Lord knows how many years right under Maribelle's eye in Maribelle's house. Everybody knew but Maribelle.'' She heaved herself ponderously to her feet. ''Whetted your appetite, haven't I?''

''Yes, ma'am, you have.''

''Good. Then you'll have to come back. Not often I get a gentleman caller as handsome as you.''

On the front porch, she said, ''Never showed you that caricature. Next time I'll have it out.'' She stood under the dripping eaves of her antebellum cottage and watched him drive away. He could see her in his rearview mirror until he turned the corner onto the paved road.

The more he learned, the more he didn't know. There was no one left alive who could tell him whether David had told his father about his marriage to Michelle. No one who could tell him whether or not Conrad tried to get a quiet annulment. Maybe that was why David was so miserable on his wedding day.

As he said "I do," David must have known he was committing bigamy. He must have spent the rest of his life looking over his shoulder. No wonder he lost his grip when Michelle finally showed up on his doorstep. The killing was looking more and more like manslaughter and less and less like murder one.

CHAPTER TEN

PAUL PICKED UP a pizza and a six-pack of beer on his way home from Wilda Mae's. He ate his solitary dinner on his upstairs porch in the twilight.

He loved this porch. He almost expected to see a tiger creep through the jungle beneath. After he ate he called Giselle and reported his meeting with Wilda Mae word for word.

"When Michelle appeared, your father must have really lost it," Giselle said.

"If he hadn't hidden her body, he probably would have gotten off with a couple of years for manslaughter. Down here he might even have received just probation."

"Probation? Are you serious?"

"In those days and with that family, dead serious."

"Come home, Paul. I feel like you're in the middle of some weird Southern-gothic epic down there."

"Sometimes I do, too. But I like it. I like the people. I've even developed a grudging kind of affection for my half brother, although his mother makes the hackles rise at the back of my neck. I'd always heard Southern women were formidable. That doesn't begin to describe them. Next to Karen Lowrance, Tante Helaine was a marshmallow."

Giselle laughed. "I don't believe it."

"Trust me."

After he hung up, he realized he hadn't gotten that list

of estate buyers from Trey. He was about to pick up the
telephone to call him when it rang.

"Hey."

Ann's voice. His heart sped up. "Hey, yourself."

"Trey left me this gigantic printout this afternoon to
give you and I forgot. Can I bring it over now?"

"Stay where you are. I'll be there in five minutes." He
hung up before she could protest.

He remembered to take a flashlight with him. He
splashed through puddles like a kid. Two kisses and he,
Mr. Sophisticated, was acting like a teenager. He ran up
her steps and banged on her door.

"It's open."

He was met by Dante, the dog's entire body wiggling
in delight at seeing him, although his face still looked like
Buster Keaton on a bad day. Paul ruffled the dog's ears.
"Hey, Dante, old man."

"I'm in the workroom," Ann called. "This is delicate.
I can't stop."

He stood behind her table and watched her work. She
had on heavy gloves and was pouring a viscous gray liq-
uid into a six-foot-length of plaster mold. She didn't look
up. "Don't speak until I'm through."

He liked the way the lights over her table turned her
brown hair into the shining red-brown of an otter's pelt.
He liked the way she concentrated.

After five minutes, she put down the pot she'd been
holding, shoved the safety glasses to the top of her head,
pulled off her gloves and said, "Okay. Now you can
talk."

"What are you doing?"

"Casting new crown molding to replace the areas that
are split and broken in your dining room. The pour has
to be just right or it doesn't fill in all the cracks."

"Where did you learn to do things like that?"

"I had six years in Washington and New York working with people who make me look stupid and clumsy."

"I'll never believe that."

"They taught me a lot. I still work freelance for both the studios I had full-time jobs with."

"Is that why you were in Buffalo?"

"Right. I am really good at golf leaf, although I hate doing it—one sneeze can cost your client a thousand bucks." She came around the table. "Sorry I forgot to bring you Trey's printout. He brought it over this morning, but you'd already left, so I brought it home in case the boys decided to use it for cleaning brushes or something."

"I'm glad you forgot it. Gives me an excuse to come over here."

"Where did you disappear to? Surely you weren't flying in this weather."

"I went to the library. Some more research."

"Someday you'll have to tell me what you're researching so diligently."

"Someday maybe I will." She hadn't invited him to sit down, so he stood awkwardly with the printout in his arms threatening to disgorge itself onto the floor.

"So, uh, would you like a drink?" The offer was grudging, but Paul wasn't about to look a gift horse in the mouth.

"Some of that white wine would be nice."

She poured them each a glass and brought his to him. He sat on the couch. She sat in the chair. He sipped. She sipped. Silence.

"So, you're going to try to buy back the chandelier?" she asked.

"Depends on how much they paid for it in the first place."

"I guess." More sips. He was certainly a sparkling conversationalist. He wanted to tell her the truth, tell her about his quest, explain to her that he didn't want to hurt her or her family, but that he might. Tell her not to trust him. Only to love him.

Suddenly they both began to speak.

"You first," he said.

"My mother wants to know if you'd like to come to dinner this Sunday at my grandmother's."

"I'd like that if I wouldn't be intruding."

"Of course not. I thought maybe you and I could go visit Miss Esther after dinner."

"Miss Esther? Refresh my memory. I've met so many people."

"She worked for the Delaneys most of her life. She wound up looking after Miss Addy full-time until she died."

"I remember. Yes, I'd like that."

"She's retired and living on a very nice pension from Aunt Addy, but both her sons live in Cincinnati or Cleveland or one of those cities. I don't know how much company she gets. She knows everything there is to know about the Delaneys."

"Wonderful. You will come with me, won't you?"

"I don't think she'd let you into her house if I didn't."

"Thanks for both invitations. What time is dinner?"

"About one."

"Where does your grandmother live?"

"You'd never find it alone. It's in the country. You can drive us both. I'll direct you."

He hadn't yet gotten used to eating dinner in the middle

of the day and supper in the evening. "I have an invitation for you, too."

"Not another dress-up-and-go-to-town dinner. Paul, I just don't have time."

"Trey invited me and his 'kissin' cousin' to dinner Wednesday night."

"He didn't mention it today."

"I guess he wanted me to ask you. So what do I tell him?"

He could see her hesitation. "Sure, I guess so. Why not?" More hesitation. "Paul, you do realize that my mother is going to put you under a microscope when you come to dinner, don't you?"

"I hadn't."

"She will."

"Why?"

"If a man is…eligible, my mother is going to check him out as future son-in-law material. I'm sorry. I had to warn you."

He started to laugh. "My *tante* Helaine used to put every pimply-faced adolescent who wanted to take out one of my sisters through hell. I know the drill."

"I didn't know you had sisters."

"Two. They're actually my cousins, but Tante Helaine raised all three of us, so I consider them sisters. Giselle is four years older than me, and Gabrielle is two years older."

"Are you close?"

"With Giselle, as close as we can be, considering we don't see one another often enough. We talk on the phone almost every day. With Gabrielle…" He shrugged. "She always resented me. She had to move into Giselle's bedroom when my…when I moved in."

"Why do you say *Tante* Helaine? A holdover from your French heritage?"

"Tante Helaine was born and raised in France. I spoke French before I spoke English. It's the French word for aunt."

"I know. What happened to your parents?"

"My mother...died. My father..." He left it dangling. She would assume he'd divorced them.

"Were you happy? Did they treat you well?"

"They were wonderful. Uncle Charlie taught me to play baseball and basketball, although I'm not tall enough to be any good. Tante Helaine taught me to cook. She said men make the best chefs."

"She wanted you to become a chef?"

"Possibly. But I always knew I wanted to fly."

"But didn't you say you grew up in Queens?"

"Queens and barely middle-class. Somehow I managed to wangle an appointment to the Air Force Academy. I've been flying ever since."

"But you stopped."

"Not flying, just flying big transports. Uncle Charlie would be upset if he knew how screwed up my right arm is. He wanted me to be a major-league pitcher."

"Do you mind talking about it?"

"As a matter of fact, I do. It's over with. I made out better than the other two guys. I can still fly. They can't."

"Was it a crash?"

"It was a crash that didn't happen, thank God. Look, let's drop it."

"Sure. Sorry." She stood. "More wine?"

He wasn't about to leave any sooner than he had to. "Thanks."

When she handed him her glass, he asked, "What about you? Tell me the story of your life."

"Bor-ring. I got a master's in art history—heaven only knows why except that I've loved art all my life. I eloped with a guy who had big dreams and no discipline. I stuck with him through six years and so many infidelities I lost count, and when I couldn't take it any longer, I quit and came home to my family to lick my wounds."

"How could any man in his right mind be unfaithful to you?"

"Travis would have been unfaithful to Cleopatra. She would have chopped off his head, which is what I should have done."

"You say you came home. Where from?"

"New York. A job I loved, friends I adored, a city that thrilled me."

"So why'd you leave? I mean, a divorce doesn't necessarily mean you uproot your whole life, does it?"

"I'm basically a country girl. Besides, I like things clean. I still get the excitement when I do a job in a big city, but when I do I'm living on an expense account. That's a bunch better than a cold-water walk-up. Where did you live before?"

"A high-rise in New Jersey." He put his glass on the coffee table and took a deep breath. "Look," he said, "I don't know what I've done to upset you, but I wish to God you'd tell me so I can fix it. Here we sit talking like total strangers with a four-foot coffee table between us when what I want to do is haul you out of that chair and into my arms. Maybe I should just do it and stop asking permission."

She jumped up and set her glass on the kitchen bar. "You haven't done anything. It's me. I look at you and I think what could you possibly see in a country girl like me, anyway?"

He had her in his arms before she could turn around.

He swung her to face him and wrapped her so tightly that her hands came up against his chest. "What did that bastard you married *do* to you? How could you not know that you're the most beautiful, the most desirable—"

"Stop."

He kissed her. Fiercely at first to capture her lips. Then he tasted her gently, sweetly, savoring the white wine that still lingered on her tongue, gently nibbling that sensuous lower lip, kissing her eyes, then drawing his lips along her cheekbone to her throat.

After a moment's resistance she came to him. She felt so soft. Women had no idea how exciting that softness was to a man. He fought with his conscience for all of thirty seconds. His conscience lost.

ANN KNEW she shouldn't be kissing Paul. She'd made herself promise to keep him at arm's length. But it had been so long since a man had held her in his arms, kissed her.

Actually, nobody had ever kissed her that way. She felt her body resonate, begin to come alive all the way down to her toes. When she responded to his kiss, it was as though she'd been desert dry and suddenly he'd opened a tap that flooded her with sensation and longing. She didn't remember when she'd begun to want him, but that didn't matter any longer.

She wrapped her arms around him, fitted her body against him, felt his hands cup her bottom and pull her toward him. He was aroused.

Well, so was she. When he slipped his hand under her shirt and unhooked her bra, then slid it and her shirt over her head, she nearly sobbed at the release. And when he began to stroke her breasts, to circle her swollen nipples with his fingers as gently as snowflakes, she could only arch her back, close her eyes and abandon herself to his touch.

She took off his shirt and clasped him naked breast to naked breast. Too late to pull away, too late to stop the inevitable.

But she didn't want to stop. He hooked his finger in the waistband of her jeans, unzipped them expertly with one hand and pushed them over her hips. He ran his lips and tongue down her body, then bent to pick her up.

She heard his quick intake of breath. His bad arm.

She stepped out of her jeans and took his hand, swept aside the curtains that hid her bed and led him there.

"I want…" he began.

She held him and whispered, "It's all right," against his ear. She lay back and pulled him with her so that he knelt on one knee at the side of the bed.

He stripped quickly and pulled a condom from the pocket of his jeans.

She caught her breath at how beautiful he was in the pale light. He bent over her once more and with aching slowness began to ease her panties down.

She didn't want careful or slow. She wanted him *now*. All she could say was "Please, please," but it was enough.

He took only a second to put on the condom, then came to her with the same urgency she felt.

She lost track of time, of body, of mind, until there was nothing but the joy of having him inside her, meeting the thrust of her hips with his, faster and faster until she thought she'd die if she didn't reach the top. She heard herself cry out, and then he hurled her over the crest with so much pleasure it was nearly pain. A moment later when she felt him spasm, she climaxed again.

When she began to breathe normally again, she held him in her arms, wanting to keep him there forever.

Eventually, however, he slid up beside her and pulled her to him. She played with the dark curls on his chest and for a moment thought how little she knew of him. She no longer cared. All that mattered was that he lay beside her, holding her, his breath soft against her hair. She felt exhausted. She could barely keep her eyes open....

She awoke when she lost the sensation in the arm that was trapped underneath him. She slipped it out, then silently raised herself to look at him.

Watching him sleep was a guilty pleasure. For the first time she studied his right arm and shoulder. The scars were neat and straight, the result of surgery. They circled around his upper arm and shoulder and continued until they disappeared over his back. Whatever had happened must have crushed the bones at the point of the shoulder. She winced even to think of the pain he must have endured.

She touched his cheek softly so as not to wake him. She longed to know everything about him.

He let out his breath and turned toward her without waking. She fitted her body against his and let sleep take her again. For the first time in years she felt utterly content.

Her eyes blinked open. Dante! She hadn't given the dog a thought once she'd begun concentrating on Paul. Had he quietly been destroying the studio out of nervousness or jealousy? He hadn't been for his walk. He must be miserable.

As much as she hated leaving the comfort of Paul's body, she slipped out of bed and through the curtains. Dante sat by the outside door with a puzzled expression

on his droopy face. He didn't move toward her. He must
be desperately in need of a walk.

She slipped on her jeans and her shirt without under-
wear, slid her feet into the rubber boots she kept beside
the door, picked up her flashlight and eased the back door
open.

Dante dashed through, down the stairs and into the
bushes across the alley. She left the door behind her
slightly ajar and slipped down silently behind him.

She'd left a warm bed. The night air was cold. She
hugged herself and prayed Dante would finish quickly.
She didn't want to call him.

As she walked down the alley after him, she saw head-
lights pass the opening at the end. A squad car.

"Please don't let it stop," she prayed.

A moment later, however, a car door slammed and
Buddy Jenkins in full uniform, hands hooked in his Sam
Browne belt, walked down the alley toward her.

"Out kinda late, aren't you, honey?"

"Hey, Daddy. Dante needed a potty break."

Sometimes when he found her working in the middle
of the night, her father would come up and have a glass
of tea or a cup of hot chocolate with her. Tonight was
definitely not the night.

"Come on, Dante," she called, and yawned so wide
that she nearly dislocated her jaw in hopes that her father
would get the hint.

"Aren't you cold, baby? You ought to go back inside."

"I'm fine, Daddy. Dante, drat it, come *on!*"

She could tell her father was itching for an invitation.
They'd grown close for the first time in their lives after
she moved back to Rossiter and began to work with him.
He and Travis had disliked one another on sight, a situ-
ation that had only worsened with time. She hardened her

heart. "I'd love to ask you up, Daddy, but I'm exhausted. I'm going straight to bed."

"Oh, okay."

She hated the disappointment in his voice. Before she could hem and haw further, however, Dante trotted up.

She didn't really want to get close enough to her father even to kiss him on the cheek. The last thing she needed was for him to catch a whiff of what she'd just been doing and put two and two together.

She grabbed Dante's collar and almost raced up the stairs. "Sorry, Daddy, but I'm about to drop."

"Sure, honey. You get some rest."

He watched until she'd gone in her door, waved to him and shut it firmly against him. She turned the dead bolt as quietly as she could. Dante stood by her with his tail wagging. She patted his head, gave him a mammoth dog biscuit from the cookie jar on the kitchen counter, pulled off her boots and her clothes and tiptoed back to bed.

As she slid in, Paul said, "Damnation, woman, you're freezing!" He propped himself up on one elbow.

"Dante needed to go out."

"Do you usually talk to Dante that way?"

"Gee, what big ears you have, Grandmother. I was talking to my father. He was angling for an invitation to come up for hot chocolate."

Paul flopped onto his back. "He'd probably have shot me."

She leaned over him. "I was thinking more along the tar-and-feather line. Ever been ridden out of town on a rail? I've heard it's extremely uncomfortable."

Without warning he grabbed her and flipped her onto her back. They laughed and tussled for a moment, then their eyes caught and held.

This time when they made love they did it slowly, savoring the taste and touch and scent of love.

As they lay tangled together in the afterglow, Paul said sleepily, "I think I'd better go. You don't need everyone in Rossiter seeing me walking across the square at six in the morning."

"Thinking of my reputation?" she asked.

"And mine," he said.

"Yours will be enhanced immeasurably."

"I'll have that engraved on my tombstone after your father shoots me." He kissed the top of her head. "I'm serious. As much as I'd like to stay here forever, I should sneak out like some prowler, slide home in the shadows and pray that your dad's squad car doesn't make another pass through the square until I'm safely in my own house." He slipped out of bed. "You do have a bathroom in this place, don't you?"

"To your left just past the arch into the workroom." She started to get up.

"No, stay." He caressed her cheek, picked up his clothes and went in search of the bathroom.

He came back fully clothed and sat on the edge of the bed so he could take her in his arms and kiss her. "Good night, country girl," he whispered.

A moment later she heard the dead bolt turn, the door open and close after him, then his footsteps on the staircase.

She stretched contentedly. It was amazing how different sex could be when it was just sex—no matter how great—and when it was love.

Her eyes opened wide. Not love. Not with Paul Bouvet. He was a man without roots. There was nothing for him in Rossiter. She'd suspected for some time that he had a secret agenda. She just didn't know what that agenda could be.

CHAPTER ELEVEN

PAUL WAS UP in the air dusting crops by the time Ann got to his house the next morning, so she didn't see him all day. She thought of him every time she moved. She worked with a stupid grin on her face even when the first batch of scamoglio plaster she'd mixed for the stairwell turned out looking more like cow poop than marble.

When she got home, she found a florist box on the landing from a very chic Memphis florist. After she let herself and Dante in, she tore the paper off the box to find a dozen pale-peach roses.

"At least he has more imagination than to send red," she said to Dante. She picked up the card. "I considered buying these from your downstairs neighbor, but I thought it might raise a few eyebrows. Love, Paul."

The love part was undoubtedly what men like Paul always said the morning after the first night with a woman.

"He's not talking love-love, Dante," she said. "I kind of wish he were. He's talking thanks-for-a-great-roll-in-the-hay love."

She decided the crown molding should have set well enough to be pulled apart, so she spent the next hour carefully removing it from its mold and cleaning up the small imperfections with dental tools. The work was sufficiently absorbing to keep her mind off Paul.

At five-thirty she called her mother and invited herself and Dante to dinner. She refused to sit in her apartment waiting for Paul to call or show up at her door. She'd had one great night. That did not make a commitment.

Two nights with Paul, and she knew she'd be lost forever. She'd vowed no more hunks, no more unknown quantities, no more risky relationships. Then she'd allowed herself to fall for a man who embodied all three.

Well, she'd let her mother investigate his background at Sunday dinner.

WITH TREMBLING FINGERS, Karen Lowrance tore open the envelope from the private detective Trey had hired. She scanned the single sheet of information, and with every word she grew more and more frightened. Across from her Trey eyed the report avidly, but kept silent.

The report said that Paul Bouvet was the son of a Frenchwoman named Michelle Bouvet, present whereabouts unknown. Father unknown, although Paul had dual citizenship when he came to the U.S. with his mother, which meant that the father must have been an American. Although both the French and American governments undoubtedly knew more, neither was being cooperative. Because the detective had no information as to precisely where in France Paul Bouvet had been born, he could not locate his birth certificate to ascertain the name of the father listed thereon.

"Damn!" Karen said. "I should have told him to look in Paris."

The report added that should the client want more information, a trip to France might be necessary. Such a course might not be productive and would be both time-consuming and expensive.

"I'll just bet it would," Karen muttered. She poured herself another small shot of bourbon, then set it down on the table beside her and ignored it. She needed a cool and sober head to plan how to proceed.

The report further stated that this Michelle Bouvet had brought him to the United States when he was five. They'd lived with her sister, Helaine, and her American husband, Charles Humber, in Queens, New York. Bouvet's mother had disappeared a year later. There was still an open missing-persons file on her.

Seven years later Charles Humber had petitioned the courts to declare Michelle Bouvet legally dead and to allow him to adopt Paul formally. Since Paul had been living with the Humbers most of his life, and since apparently Mrs. Humber was Ms. Bouvet's closest relative, the petition was granted. Paul Bouvet, however, had retained his mother's name.

Karen passed over his school records, his appointment to the Air Force Academy and his subsequent service.

Close to the end of the report, a sentence caught her eye. "Because of injuries received in the accident, Mr. Bouvet can no longer fly transports, but maintains a Class III commercial pilot's license."

He owned the house in Rossiter, which he was currently renovating, a nearly new silver BMW and a Cessna 182 aircraft currently hangared at Morrison Airfield.

She dropped the page on the ottoman that served as a coffee table and began to worry one of her long fingernails with her teeth. When it split, she bit it off with an oath. Now she'd have to get a new acrylic tip.

"Okay, Mama. I've been forbearing long enough. I want to read that report. What the hell is the problem with this guy? Is he going to blow up the cotton gin or something?"

She'd hoped to have proof, but the DNA results hadn't come back yet. Still, she was ninety-nine percent certain that Paul Bouvet was, in fact, her husband's bastard son. The dates were right. He must have been conceived just before Paul came home to Rossiter and married her.

Paul Bouvet was only a year or two older than her Trey. And much smarter, she suspected. Trey was a good son, a loving husband and father. He was even a fairly good businessman, as long as he stuck to cattle, cotton and soybeans.

Get him outside his area of expertise and he was hopeless. He'd grown up in a world of privilege and family that left him ill prepared for the real world. So far his greatest challenge had been to keep a high enough grade-point average in college to stay in his fraternity house. And he'd barely accomplished that.

Even with the men who worked for him, he had absolutely no people skills. Karen couldn't count the times she'd had to smooth over Trey's shoot-from-the-hip decisions. She was still very much an active partner in Delaney Farms. If Paul Bouvet sued for a portion of the estate, she'd lose nearly as much as Trey.

There was still a possibility she was wrong. Any jury in the world would laugh her out of court if she said she'd recognized her husband in this stranger at first glance.

If she told Trey her suspicions now, he'd either panic and do something irreparably stupid, or he'd fall all over himself making his new *brother* welcome.

Neither was acceptable.

She made a decision to keep as much as possible from him until the DNA results came back, even if she had to lie. According to her doctor, the testing should take no more than a week. If Paul Bouvet's DNA and Trey's DNA proved that David Delaney had fathered both of them, then she'd have to tell Trey and try to make him understand how dire the consequences could be for them all.

"This report is worse than useless," Karen said, tossing the remaining pages onto the ottoman.

"Mother, I feel as if I've gone along with this blindfolded, but if there's a problem, then we have to face it together. Did Daddy have debts we don't know about? Did he commit some crime that hasn't come to light? Frankly, I can't believe if he was playing fast and loose with the SEC, they wouldn't have investigated us a whole lot sooner than this. Is this guy some kind of hit man? Did Daddy borrow money from the mob?"

"Don't be ridiculous."

"I'm not being any more ridiculous than you are. And what's this business about his toothbrush? There's only one reason you'd want that."

"Trey, you're going to have to trust me for a few more days. I've got some investigations of my own going."

"Not good enough. What? Is this some long-standing feud from way back in Ireland six generations ago?"

"Now you really *are* being ridiculous."

"Then some personal feud."

That was a little too close to the truth for Karen. "All right," she said. "We're not only dealing with possible financial repercussions of something your father may or may not have done before he died, we're also dealing with the possibility of scandal that could compromise the entire family."

"And you expect me to sit by without knowing any more about it than that?" Trey shoved back his hair in exasperation. "You and Grandmother handled the business after father died. I didn't start running things on my own until after college. By then all the estates were probated, the tax audits done. How come this is coming out of the woodwork after all this time?"

"I honestly don't know." Karen leaned her head back

against the sofa. "That's the only thing that gives me hope I might be wrong. Why wait this long?"

"I'll give you twenty-four hours, then you have to tell me."

"Give me a week."

"Mama!"

"A week, Trey. By then either this will have all blown over or we'll have to start making plans to get rid of this man."

"I've never heard you talk like this," Trey said. "You sound as if you're talking about killing him." His voice had risen dangerously.

"Of course I'm not." It might yet come to that, but Trey would not be told if it did. "He must be made to feel uncomfortable in Rossiter. He might even wind up in the hospital." She dropped her head into her hands. "For the first time in my life, I wish another human being would simply vanish off the face of the earth. Quickly." Then she looked up and laughed at Trey's horror-stricken face. "Oh, darling, I'm kidding. I got carried away." She reached across and touched his cheek. "Don't worry until we know more."

"How can I not worry, Mama?"

"Trust me. I promise I'll find some way to get that man out of our hair and our lives." She picked up her glass. "Maybe put him in a body cast for a couple of months until we're ready to deal with him." She laughed shortly.

"I'll try to find out more about him when he comes over for dinner Wednesday night."

Karen sat bolt upright. "You invited him for dinner? At your house with Sue-sue and the children?"

"You said get close to him."

"Not that close. To have him in your own house? Sometimes you don't have the brains God gave a goose."

"Ann's coming, too. Want me to cancel?"

Karen closed her eyes. "No. Let them come. Just don't let him get too chummy. And keep your eyes open."

"Yes, ma'am."

"Now go on home, honeypot. Mama's worn to a frazzle." She closed her eyes against the headache that pounded in her temples.

She vaguely remembered hearing Trey say as he left the room, "Don't worry, Mama. I'll fix it."

As he closed the door, she whispered, "Dear God. *Michelle*. To finally know her name after all these years…"

ANN WAS CAREFULLY coping the last piece of crown molding for the dining room when Paul drove in. She recognized the growl of his engine and her heart turned over.

Dante, who'd been lying on the cool tiles of the hearth, got up and trotted to the back door to greet Paul. Half-a-dozen workmen were in the house. Besides that, there still weren't any curtains at the windows, so she hoped Paul wouldn't do something like put his arms around her and kiss her. "Drat," she said as the saw slipped and took a small nick out of one edge of the molding.

"Hi."

She heard his voice behind her. Her body came alive, but she didn't turn around.

"Hey. You about finished crop dusting?"

"Yeah."

She heard his footsteps behind her, but she also heard one of the workmen's boots tromping down the staircase. She looked over her shoulder and gave Paul a small shake of her head. He raised his eyebrows, but got the message.

When he was much too close for comfort, he said softly, "I know this town is limited for takeout, so I went by the market this afternoon and picked up picnic stuff. Could I interest you in dining al fresco on my sleeping porch?"

"What kind of picnic?"

"A little wine, a little pâté, a little French bread, a few grapes—stuff like that."

"I really—"

"Don't even try to say you really shouldn't take the time."

She nodded. "All right. I'd love to. What do we sit on?"

"Aha. I picked up a couple of wrought-iron chairs and a table today. If I can get one of the guys to help me, I'll have everything set up on the porch by the time you go home, clean up and get changed."

"Are you implying I'm grubby?"

He laughed. "You have plaster on your nose."

"It's the scamoglio. This batch turned out pretty well. Want to see?"

She laid the newly coped piece of trim carefully on the dining-room floor and led him to the front hall. "Ta-da."

"I'll be damned if I can see where you've redone it."

"It'll look fantastic with a couple of coats of clear bees-wax on it." She hugged herself. "I am *so* good at this."

"Humble, too." He started to reach for her again when one of the painters walked between them carrying a ladder.

"Hey," said the man.

"Hey," said Ann. "Cal, can you help Paul carry some stuff upstairs before you leave?"

"Sure. I'm on my way out. Let's do it."

Ann smiled at Paul. "Voilà. How'd you get the stuff in your car?"

"It's in boxes. Has to be put together."

"Oh. I think I'll leave now. I can finish the molding tomorrow morning when I can see better." She grinned. "Bye."

"Bye."

Paul spent the next hour putting together his table and chairs, setting them up on his porch, adding the tablecloth and napkins and china and wineglasses and candlesticks he'd bought to help the mood. Then he quickly changed the linen on his mattress. The second day of his camp-out he'd bought a microwave and a small refrigerator, so he put the wine on ice and had a hurried shower.

He felt like an adolescent. He knew the way he wanted the evening to end—with Ann sharing that mattress with him.

He'd just put the single peach rose he'd saved from the bunch he'd given her into one of the four wineglasses he'd bought when he heard the back door open and Ann's voice call.

He went to the landing and leaned over the railing. "Come on up. Can we trust Dante around pâté?"

"Only if you keep it out of his reach," she said.

She looked scrubbed and shining. She wore some kind of gathered skirt printed with wildflowers and a white shirt that buttoned invitingly down the front. He saw no sign of a bra. His pulse quickened.

His other purchase for his indoor campsite had been shades for the tall windows on the north side so that he could change clothes in the morning without parading in front of the people in the Wolf River parking lot.

Tonight the blinds were closed against prying eyes. The

only light came from the candles. She walked past him onto the porch.

"Paul, this is lovely. It's like being in a tree house."

"That's what I call it—my tree house." He wrapped his arms around her waist and pulled her back against his chest. "You smell wonderful."

"Thank you for the roses."

"You should have roses every day." He turned her in his arms and kissed her softly. Behind him he heard Dante subside with a sigh and a thud as though saying, "Not again."

The evening was as perfect as Paul hoped it would be. He had vowed not to mention the Delaneys or Rossiter or his family. They talked about flying and art restoration and plays and ballets and music. They drank the wine and ate the pâté and took Dante for a tour around the overgrown garden, then came upstairs, drank more wine and finally, without speaking, they took off their clothes and made love.

Afterward Paul lay on his back, watched the candles on the porch gutter, and wished he could end every night of the rest of his life like this, wrapped in Ann's warm embrace with the scent of her body and the perfume of her hair in his nostrils.

Maybe it was possible, but only if he dropped his quest right this second before he stirred up any more mud. Why not simply finish his house, move in, fly his airplane, maybe even buy the field from Hack? Was Ann worth living the rest of his life without knowing what had happened to his mother?

He'd spent more than thirty years without knowing. Most of those years he'd assumed he would never have a clue, and so had dismissed the possibility from his mind.

Why not go back to the days before Giselle found all that information hidden in her mother's closet?

He closed his eyes. He couldn't *un*know something. When he'd finally read the report from the detective his uncle Charlie had hired to try to find his mother, he knew he could never take refuge in ignorance again. He had to go on, and he had. Until at last he discovered the man who was his father.

He no longer cared about humiliating the Delaneys by revealing their scandals. He no longer wanted to take everything they owned and hand it back to them. He rather liked Trey. The guy reminded him of a bumbling puppy who hadn't quite been paper-trained.

Above all, Paul wanted Ann.

His second cousin. She had a right to know that.

But if he told her, she'd know he was a fraud and she'd leave him.

"Hey, sleepyhead, this time I'm the one to do the skulking home after midnight," Ann whispered.

"Don't go."

"I have to. Tomorrow is Sunday, remember? You're invited for Sunday dinner at Gram's."

He groaned. "Do I have to?"

"You bet you do. Now kiss me and let me go to my lonely bed."

"And leave me in mine."

"Right."

"All right. I don't renege on invitations even if they turn into inquisitions." He caught her wrist. "But only if you'll go flying with me tomorrow afternoon."

He heard her intake of breath. "Oh, Paul—"

"Say yes. I want to show you my world."

"If I have to. But no funny business."

"No funny business and we'll land as soon as you want to."

"Then, I suppose…"

PAUL DIDN'T THINK he'd ever seen so much food outside a restaurant. He could feel his arteries clogging, but as he munched his second piece of fried chicken it didn't seem to matter.

He'd learned about Ann and her family. Nancy Jenkins taught sixth grade, loved horses and old houses, had married Buddy Jenkins and never lived anywhere except Rossiter.

Buddy, born and raised in Arkansas, with no family left to speak of, had come to Rossiter fresh from a tour of duty with the MPs and had fallen in love with little Nancy Pulliam, the schoolteacher. Instead of moving to a larger town and a bigger job, he'd wound up as a small-town chief of police. He'd started restoring old buildings to make ends meet, and with Ann's help and inspiration, he'd taken enough classes and studied under enough master craftsmen to become an expert in his own right.

"Now," Ann's mother said as she served Paul his second piece of pecan pie, "tell us about you. How on earth did you end up in Rossiter?"

He'd worked on his story, but this was his first chance to trot it out in public. He glanced at Ann, who gave him an "I told you so" smile.

He took a deep breath. "I was at loose ends and looking for a new project."

"But in Rossiter? How on earth did you even know the house was for sale?"

Now for the first bold-faced lie. "I've always been interested in antebellum mansions—"

"Honey, I hate to tell you this, but the war ended in

1865," Nancy Jenkins said with a smile. "The Delaney house is a whole lot younger than that."

"I do know that, Mrs. Jenkins." He grinned back at her. "But at this point and in this area it seemed to me that all the really good stuff was already snapped up. Either that or way beyond repair."

"So you were looking for a place?" Buddy asked.

"Actually, I was being a pain to my family in New Jersey. My sister Giselle suggested I take a trip—a very long trip, I think, is what she suggested. I decided to drive to New Orleans, maybe stop at Natchez and Vicksburg along the way, maybe see some Civil War battlefields."

"Down here, I'll have you know we refer to that war as the Northern Aggression," Gram said. "More tea?"

"No, thank you, ma'am." He was about to float away already. "I was driving from Shiloh to Memphis and passed the sign for Rossiter. I turned in because I was hungry and looking for a place to eat. I passed by the For Sale sign on my way to the café. Believe me, I had no intention of buying that house. I just asked to see it to pass a couple of hours so I wouldn't have to check into my motel too early."

Sounded plausible to him. He hoped the others bought it.

"Goodness! You are a real man of action," Nancy said.

"Probably more like crazy," Buddy snorted.

"So what does your family think of your move?" Nancy asked.

"I only have a couple of girl cousins left, both of whom I consider sisters, since their mother raised me. Giselle is actually my first cousin."

"Ann told us your mother died young."

He stiffened. "Yes."

"And your father?"

"Left us."

"Oh, I'm so sorry." Nancy really sounded sorry. It wasn't simply chitchat. "And you've never married?"

He caught Ann's eyes raised to heaven and heard her groan under her breath.

"Not so far. Too busy."

"But you're not too busy now, are you? That is certainly a big house for one person."

"Yes, it is."

"Mother," Ann snapped, "knock it off."

"I don't know what you mean."

"You darned well do. Come on, let's help Gram with the dishes."

After lunch he tossed a baseball left-handed with Buddy for a while.

"Ann was one hell of a softball pitcher," Buddy said as they sat on Gram's front steps to cool off. "Couldn't run worth a damn. I told her Babe Ruth hit home runs because he didn't like to run, so she started doing the same thing. That was before she went off to college and took up art restoration. And met that idiot she married."

When Ann came out to tell him the kitchen was finally clean, she carried two large covered plastic dishes that he assumed were leftovers from dinner.

He turned to Buddy. "We're going flying."

"But first we're going to drop in on Miss Esther," Ann said. "Don't tell me you forgot. Then if we have time, maybe you can take me flying."

"You promised."

Buddy stood and from the second step of the porch loomed over Paul. "You all be careful." Paul understood the words were as much threat as warning.

"Yessir."

MISS ESTHER'S little cottage was down the street and around the corner from the Delaney house. It was newly painted white. The lawn and shrubbery were immaculate, and he could see perennials beginning to sprout in the flower beds.

Miss Esther answered the door with her hat on. "I know y'all finished church a while back, but your church and my church put a different time limit on Sunday services." She looked down at the covered plastic dish. "Don't tell me that's Sarah Pulliam's fried chicken."

"And half a Dolly Madison cake. She says she hopes you like them."

"Indeed I do. Come in and sit down while I put these in the icebox and get out the ice for the tea." She beamed at Paul.

"Can I help?" Ann asked.

"It's all ready. Just be a little minute."

The cottage was small, the furnishings no longer new, but every bit of wood shone with polish. The wood floors sparkled. On a table by the window sat at least twenty pots of African violets, most in bloom. On another table stood at least as many framed photos of what must be Miss Esther's family.

She came in with a heavy tray, but when Paul tried to take it from her, she shooed him away. "I can carry a tray, young man. I been doing it all my life."

Paul had no idea how old she was. She was thin, but there was no stoop in her bony shoulders and her white hair was twisted into a fat bun on the back of her head.

She sat in a Lincoln rocker on the other side of the coffee table, settled them with their iced tea and homemade shortbread cookies that made Paul wish he hadn't eaten so much Sunday dinner, and said, "I am glad you called. I have been meaning to stop by and see what all you're doing to my house, but I been too busy getting the garden ready to plant."

"We're a long way from finished, Miss Esther," Ann said, looking ruefully at the cookies. "But come by any time."

"Yes, please do," Paul echoed.

"Now that we've taken care of the chitchat, tell me how come you two are visiting a worn-out old black lady on a fine Sunday afternoon."

"You don't look worn-out to me," Paul blurted.

Miss Esther stared at him a moment, then burst out laughing. Paul blushed.

"I'll bet you want to know about the folks who lived in that house before you bought it, don't you?"

"I've already found out a good deal about them, but I thought you might fill me in on the last generation and how the house came to be in such bad shape."

Miss Esther shook her head. "Miss Maribelle left that house and a trust fund to Miss Addy for her lifetime. It was plenty to take care of what needed to be kept up, but Miss Addy wouldn't spend a dime on the house. And pretty soon, she started going downhill. The doctors called it 'senile dementia,' whatever that is. So far as I was concerned, she just got crazier and crazier. Sometimes I swore I was gonna walk out and make Mr. Trey hire a real nurse."

"But you didn't," Ann said.

Miss Esther sighed. "Couldn't. I spent most of my life looking after the Delaneys. Mr. Conrad—that's Miss Maribelle's husband—gave me this little house free and clear when the few black folks in town all lived north of the railroad track. After he died, Miss Maribelle kept me on and hired help for me when I needed it."

"I've heard Maribelle could be difficult," Paul said.

"Huh. She could get up on her high horse, and she had a bad temper that just come outta nowhere sometimes. She never would apologize, but every time she flew off the handle, she always tried to make up for it afterwards. She gave me my first African violet. She felt so bad about bringing young Mr. David home from France and making him marry Miss Karen, she had those windows put in the ceiling of the old summerhouse and fixed it up so he could use it to paint in."

"Why didn't the house pass to Trey when Maribelle died?" Ann asked curiously. "Maribelle left him everything else."

Miss Esther looked away. Paul saw her gnarled old hands grip the arms of the rocking chair. "Miss Addy made her promise, even after Miss Maribelle found out about Miss Addy and Mr. Conrad."

"You knew about that?" Ann said with a gasp.

"Let me tell you one thing, child. Servants know nearly all there is to know about the people they work for. Those people do not know one solid thing about them. Remember that." She nodded to punctuate her words. "For years Miss Maribelle treated Miss Addy like the poor relation she was letting use her piano to teach lessons. Toward the end that changed. Miss Addy seemed to get the upper hand. Don't know how. Maybe something to do with Mr. Conrad. Anyway, Miss Addy had no intention of leaving that house if Miss Maribelle died, so they fixed it up between 'em so she wouldn't have to. If you want to find out any more, best find Miss Addy's journal."

"Journal?" Paul said, and glanced at Ann.

"Either it got thrown out or went in the estate sale," Ann said. "We haven't found a journal."

"Of course you haven't. She hid it." The old lady laughed and rocked furiously. "Then when she got so

crazy, she couldn't remember what she'd done with it. I
used to find her wandering around the house barefoot in
her nightgown in the middle of the night pulling out drawers and looking in the backs of closets. She used to say
to me, 'Esther, we have to find it. It's the third one. I must
destroy it.' I'd calm her down, and a month or so later
off she'd be again.''

''What did she mean, the third one? And why did she
want to destroy it?''

''Don't know. She never did find it, though, 'cause the
night she died she held my hand and made me promise if
I found it I'd burn it without reading it.'' Miss Esther
sniffed. ''Guess she didn't want nobody reading about her
goings-on with Mr. Conrad.''

''What happened when Uncle David got killed?'' Ann
asked. ''Who got the money and the businesses then?''

''Miss Karen got some insurance money and some of
the business, but most of it went to Mr. Trey. She got the
house—''

''I thought Maribelle got the house,'' Paul said.

''Not the Delaney house, Mr. David's house—the one
he built for Miss Karen after they got married. The house
out on the land. Mr. Trey's house it is now. I hear tell
he's done added on and added on—even got him a swimming pool. Mr. David and Miss Karen didn't live with
Mr. Conrad and Miss Maribelle but a year or so, even
though Mr. David spent a good many more nights sleeping in that studio in the backyard than at home. Didn't go
to his own house any more than he had to. I fed him as
many breakfasts after he moved out as I did before. He
used to say my kitchen was the only place in the world
felt like home to him.'' She shook her head. ''Poor boy.''

Karen Lowrance had never actually said his father had
built her a house before he died, but Paul supposed it

should have been obvious. Karen would probably have preferred a tent to her mother-in-law's house. He'd always visualized his father's ghost in the mansion, but perhaps it stalked the halls of the house that was now Trey's, instead.

Miss Esther's voice brought him back from his musings. It took a second to catch up with the conversation. Miss Esther was talking about the Delaney business.

"'Course Mr. Trey was too young to handle the businesses after Mr. David died, so Miss Karen and Miss Maribelle took over until Mr. Trey got out of college. Miss Maribelle and Miss Karen fussed a good bit sometimes, but in the end they did real well at it."

"What can you tell us about Conrad's son?" Paul asked. "Did you ever notice any, say, strange visitors?"

Miss Esther shook her head. "Mr. David? He had his drinking buddies, but that was about all."

"No other women?"

"Son, what do you want to know that for? I declare, if Miss Ann hadn't told me it was all right to talk to you, I'd swear you were with one of those scandalous newspapers I see in the grocery store."

Paul backed off quickly. "Sorry. I didn't mean to upset you."

"Well, for your information, my Mr. David never so much as looked at another woman after he married Miss Karen. And he didn't sneak 'em into that studio, either."

"Of course he didn't, Miss Esther." Ann caught Paul's eye. "We've taken up entirely too much of your time."

"Nothing better to do. My boys are all living up north now. Don't see my grandbabies but a few times a year."

Paul put down his empty glass, reached across the table and took Miss Esther's hand. "Please come see the house. Anytime."

Miss Esther seemed mollified. She smiled at him. "I'll stop by on one of my walks."

They said their goodbyes and left.

In Paul's car Ann turned to him. "I always knew men liked to gossip, but you take the cake."

"Morbid curiosity. I'm sorry."

"Don't be. I thought it was fascinating. I wonder what Miss Addy did with that journal?"

"I'll look around. Now, about that airplane ride…"

PAUL COULD FEEL Ann trembling as he helped her into the front seat of his Cessna. "Are you really terrified?" he asked. "Because if you are…"

"In my job, I have to fly all the time. I'm always a bit nervous. I've never been in a little plane, that's all."

"I can land this one safely in a cotton field. Can't do that with a 747. We'll be fine, you'll see."

He was proud of the little silver plane. It wouldn't do barrel rolls, but it was a lovely aircraft and a pleasure to fly. He finished his preflight check, started the engine and began to roll down the grass strip. Beside him, Ann caught her breath. He took his hand off the controls long enough to touch her knee in reassurance.

The afternoon was warm and the sky was patterned with white, puffy clouds. Although they looked innocent, the thermals under them made for a bumpy ride. Ann gasped each time the engine changed pitch.

He kept his pattern simple with plenty of airspace between him and the ground. He never strayed far from the field. He wanted her to know that they could get down in a hurry if she demanded to land.

He felt her begin to relax. He pointed out landmarks beneath them and flew along the railroad tracks that bisected Rossiter. "That's called flying IFR—I fly rail-roads," he told her. She managed a small chuckle.

He wanted her to love this experience as much as he did. Maybe if she took some lessons... Hack had his in-structor-rating. He'd be happy to teach Ann. Paul could barter a few extra dusting runs for lessons if he could talk Ann into it.

They had to yell at each other to be heard, so after a time they sat side by side without speaking.

Thirty minutes was enough for her introduction. He turned back for the field and began to set up for his land-ing when without warning the engine gave a single tu-bercular cough and quit.

The only sound now was the rush of wind. A second later a coat of black oil covered the windshield.

He could feel Ann tense. He knew she was trying not to scream. "We've broken an oil seal," he yelled at her.

"Are we going to die?"

"I'm already in the glide path for the field. We're fine. She'll damn near fly herself."

No sense in trying to restart the engine. Even if he could coax it to life, he might stall. At this altitude that could get them killed.

He slid the plane onto the grass strip. It bumped a cou-ple of times, then came to a stop.

In the sudden silence he heard her inhale sharply. He turned to her and slipped his arm around her shoulders. He could see that her knuckles were white where her hands were clasped in her lap.

"Sorry, Ann. I have no idea why we should have bro-ken an oil seal. They were all just checked."

"Please, can we just get out of here?" When she looked at him, her face was ashen. "Now."

"Sure." He smiled. "I promise we weren't in any danger."

He climbed out, then helped her down. "What if we'd been over the mountains?" she asked.

It was a reasonable question. "There are plenty of landing places available almost everywhere." He felt certain Ann knew that was a lie. In the mountains or over a body of water, they would have been in real trouble. Even in this relatively flat country of open fields, setting down could have been problematic with all the trees and creeks. If Ann hadn't been with him, he wouldn't have stayed close enough to the field to simply dead-stick in. His own legs started to feel a bit shaky.

At that moment Hack hobbled up. "What the hell happened? I heard you coming in and then I didn't."

"Blew an oil seal." He turned to Ann. "Look, I really need to check this out. Are you okay to drive my car? Hack can give me a ride home later, can't you, Hack?"

"Where your manners, boy? Take the lady home. I'll start checking this out while you're gone. I want to find out what the hell happened, too."

On the way to Ann's house, Paul tried to explain how unusual an occurrence this was, how safely she could fly with him.

She listened politely, nodded from time to time, but he could see he hadn't convinced her. She climbed out of his car and trotted up her steps without a backward glance.

He stopped at his house long enough to change into the grubby clothes he wore to work on the plane.

Hack met him at the edge of the field. He was rubbing black oil off his hands. "Don't think you exactly made a convert today."

"She may never fly again. Of all the days to have this happen, why did God pick today?"

Hack sighed. "God had nothing to do with it. Come see what I found."

As he bent over the engine, Hack pointed at the oil seal. "That seal didn't fail by itself. It had help in the form of an ice pick or a pocketknife. Just enough of a hole so it wouldn't leak onto the hangar floor or show up in the preflight. It would hold for a little while, then it would split all at once. Bang. No oil pressure."

"You mean somebody actually did this?"

"Somebody who knew at least a little something about planes. Your average teenage vandal would have poured sugar or coffee grounds into the gas tank. The engine wouldn't have started in the first place. This took sophistication. Like the young lady said, if you'd been over the mountains, you'd have been in a pickle."

"Why would someone do this?"

"You made anybody in town mad?"

Paul felt the hackles rise at the back of his neck. "Not that I'm aware of."

"I better check the other planes. Whoever did this may have gone through the hangar with an ice pick. You don't want to dust crops without an engine."

"You're right about that. When could it have happened?"

"Anytime. Someone could have parked down there on the other side of the railroad tracks after I'd gone to bed and walked through the field. Not something I'd choose to do with the copperheads waking up from the winter. I wouldn't see a flashlight in the hangar from inside my trailer."

"So it could happen again."

"Not that way. While you were gone I called my cousin Johnny and asked him to lend me one of his coon dogs. Anything comes within smelling distance of this place after dark, that hound will go crazy."

"Why haven't you had a dog before?"

Hack shrugged. "My old dog died about a year back. Didn't have the heart to replace him." He looked up.

Paul looked at the grim set of Hack's jaw, the narrowed eyes, and saw why he had been a good bomber pilot. Hack Morrison made a bad enemy.

"Now I think I may just go buy me a couple of real junkyard dogs to eat up any strangers I sic 'em on."

"Who can I get to fix the Cessna?" Paul asked.

"Me, for one. I assume you can help. I got a couple of buddies at the airport downtown who moonlight. Going to take us a coupla weeks to pull the engine and the prop, tear the whole thing down and find out if there's any other damage. Not gonna be cheap, either."

"It's got to be done. When I find out who did this, I may just feed him to that hound dog."

On the drive back to Rossiter, Paul turned the event over and over in his mind. He hadn't made anybody angry, had he? Not as Paul Bouvet. And nobody knew he was really Paul Delaney. Or had someone uncovered the truth?

CHAPTER TWELVE

"ALL I ASK is that you give flying another chance," Paul said as he stood at Ann's door that evening.

"I'll have to think about it."

"Look, I know you were frightened. I was thinking that if maybe Hack gave you a few lessons so you'd know—"

"No! I mean, I don't think so."

"May I come in?"

"It's been a really long day, and it's going to be a very hard week."

"Maybe I could make it easier."

"I just want to soak in a hot tub and go to bed."

"My plan exactly."

She managed a smile. "Alone. I'll see you tomorrow."

"Will you still come to Trey's with me Wednesday?"

"Of course. Why wouldn't I? They live on the ground, not up in the air."

So on Wednesday evening with a bottle of really good wine in the back seat and Ann beside him—Dante was home alone for the evening—Paul drove to Trey Delaney's house.

"Good God," Paul said reverently. "No wonder he didn't want to live in the old mansion."

If the Delaney house was smaller than Tara, he could have tucked Tara into one corner of this shining Georgian palace with its enormous columnar portico.

"I guess Uncle David built it when times were good in the cattle business."

"I should say. Is that a tennis court?"

"Uh-huh. The swimming pool is behind the house, and the riding stables and arena are over that way, far enough so that the flies and smells can't permeate the house. Trey rides over in a golf cart."

Gleaming white fences edged the driveway. Beyond them, black Angus cattle grazed serenely. For the first time Paul realized just how rich Trey Delaney must be. To lose all this would be devastating. But Trey had no reason to fear Paul Bouvet, flyer with a busted wing. Certainly no reason to sabotage his plane.

When the white-coated butler opened the front door and ushered them through the house to the back terrace, Paul felt as though he'd stepped into a stage set.

When he met Sue-sue, he realized she was the one who'd set the stage. She wore enough gold jewelry to weigh her down if she fell out of a boat, a diamond wedding band and an engagement ring with a diamond so big it probably had a name. Like the Hope or the Kohinoor.

His fiancée had taught him to notice things about women he would never have picked up on before. Sue-sue came forward in the perfect little spring dress, wearing expensive Italian sandals on already tanned legs. Her shoulder-length blond hair looked freshly cut. He had to admit Sue-sue was gorgeous. Her trim body showed no evidence of her two pregnancies. "The kids are spending the night over at their grandmama's," Sue-sue said. "They'd just love to meet you, I'm sure. Maybe next time."

If there was one.

Sue-sue was the perfect hostess, Trey the hearty host. The conversation turned on the upcoming University of

Tennessee basketball season and next year's football. It was about the smallest small talk Paul had indulged in for years. He noticed that Ann slipped easily into her social role, although she gave him a sly wink.

No wonder Trey was a bit of a lunkhead. His wife probably never read anything more stimulating than this week's women's magazine. Then, just as he was beginning to feel smug and superior, Sue-sue turned to him and asked, "May I hit you up for a donation to our arts group? I'm president of the state board, and we're trying to set up this year's 'opera and ballet in the schools' programs."

"Don't say yes," Trey said heartily. "She'll have you down to your socks before dinner's over if you give the woman an inch."

"You enjoy the ballet?" Paul asked Sue-sue.

"Absolutely. Trey does, too, don't you? He's not so keen on opera, but he likes Puccini and he loves musical comedy. We go to New York at least once a year to see the shows, and we try to make the Edinburgh Festival at least once every three or four years. We haven't been to Stratford in Canada since little Maribelle was born. Trey says he's too busy in the summer." She turned to Ann. "Why don't you and I go this year? It's probably not too late to get tickets. My treat."

He saw Ann's smile tighten. "I can afford to pay my own way."

"Oh, Lord, honey, I never meant you couldn't! Just that it would be wonderful to have somebody as knowledgeable about theater as you to go with me. And we could shop till we drop."

The conversation became more general, and soon Paul found himself discussing the relative merits of the Tate Gallery in London and the Frick in New York. He also discovered that Sue-sue had a degree in political science from Swarthmore. So much for stereotypes. Obviously, Trey's wife wasn't nearly as empty-headed as she seemed to be.

Over dessert, Paul asked Trey, "You promised to tell me about the bear."

"Which bear?" Sue-sue asked.

"The bear on the front porch of Trey's office."

Sue-sue raised her eyebrows. "Oh, that awful thing."

"Not awful, honey," Trey said. "That bear has a history."

"I'd like to hear it, if Sue-sue doesn't mind," Paul said.

"Oh, go ahead. Ann and I are going to go get the coffee and clean up the kitchen, anyway, aren't we, Ann? Then y'all can join us in the living room."

The men were left alone for their after-dinner drink. The brandy Trey offered was excellent.

"Now ol' Smokey Joe stood out in front of an old drive-in on the road to Whiteville," Trey said. "Used to be a wooden Indian, too, but nobody knew what happened to it. One night my granddaddy and a bunch of his fraternity buddies up for the weekend were drinking and hoo-rawing and Granddaddy decided it would be fun to steal that bear." He chuckled and shook his head. "So they did. Piled him in the back of Granddaddy's convertible and hid him in the summer kitchen."

Paul realized Trey was a born raconteur. His liking for the man increased.

"Didn't take the sheriff thirty seconds to figure out who'd done it," Trey continued. "The man who owned the drive-in refused to press charges, so the bear went back home and Granddaddy and his friends spent the rest of the weekend picking up trash alongside the highway as punishment.

"After that, of course, it became a tradition to steal ol'

Smokey Joe at least once a year. He always showed up back at the drive-in a couple of days later, of course. Finally the owner just gave up and didn't even call the sheriff when ol' Smokey Joe turned up missing.'' Trey shook his head and sipped his brandy. ''Hard to believe it, but my granddaddy must have been a caution when he was young.

''Anyway, the owner died, and the man's son decided to sell the place. He called my daddy, because by that time Granddaddy was dead, and offered to sell him the bear.'' Trey chuckled again.

''Daddy said he'd buy him, but he wanted to steal him one more time. So he and Buddy and my great-uncle Harris Pulliam drove over there at two in the morning, left a check in the man's mailbox and stole Smokey Joe for old times' sake. He's been chained to the front porch of my office ever since.'' Trey shrugged and finished his brandy in one gulp. ''The younger generation hasn't heard that story and I don't want 'em to. First thing I know, they'll be stealing him again right off the front porch at the office.''

The story reminded Paul that he was and would always be a complete outsider in this family. His father would remain a stranger no matter how much Paul learned about him. This culture, this heritage, that was bred in Trey's bone would forever be foreign to *him*. Paul managed a grin. ''Great story.''

''Now, shall we join the ladies?''

About an hour later, as Ann and Paul were finishing their coffee and making a move toward leaving, Trey turned to Ann. ''You haven't been hunting with us since January. Shame on you.''

''No time. First I was in Buffalo digging my way out of snowdrifts, then I went to work on this job.''

"This Saturday is the last hunt of the season. You have to come," Sue-sue pleaded. "Saga's fit and ready to go." She turned to Paul. "Do you hunt?"

When he said no as politely as he could, he heard Ann say, "But you're going to try it, aren't you?"

"I hadn't planned on it."

Her grin was devilish. "You made me go flying. Getting you up on a horse in return is the least I can do."

"We've got a lovely crossbred gelding who'd be perfect for you," Sue-sue said.

"His mama was a Belgian draft horse," Trey continued. "He's quite placid. He wouldn't flinch if you set off a bomb under his feet."

"You could ride second field," Ann said. "All you have to do is sit in the saddle and walk along with all the other old fogies."

"I don't have the proper clothes."

"Heck, you can borrow some of mine," Trey said. "It's an informal hunt, anyway. You and I look about the same size. What size shoe do you wear?"

Paul told him.

"Perfect. My boots will fit you, and I know my britches will. Say you'll do it." He gave Paul a smile that had a great deal of challenge in it. "Can't be a real part of the community otherwise, you know."

In the end Paul agreed to ride the unflappable horse, took home a pair of Trey's riding boots, some boot hooks to pull them on, a boot jack to get them off, a pair of britches and a velvet hard hat to protect his head should he fall off.

"Which you won't do," Trey said. "Nobody falls off Liege."

As they drove away from the house, Trey and Sue-sue's

arms around each other's waist, waving them goodbye, Paul said casually. "I hate you."

"Can't imagine why. I don't get mad, I get even. You scare me, I scare you back. Seriously, you'll have a wonderful time, I guarantee it."

SATURDAY MORNING dawned clear and chill with a brisk wind blowing out of the north. The weather report said the temperature would only reach fifty-five degrees.

Ann showed up at seven in the morning with coffee and sweet rolls hot from the café. "I've come to help you dress," she said.

She looked fantastic. Despite the fact that Trey had said informal, she wore what Paul assumed was the entire costume, including a stiff white shirt with a white stock wound around her lovely throat and pinned with a gold pin.

They took their breakfast out on the porch, despite the cold. "Know what the stock is for?" she asked. "It's to use as a sling or a tourniquet."

"That makes me feel really comfortable."

"Don't be grumpy. Tally-ho."

The area around the Delaneys' pristine stable block was full of trucks, SUVs, horse trailers, horses and riders.

Paul's heart sank. Over at the side, four or five carriages sat ready to depart, their horses already hitched. "Can't I ride in one of them?" he asked plaintively.

"Nope."

Trey and Sue-sue were nowhere in sight. To Paul's untutored eye, Ann's horse, a tall bay gelding that Ann said had once been a race horse, danced and snorted like a dragon. Paul's own horse was immense. "The things I do for love," Paul whispered.

"Give me a leg up," Ann said. They had arrived late,

largely because he had hung back as long as possible. Both first and second fields had begun to move off across the field. "You use the mounting block to mount. I'll ride with you until you feel comfortable, promise."

He climbed onto his horse clumsily and fitted his feet into the stirrups.

"Okay?" Ann said, and walked away from him. After her horse had taken half-a-dozen steps, she stopped him and jumped down. She called to a nearby groom. "He's lame."

"*Si, señora,*" the groom said. "Yesterday he was sound, but he's lame on his front leg again this morning."

"Okay, Marco. Better untack him and put him away." She turned to Paul. "You lucked out. I can't ride."

He slipped out of the saddle. "Sure you can. He may not be a fire-breathing dragon, but I'll bet my horse isn't lame."

She looked at the Belgian with longing.

"Go on."

"What will you do?"

"I heard that," said a tall, gray-haired lady in a feathered hat. "He can ride with me in my Meadowbrook cart. I hate driving alone."

Ann's face became wreathed in smiles. "Paul, this is Mrs. Adler. She follows the hunt in her carriage."

"Uh, how do you do?"

"At the moment, I'm in a hurry. Climb aboard, young man, and hold on tight."

Ann had already mounted and was trotting toward the fast-vanishing hunters.

After ten minutes with Mrs. Adler, Paul devoutly wished he'd stayed aboard his Belgian. Her big gray horse had a ground-covering trot. The ground, however, was bumpy. Mrs. Adler seemed determined to catch the main body of the hunt before they were out of sight.

Paul knew how Ann must have felt clinging to his aircraft for dear life. He swore that if he survived the morning with Mrs. Adler, he'd never go near a horse again.

As they topped the rise, he heard the call of a hunting horn. "They're away! Come on, Delta." Mrs. Adler popped her reins against the flanks of her horse. A moment later he broke into a canter.

Several times he was sure Mrs. Adler would fly right out of the cart, but she always landed back in her seat with a thump, the reins secure in her gloved hands. He clutched the sides of his seat and prayed.

Below him he could see the hunters galloping across a broad meadow divided in several places by barbed-wire fences. "They jump barbed wire?" he yelled at Mrs. Adler.

"Don't be ridiculous. There are wooden jumps let into the fence at intervals. Watch." She pulled the cart to a halt within hailing distance of the other carriages. He was afraid he'd have to pry his fingers loose from the edge of his seat.

Below him the hounds were running full out and the riders weren't far behind. He spotted Ann on the Belgian flying over the ground. This was the placid horse they intended him to ride?

The hunters began to pour over the jump like gravy out of a boat. Ann was close to the tail end of the group. She galloped down to the fence, the Belgian left the ground, and without warning something went wrong. One minute Ann was in the saddle, the next she was flying off the right side of her horse to land out of sight on the other side of the fence.

Paul stood up and shouted her name.

"Oh, dear," Mrs. Adler whispered.

The forward force of Mrs. Adler's Percheron knocked Paul back in his seat. This time he didn't begrudge Mrs. Adler's hell-for-leather driving technique. At the foot of the hill hounds were milling about baying at nothing in particular, and riders were off their horses.

Paul vaulted out of the cart before it came to a full stop. He raced toward Ann, his unfamiliar riding boots slipping and sliding on the wet grass.

He saw Trey and several riders bending over Ann's prostrate form on the other side of the jump. He shoved through the crush of riders and climbed over the fence, hopped across the ditch and knelt beside her. He grabbed her gloved hand. "Ann, my God, Ann." Out of the corner of his eye he caught the unflappable Belgian chomping grass. There was no stirrup hanging from the right side of his saddle. Paul looked around. Just behind him he spied the stirrup and the leather that should have held it on the saddle.

Ann opened her eyes, took a deep breath and said, "There. I thought I'd never breathe again." She started to sit up, but Trey held her down. "No, you don't."

"I'm fine, Trey. I just got the wind knocked out of me. What the hell happened?"

"I'm going to kill somebody over this," Trey said grimly. He held Ann's other hand. "You must have broken a stirrup leather. That's not supposed to happen in my barn."

"Well, for Pete's sake." She smiled up at Paul. "Okay, we're even."

"Not even halfway," he said grimly. "We need to get a cervical collar on you. Can you feel everything?"

She rolled her eyes. "I never lost consciousness, just my breath. I never hit my head—the hard hat took the brunt of the fall. I fell flat. My dignity and I are equally bruised, but that's the extent of the damage." She pulled herself to a sitting position. "Now, can somebody catch my horse and lend me a stirrup leather?"

Paul reached behind him and pulled the broken half of the leather free of the stirrup. While everyone concentrated on Ann, he stuffed both parts of the leather under his sweater. "You're not going to keep riding, are you?"

"First rule of riding, always get back on the horse." She touched his cheek. "Don't worry. I'm just going to ride back to the barn with you and Mrs. Adler if she'll take you."

"Of course I will, dear," Mrs. Adler said from her perch. "This is quite enough excitement for one day."

No one had an extra stirrup leather, so Ann and her horse ambled back to the barn with her legs dangling at his sides. The horse wasn't even breathing hard.

Paul noticed that the grooms had made themselves scarce. So he pulled off the saddle himself, let the big animal into an empty stall, hung saddle and bridle on the closest rack and found Ann leaning against Mrs. Adler's cart.

"You mind taking me home now? I'm starting to stiffen up."

He thanked Mrs. Adler, patted her horse and helped Ann to his car. For the second time he realized he'd never be able to carry her. Not even across a threshold.

He was halfway to her home before he realized the implications of that.

After he put Ann under a hot shower and rubbed liniment all over her body, already beginning to turn interesting shades of puce, he sat down to wait until she fell asleep.

As soon as he heard her regular breathing, he walked

into the workroom, turned on the big lights over the work-table and took the two halves of the stirrup leather from under his sweater.

It was only a fluke that Ann had been riding the Belgian. If Paul had broken a stirrup leather unexpectedly even at a walk, he'd have fallen off. Unlike Ann, he probably would have been hurt.

He might have reinjured his right arm. Falling off the right side of the horse, he would instinctively have reached to break his fall with his right arm. He winced at the prospect of the pain and damage that might have caused.

The reason for the breakage in the leather was easy to spot once he looked for it. Someone with a very sharp knife had scored the underside of the leather without cutting through to the top. Anyone saddling the horse wouldn't have seen it unless they examined the leather carefully.

His father had broken his neck jumping over a fence on a hunt.

Coincidence?

When the phone rang, he grabbed it on the first ring and heard Mrs. Jenkins's voice. "Is Ann all right?"

He turned his back and cupped the phone so as not to wake Ann. "She's bruised and she's going to be stiff, but I think she's okay."

"Good. The idea that she could go first field when she hasn't been on a horse since opening hunt. I swear, sometimes I don't know what she's thinking. Is she asleep?"

"Yes."

"Stay with her, will you? I'll head Buddy off so he doesn't come barging in and wake her up. We'll bring over supper for both of you. Say, about six?"

"You don't have to do that."

"I realize that. Don't forget Dante needs his walkies."

"Yes, ma'am."

He hung up and looked at Dante, who sat by the back door expectantly. He found the dog's leash, checked Ann's breathing once again and slipped out the door with Dante. As he was crossing the street toward the little park, a squad car slid to a stop in front of him.

Buddy stuck his head out the driver's-side window. "How's my daughter?"

Paul repeated what he'd told Ann's mother. Buddy nodded and drove off without a word. The way information passed around this town, he wondered whether Buddy knew he and Ann had been sleeping together.

For a moment he considered that Buddy might have been the one to set up the plane and the riding accident. He had no way of knowing he'd be putting his own daughter in danger.

He dismissed the idea at once. If Buddy had a problem with him, he'd haul Paul into the backyard and deck him.

Ann was still asleep when Paul went back inside with Dante. The dog padded over and carefully climbed onto the bed to snuggle against Ann protectively.

When Ann awoke and started to get up, she groaned. He went to help her, but she pushed him away. "Got to do it myself. Oh, boy."

"Can I recommend a course of treatment?"

"And that would be what, Doctor?"

"Doctor dear, to you."

"Okay, Doctor dear."

"Twenty minutes of ice, twenty minutes of heat. Alternate on the sorest spots. Then another hot shower, another round of liniment, and you let me give you a massage."

"Sounds lovely, except I don't have either a heating pad or an ice pack."

Not for the first time, Paul realized how limited Rossiter was for anything more exotic than eggs and butter. "I'll be back soon," he said. "Oh, your mother's bringing dinner here for both of us. Is that okay?"

"Sure." She hobbled to the overstuffed easy chair and gently lowered herself into it.

He stopped by his room long enough to change from his borrowed boots and riding britches to jeans and sneakers, then he broke speed limits to town and back. During the entire drive he cursed whoever had cut that leather.

CHAPTER THIRTEEN

PAUL SHARED the soup, sandwiches and brownies that Nancy Jenkins had brought with Ann and her parents, then settled Ann in her big armchair with both heating pad and ice pack.

"Don't forget," he said, "twenty minutes hot, twenty minutes cold. It's what got me through years of baseball."

"Thanks, Doctor." She looked over his shoulder to where her parents were cleaning up the kitchen and rolled her eyes. "Send them home. Say I want to go to bed."

"Would I be telling the truth?"

She whispered, "Are you some kind of sex maniac?"

"I'll be happy just to hold you and kiss your boo-boos." He grinned down at her as she slapped at him.

"Well, baby," Nancy Jenkins said, "you're in good hands. Buddy and I are out of here. I don't suppose I'll see you at church tomorrow."

"I don't suppose. Thanks for coming."

Paul saw her parents out and took Dante for a walk. He was growing fond of the big mutt.

Ann was still in her chair when he returned. "I think I'm going to sleep right here," she said. "It's better when I'm not flat on my back."

"I'll remember that," Paul said.

Her eyes opened wide. "Listen to you."

"Just trying to cheer you up."

"Well, don't. I want to feel pitiful, at least for tonight.

You know, the first thing I thought while I was flying through the air was that all these people were watching me make a fool of myself.''

''You had help.''

''Liege didn't do anything...'' She stared at him, then said quietly, ''That's not what you meant, is it?''

Paul hadn't planned to tell her about the cut leather and certainly not about the sabotaged plane. But, dammit, if someone was trying to maim or kill him, she might inadvertently walk into another setup meant for him without getting off so lightly. Earlier he'd hidden the stirrup leather in Addy's button box. Now he went into the workroom, moved the buttons he'd carefully laid on top and brought both pieces of leather back to put into Ann's lap.

''So?''

''Look at the underside.''

She turned both pieces over. She caught her breath. ''Do I see what I think I see?'' She sounded very small and frightened.

''If you see that someone slashed halfway through the leather so that it would break under pressure, then yes, you do.''

''It was on the right side, wasn't it? A rider mounting from the left wouldn't put any pressure on that stirrup until he was getting set to take the first jump. If it's a practical joke, it's a dangerous one.''

''I don't think it was a joke.''

Her eyes grew round. ''I wasn't supposed to be riding Liege. I was supposed to be on Saga.''

''Right.''

''You think it was aimed at you? Paul, we may not accept incomers as natives until the second generation, but we don't try to assassinate outsiders simply because they move to town.''

"That's not all." He told her about the sabotage to the oil seal on his Cessna. "Expensive to repair and dangerous—although we were close enough to the field that we weren't in real danger. Hack called me yesterday to say he'd found a puncture in the oil seal on the Stearman, too. It hasn't been flown recently. There was no engine damage, but I fly low and slow with a full load of fertilizer. With a punctured oil seal, I wouldn't have had time to react to an engine failure."

"Hand me the phone. We've got to tell Daddy."

He put his hand over the telephone. "Tell Daddy what? Somebody doesn't like me? We can't truly prove the incidents were sabotage and not some kid's idea of a prank gone wrong."

"Both incidents? I thought you didn't believe in coincidences."

"I don't, but juries do."

"Whoever it is could try again."

"I'm on guard now. I don't think he's trying to hurt anybody but me, but you'll be safer if you keep your distance from me, at least in public. In private is another matter."

"Don't joke."

"I'm not joking. I can look after myself, Ann, but not if I'm worrying about you. Be careful."

"I promise." She shivered. "It's time for the heating pad. Do you mind if I come over there to the couch and let you take its place?"

"My pleasure." He helped her up and settled her against him on the couch with her quilt over them both.

"Um. You've got more heated area than a heating pad," she said drowsily.

"Parts of me are considerably hotter, too."

After a few minutes she asked, "What are you going

to do about the...pranks, jokes, attacks, whatever they are?''

''Don't know yet.''

''Maybe you should go on a vacation someplace until the house is finished.''

''You want me to?''

She tilted her face so that she could kiss the underside of his jaw. ''I want you here. But I'd prefer you alive.''

HE FINALLY EASED Ann into bed about midnight and lay down beside her without undressing. Dante came over, licked the hand he'd trailed over the side of the bed, then lay down on the floor with a sigh.

Paul planned to lie awake and work out the identity of his attacker, but the day had been too long and he was too comfortable lying by Ann's side. He fell asleep. He didn't hear Ann get up. The aroma of good coffee finally forced his eyes open.

''Good morning, lazybones.''

He groaned. He was certain his belt had left a permanent crease in his waistline.

''I will kiss a man with whiskers, but I draw the line at unbrushed teeth.''

He opened his eyes. ''I expected you to be too sore to move.''

''Your therapy must have worked. I'm hardly sore at all.''

''You passed your aches on to me,'' he said. ''Give me that coffee this instant, woman.''

He borrowed a new razor and toothbrush from Ann and took a long shower. He suspected his aches came from his wild carriage ride with Mrs. Adler. He dressed, but padded back to Ann's kitchen barefoot. ''Thanks for the new toothbrush. Now you can kiss me.''

The kiss turned long and passionate. He pulled her tightly to him, at which point she yelped and drew away. "I'm still a *little* sore," she said.

"Feel up to driving into the city for breakfast?"

"The café's not open, so either we eat dry cereal or we go hunting for bacon and eggs. I'm game."

"I have to stop by the house to change clothes." He turned back to her. "Speaking of toothbrushes, the craziest thing happened the other day. My toothbrush disappeared. It was there in the morning and not there in the afternoon."

"One of the workmen probably used it to clean grout or something and didn't want to admit it."

"Hmm."

"Dante, stay. You've had your breakfast."

During the brief moments before sleep overcame Paul the previous night, one name had come into his mind. Karen Bingham Delaney Lowrance. Had she guessed his identity? Was she behind these…accidents?

Paul had always assumed that his father had killed Michelle on his own. The more he learned about his father, however, the less likely it seemed that he was a murderer. He seemed too weak, too feckless. But he could have had help.

Karen seemed quite capable of committing multiple ax murders if she felt they were necessary. Getting rid of one young Frenchwoman who threatened her and her family wouldn't have required more than a moment's consideration.

Could Michelle have met Karen instead of Paul? Karen had been charm itself when he'd interviewed her, yet she might be trying to kill him. His unsophisticated and romantic young mother would have been easy prey. Especially if Karen had offered her consolation, sympathy, even assistance.

Had he spent his whole life blaming his father for a murder he did not commit?

He spent a comfortable, lazy Sunday with Ann. He missed sharing the Sunday *Times,* but the local newspaper wasn't bad. They put Dante into the back seat of Paul's car and drove down back country roads and lanes for a couple of hours while Ann showed him some of the sights. She directed him to LaGrange, where several pilots had restored a number of elegant houses much older than his. Paul couldn't remember ever feeling as content. They drove all the way down to the Mississippi River, which was in flood and therefore considerably mightier than it would be in the summer.

Finally they picked up a couple of steaks to grill on Ann's back stoop.

And that night they made wonderful love.

They had agreed that if Paul left before six-thirty in the morning, when the café opened, he could make it home without arousing suspicion, then meet Ann for breakfast at seven-thirty as though they had not seen one another since yesterday.

It might have worked, except that a Rossiter squad car driven by a cop Paul did not know saw him cross the square and waved as he drove by.

Busted. No doubt Buddy would be informed before he got to the job site to check on the progress of his crews.

Paul didn't care about his own reputation. He did worry about Ann's, however.

Maybe the entire town had banded together to get rid of him before he became the second man to ruin Ann's life. No. That was absurd.

After breakfast, as he and Ann strolled back to the

house, he looked up at the shining front facade and said, "I had no idea it could possibly turn out this well."

"We're not nearly finished. And you'll have to get rugs, window treatments, real live furniture—"

"Window treatments, at least. When I sell it…"

Ann stopped dead. "When you *sell* it? You plan to sell it?" She looked horrified.

"I mean if…if I sell it," he stammered.

"You said when."

"People do sell houses, Ann."

"You're doing this on speculation? To make big bucks off your investment, then move on to the next old house?"

"Look, let's talk inside. Out here on the sidewalk is too public."

"Suits me if everybody hears. If I ever owned a house like this, I'd *never* sell it. Not for a billion dollars. My God, I've put my heart and soul into this restoration and so have my father's crews. We've opened our houses to you, not to mention our beds—"

"Ann—"

"Because we thought you were going to be here in Rossiter, a part of the town."

"Ann, calm down. We're fighting over a word, a single word."

"So you're not planning to move?"

What could he say? "Not anytime soon, but things change. That doesn't mean my feelings for you or Rossiter will change. Dammit, I love you!"

A grizzled carpenter just climbing out of his truck grinned and said, "Good for you," and walked into the house.

"Oh, glory," Ann said. "That'll be all over the county by noon. *What* did you say?"

"I said I'm in love with you. I don't know what that means, and I definitely did not intend for it to happen, but it did."

"Oh."

"So let's just play it as it lies, all right?"

"What if I love you back?"

Paul closed his eyes. "I thought I had everything figured out. Now I don't know anything. Whatever happens, remember that at this time and forever, I do love you. You got that?"

"Right." Her eyes were curious.

"Now, I have to go dust my last two crops and you have to go do…whatever it is you have to do."

"Okay."

"I am now going to kiss you in full view of the entire town of Rossiter." He pulled her to him and did precisely that. Then he trotted around to the back of the house, climbed into his car and drove off at a pace that would have earned him a traffic citation if Buddy had been watching.

ANN SUSPECTED her father's guys were snickering at her behind her back, but nobody had the nerve to mention Paul's kiss. She decided to play it safe and eat lunch at home rather than risk going to the café.

After eating her tuna sandwich, she curled up on the couch with Dante beside her.

Paul's kiss should have left her with a pure champagne high.

Instead her elation was tempered by unease. She'd learned to trust that instinct—first in her work, then eventually in her life. She could look at a painting and sense a hand, an expression, even occasionally an entirely different painting, invisible beneath layers of varnish. She'd be willing to give long odds that something was concealed beneath Paul's surface.

She scratched Dante's head. He edged closer.

"I'm being silly and oversensitive," she told him. "Travis conned me so often that I can't trust any man."

Dante moaned.

As a cop, Buddy knew about identity theft. Before he'd signed the contract he'd checked Paul's identity and credit rating. He was precisely who he said he was. He wasn't lying when he said he'd never been married, and he wasn't supporting any children.

"Maybe he's the sort of guy who has to have an adoring female at all times and considers me the best choice of a limited lot. Does he fall in and out of love as easily as Travis did? Will he convince me to give him my love, my trust, then walk away the minute my job is finished?"

In a town like Rossiter, everyone would know. She'd already suffered enough sorrowful glances when she'd divorced Travis. She couldn't endure any more pity.

But Paul seemed serious. He must know that if he dumped her, Rossiter would line up on her side.

Lord, what a prospect!

She shoved Dante off her lap.

"I need a project for the afternoon that does not involve dental picks. If Aunt Addy's journal hasn't been sold or destroyed—if it's still in the house somewhere—I am darn well going to find it."

Presenting Paul with Addy's journal would serve as the perfect apology.

CHAPTER FOURTEEN

AFTER LUNCH Ann got busy with the tile replacement in the front bathroom of the mansion. There was no time to consider possible hiding places for Aunt Addy's journal. She would give it more thought later.

She decided that she had no right to force Paul to talk about his plans for the future. Maybe she should just take Marti's advice and enjoy the moment.

She and Paul had another picnic on his porch that evening and were sharing an after-dinner apple when his cell phone rang.

"Giselle. Hi. Sorry, I know I should have called before this." He looked at Ann, got up and walked through his room and into the hall beyond.

Why was he so secretive? He'd already said Giselle was the sister-cousin he got along with. Ann couldn't bring herself to eavesdrop, but she wanted to. He talked for fifteen minutes, and several times when he raised his voice, she did understand the words. "I'm as confused as you are," he said once.

"I think I may have figured this out wrong from the beginning," he said.

Figured what out?

He came in and sat down beside her on the porch again after he'd hung up. "My sister Giselle. I told you about her. She's annoyed because I haven't been keeping in touch the way I promised."

"Will she visit you when the house is finished?"

He looked startled. "I hadn't given it any thought. I suppose under the right circumstances she might." ·

Ann shivered. She'd borrowed one of Paul's plaid shirts for warmth, but it only fell halfway down her thighs. The rest of her was getting colder by the second.

He pulled her up and into his arms.

"Come on, I'll clean up this mess tomorrow morning before I head out to the airfield."

"I thought you said you were through dusting?"

"For the moment. Now I'm working on the Cessna with Hack. It's one hell of a job." He thought for a minute. "Who around here can fly a plane?"

"I don't know—some of the farmers, I guess. The airline pilots obviously can, maybe some of the doctors can, as well. Hack would know who has a private plane."

"Only if they park them with him." He nearly asked about Karen Lowrance, but she'd be too smart to sabotage his plane herself. She'd hire someone.

Later, as Ann lay in his arms in the rosy glow of their lovemaking, she asked drowsily, "Tell me about your mother."

"My mother? Why?"

"Because I want to know everything about you."

"She disappeared when I was very young. End of story."

"No, it's not. Don't you have any keepsakes, any pictures?"

"Only one. I'll show it to you sometime." He sounded drowsy.

She sat up. "How about now?"

He groaned. "All right, but it's just an old photo." He dug around in his suitcase and came up with a framed eight-by-ten, black-and-white photo of a woman holding a child in her arms.

"That's you, isn't it? Look at all those long curls. You wouldn't last two minutes in a day-care center." She took the picture from him. "You have her dark hair." She returned the photo and waited for him to come back to bed so that she could spoon against his back. It wouldn't have been politic to tell Paul that his mother looked as though she'd been rode hard and put away wet. She looked too thin to be carrying around a bruiser like her son. Still, there was something familiar about that photo…

She took Dante out and slipped home before dawn. Something about that photo nagged at her, but it wasn't until she was standing under her own shower that it hit her.

She jumped out of the shower and ran into her workroom naked. The pictures they had taken from Uncle David's studio were carefully stacked on one of her work counters. She pulled the Paris street scene aside. There she was—the girl with the wind in her hair. She looked young and joyful in this sketch, while the woman Paul had showed her looked desperately tired and much older. But bones didn't lie. The girl in this sketch was Paul's mother.

One by one she looked at the other sketches, and then the sketch of the girl naked and obviously sated with love-making.

She threw on clothes, tied a scarf over her damp hair, grabbed Dante's leash and her keys and walked across the square to the mansion.

Paul's car wasn't in the parking area. He must have gone to the airport early. She ran home, jumped into her truck with Dante and peeled out just as her father pulled up. As she passed him, he yelled out his window, "Slow down!"

She stabbed the brakes and kept to a sedate thirty miles an hour until she reached the highway. Then she floored it. If her father was checking on the house, he wasn't aiming his radar gun down the highway.

By the time she bumped over the railroad tracks in front of the airfield and slid to a stop beside the hangar where Paul kept his plane, she was furious.

She saw him leaning into the engine compartment chatting to Hack. She stomped over to him.

"Hey, Ann, honey," Hack said. Then his eyes widened. "Uh-oh."

Paul came out from under the cowling and turned to her. "Ann? Hi. Something wrong at the house?"

"You're damn right something's wrong."

He blinked. "Huh?"

"Get down from there. We have to talk."

"Now?" He glanced at Hack.

"I could use a cup of coffee," Hack said. He backed away and limped toward his trailer.

Paul wiped his oily hands on the towel hanging from his belt and reached for her.

She jumped back. "Don't you touch me, whoever the hell you are."

"I beg your pardon? Ann, what's gotten into you?"

"Did you think that photo was so old and faded I wouldn't make the connection? Did you think she'd changed that much?"

"I...I don't know what you're talking about."

"You damn well do. The girl in Uncle David's sketches is your mother." He started to respond, but she held up her hands, palms front. "Don't bother to deny it."

He hung his head. "No, I won't." He turned away.

"Damn! I was half-asleep when I showed you that picture. I wasn't thinking."

"Maybe other people wouldn't have caught the resemblance, but I'm an art restorer! I spend my life dealing with faces." She took a deep breath. "Who the hell have I been sleeping with?"

"I know I should have told you, but I still haven't discovered what I came to find out. There didn't seem to be any right time, and I didn't want to drag you into my problem."

"What problem?" Ann screamed. "Who *are* you?"

"Calm down, just calm down." He realized that behind her Dante was standing at attention and the hair on his back had risen. "Tell Dante I'm not going to attack you."

She turned. "It's okay, Dante. Sit."

The dog did as he was told, but he stayed alert.

"Now, can we go someplace where we can talk?"

"What's wrong with this place?"

"It's a long story."

"There are a couple of folding chairs over there. I'm not going anywhere until I know who I'm going with."

"Fine," he snapped. He brought over the chairs.

She sank into one. He stood in front of her with his hands in his pockets and a defiant look on his face. Like some kid who's been called to the principal's office, she thought. But he was no kid.

He told her everything. His mother's marriage, his birth, coming to America, her disappearance, his adoption, his lifelong certainty that his mother had been murdered by the man who'd abandoned her. He told her that he'd finally discovered evidence that led him to Rossiter and David Delaney. "The house's being for sale was coincidence," he said. "I only planned to come down here long enough to substantiate my suspicions, but then buying and restoring the house seemed like the perfect cover. It gave me a reason not only to live here but to ask questions about the family.''

"Cover? That's all it was? A cover? All that guff you handed my mother about Shiloh and Civil War battlefields was lies? You're spending a quarter of a million dollars on a cover story?''

"Much more than that. I planned to throw the house— throw myself—into their faces. I wanted to destroy the Delaneys. I wanted the world to know that David Delaney was a bigamist and a murderer. I wanted them to admit that Trey was illegitimate. I wanted them to acknowledge me as David Delaney's firstborn legitimate son. I even considered contesting the disposal of my father's estate, but I decided against it. I could have, you know. I checked. The will leaves nearly everything to Paul David Delaney's first legitimate male heir. That's me, not Trey Delaney.''

Ann gaped at him.

He looked at her grimly. "Most of all, I wanted to find where your dear uncle David hid my mother's body after he killed her. I wanted to give her a proper burial with a tombstone that reads, 'Here Lies Michelle Bouvet Delaney, wife of Paul David Delaney, mother of Paul Antoine Bouvet Delaney.'''

"What did you plan to do with the house after you accomplished what you wanted to do? Burn it down and dance on the ashes?''

"I planned to sell it right out from under them.''

"You're crazy, you know that? I've been sleeping with a crazy man.''

He dropped into the chair opposite. "Yeah. I'm beginning to think you're right.'' He dropped his head into his hands. "I'm beginning to think I was wrong.''

"Uncle David really wasn't your father?"

"Oh, he was my father all right. I'm just not sure he killed my mother."

"How do you know he was your father, just tell me *that*. You said yourself it's been over thirty years, and all of a sudden new evidence pops up? Give me a break."

"Not new. Giselle and I simply didn't know it existed."

"This I gotta hear."

"To understand, you had to have known Tante Helaine. She looked tough and she ran that family with an iron hand, but she was a French immigrant married to an American without money or connections. She had the French hatred of authority, bureaucracy and most of all the police. She'd lived through the war. She had plenty of reason to be afraid of the police."

"Not American police."

"Any police. She believed the only way to survive was to stay below the radar. She was terrified that she'd commit some infraction that would get her sent back to France and away from Uncle Charlie and us.

"My mother and I were living with Tante Helaine and Uncle Charlie, and my mother was working in Tante Helaine's bakery. But Maman spent every free minute she had at the library, poring over old telephone books, newspapers—anything she thought might help her find my father. I was too young to know all this at the time, of course. Tante Helaine told me later. All Maman knew about this Paul David Delaney was that he was from a small town somewhere in the mid-South and that his people had money."

"She wanted him to support you."

"She wanted him *back*. She believed that his family

was preventing him from returning to her and that he still loved her. Once he knew he had a son..."

"Lord."

"She wasn't quite twenty-five years old."

"My God. In that photograph she looks forty at least."

"She was worn-out. I can't remember ever seeing her smile. She was tired all the time. But she never stopped loving him. Times were different."

"They certainly were."

"One day she left a note for Tante Helaine saying that she thought she knew where my father was and that she was taking what money she had and going to him. She said she'd let Tante Helaine know more when she was certain, but that she had to catch a bus. She took one small suitcase and walked out the door."

"Where were you?"

"All three of us, Giselle and her sister, Gabrielle, and I, were at the bakery with Tante Helaine. It was Maman's day off—the day she usually spent in the library." He raised his eyes. "That's the last we ever heard from her."

"Did you go to the police?"

"Uncle Charlie filed a missing-persons report over Tante Helaine's objections. She said they'd ignore him. She was right. The police said Maman was over eighteen and had probably just deserted me and run away with a lover. They filed the report, but that was all."

"But surely she would have written or called?"

"She'd have written. She wouldn't pay for long-distance charges." He sighed and stretched his legs out in front of him. "Anyway, Uncle Charlie petitioned for custody. Tante Helaine pitched a fit. Not that she didn't want to keep me. She was afraid that if the authorities knew I existed, they'd drag me off to some foster home. At that point Child Services were so backed up they'd probably have given custody to a dealer in international prostitution. Seven years later Uncle Charlie forced her to have Maman declared dead. They adopted me.''

''They loved you.''

''Tante Helaine couldn't show love, but I think she did love me. They handled me in different ways. Uncle Charlie told me to get on with my life, forget about Maman because we'd never know. He said the best way to thumb my nose at my father was to be something really special so he'd be sorry he'd deserted me.''

''Good advice.''

''Tante Helaine drummed it into my head that my father was a monster, that he'd run away from Maman and hidden from her, and that when she did find him, he killed her. She was sure of it. As time went by, so was I. Until six months ago all I could do about it was swear revenge. Then Tante Helaine died, and I offered to help Giselle clean her things out of the apartment so that it could be sold. Uncle Charlie had died years earlier of lung cancer.

''In the very back of Tante Helaine's closet, hidden behind a hundred pairs of old shoes, was my mother's suitcase. It had been held for a year after she disappeared in the 'left luggage' area of the bus station in Memphis, then opened and sent to the person whose name they found inside—Helaine.''

''And your mother had left all the information she'd gathered inside?''

He shook his head. ''It wasn't that easy. All Maman's papers were there—my birth certificate, her marriage certificate, immigration papers, certificates of dual citizenship for the son of one Paul David Delaney, American citizen, address unknown.

''But that wasn't all. Giselle and I didn't know it until we opened that suitcase, but after Maman disappeared Uncle Charlie had hired a private detective to find her. Apparently Tante Helaine made him fire the guy when he'd barely gotten started. As far as she was concerned, it was stirring the waters and might bring unwanted attention from the authorities. She'd seen children taken away in the war. When I talked to the detective—''

''You found him?''

''He's retired, but his son is running the business. He said Tante Helaine was certain from the beginning that my mother was dead and that my father had killed her. She refused to entertain the idea that she might have run off because she wanted to get away, or that she'd been murdered in some random incident on the road. He was investigating only six months after Maman disappeared, so he didn't have that suitcase to work from.''

''Did he find her?''

''He managed to trace her as far as Memphis. He made a list of seventeen Paul Delaneys within a hundred miles of the city, because Maman's Paul had said he was from a small town. That's where he quit when Tante Helaine fired him.''

''But you went on?''

''Tracing people is much easier now with the Internet. Within two days I had narrowed it down to two Delaneys in this area. One was dead. The other was alive. I flew down and met him. He was a small, dark man. Nothing like my father in the only picture I have of him. He also didn't have an artistic bone in his body and had never been to France.''

''So you came to Rossiter?''

''That was where the other Delaney lived—the one who'd died. I knew this was it the minute I drove into town and saw the house. My father had told my mother stories about the wonderful house he grew up in.'' Paul paused. "I didn't get angry until after I went through it with the real-estate agent."

"You felt shortchanged because you hadn't grown up rich and privileged?"

He turned a cold eye on her. "I got angry when I discovered he'd married another woman two months after he came home and had another son less than a year after that. A child raised with wealth and privilege and, most of all, two parents. I got angry because I knew what a difference child support would have made to my family. Tante Helaine and Uncle Charlie took a boy with no assets and no prospects into a family where both of them worked sixty to seventy hours a week and sweated every bill."

"Uncle David didn't know about you."

"Maybe he did, maybe he didn't. My mother planned to tell him when she met him."

"No wonder Trey tried to kill you."

Paul shook his head. "Couldn't have been Trey. He doesn't know who I am."

"Well, somebody sure did, and Trey's the logical candidate. You said it yourself—you could take everything he has, everything he's worked for. If Aunt Karen told him…"

"She doesn't know, either. Nobody down here did until now."

"Want to bet she knows what you ate for breakfast a year ago?" Ann said. "When Uncle David got killed, Trey was a child. Aunt Karen and Aunt Maribelle ran the business. Trey's been under the thumb of some woman or another his entire life. Now Sue-sue's taking over. He loves his family more than anything in the world. He'd kill you or anybody else if he thought they were threatened."

"Please believe I wanted to tell you all this before."

Ann laughed, but there was no amusement in the sound. "If you'd wanted to, you would have found a time and a place to do it. You would have trusted me if I'd mattered to you. What was I, a small-town diversion to keep you relaxed until you dropped the bomb on the Delaneys?"

He started to speak, but again she held up her hands. "Not one word. I don't want to hear it. Not now, not ever. Now you listen to me, because this is what is going to happen. I will finish my part of your restoration. I don't have much left to do, anyway. I've been putting off a job on a prairie house in Des Moines. I'm going to accept it. It should last at least three months. When I get back, you will have had your mudslinging fest with the Delaneys and have gotten your pound of flesh. After that, I suggest you sell the house. If you don't get an offer right away, give the listing to Mrs. Hoddle—she'd love to sell it for you. Then you go on back to New Jersey and leave us country folk alone."

"I won't let you just walk away like this."

She surged to her feet, snapped her fingers at Dante and started toward her truck. "I swore I'd never let another man use me. Travis used me for money, you used me for information. Same thing. I hope you find your mother's body, but I can tell you this right now. Paul David Delaney never killed a fly, much less the woman he drew in those sketches. A woman he obviously adored. You better go back to the drawing board before someone really does kill you."

She ran for her car. He could have stopped her, but he made no move to go after her. He sank into his chair and put his face in his hands. The worst thing about it all was that she was right. He'd wanted revenge. And all he'd done was alienate the first woman he'd ever truly loved— the woman he wanted to spend his life with.

Hack slunk around the edge of the building. "Bad, huh?"

"The worst."

"Give her time to cool off, then send her some flowers."

"Flowers won't cut it this time."

"The woman is in love with you, son."

"And I'm in love with her."

"Then what's the problem? Nobody's bleeding, nobody's dead. Anything else you can fix."

"Unfortunately somebody *is* dead, and I no longer know what to do about it."

CHAPTER FIFTEEN

ANN CAREERED around the curves on the back road barely registering the wild dogwood that had burst into bloom almost overnight. The grief she felt was too deep for tears. She drove up her grandmother's gravel driveway, slammed on the brakes, skidded to a stop and jumped out of the car while it was still rocking.

Dante followed her. He'd sensed her misery and had refused to stay on his side of the car. She'd driven most of the way with his huge head in her lap, nearly blocking the steering wheel.

Sarah Pulliam was digging the winter weeds out of her flower beds. She rose stiffly, pulled off her cotton gloves, adjusted her wide-brimmed straw hat and came forward with a broad smile on her face. "Ann, how nice—"

She froze, and a moment later rushed to Ann and took her hands. "What's happened? Is it Buddy?"

"No, Gram, it's not Buddy and it's not Mama. It's me."

She'd thought her grief and anger too deep for tears. When she began to sob so hard that she had to gulp to catch her breath, her grandmother's eyes widened. "Come in. Tell me."

"I promised him I wouldn't tell." She sniffed. "He lied through his teeth to me. I don't see why I should feel obligated to keep my mouth shut." The tears started again. "I've got to talk to *somebody*."

Her grandmother ushered her into a bentwood rocker on the front porch and sat in another rocker opposite her. Dante sat as close to Ann's rocker as possible. "Are you pregnant?"

"What? No. Why would you think that?"

"When two people do what you two have been doing, the result is often pregnancy."

"You know?"

"The whole county knows. Maybe the whole state. My gracious, child, where have you lived all your life?" Sarah sniffed. "So you're not pregnant. Then what is it? I thought he was such a nice young man. Obviously I was wrong. What kind of a rat is he?"

Between sobs and gulps, Ann blurted out the entire story.

Sarah listened without saying a word, but the longer Ann talked, the faster her rocking chair rocked.

"So that's it," Ann said at last. "He wanted information, and I sure supplied it. I even took him to see Aunt Karen and Miss Esther. What an idiot I am. I should have known a man like that had to have a hidden agenda. When will I ever learn?"

"You love him, I take it."

"Yes, I do." Ann took a deep breath. "But I got over Travis. I'll get over him."

"This one's not like Travis. Travis was a dream that turned into a nightmare."

"And this isn't?"

"He behaved like a scoundrel, but he had a reason. Was it a good enough one? I don't know. Did he actually tell you any bald-faced lies?"

Ann thought back. "No...I'm not sure. Right now I can't remember which parts he actually told me and which I inferred."

"I've seen the way he looks at you. He didn't lie about that. He's in love with you."

"Yeah, right."

"Listen to me. I knew Harris Pulliam was the one the minute I saw him climb down off his log skidder at the logging trials. I think he knew it, too. If Paul Bouvet—or Delaney or whoever he is—is the one for you, then work it out."

"I can't."

"You can. You feel betrayed and just plain dumped on as a woman at the moment when you were finally getting your self-esteem back. Tell me, what would you have done if your mother had just up and disappeared and you felt certain she'd been murdered?"

"I wouldn't have to do anything. Buddy would do it. And woe betide the man who killed her."

"This young man comes from a set of circumstances that might have turned him into a bank robber or a drug dealer. Instead, he's a hero. I finally placed his name. That plane accident he got hurt in made the newspapers at the time."

"I never saw it."

"When you're in the middle of a job, Ann, the world could fall down around your ears and you wouldn't find out about it until they dug you out of the rubble. I don't remember all the details, but he saved his plane and some lives. Does that sound like a scoundrel and a cad to you?"

"Pilots are notorious with women, Gram. Even I know that."

"Tell that to those pilots in La Grange and their families. There are womanizers in every field. My point is, he came down here as much for closure as for revenge. And the better he got to know us—the better he got to know *you*—the more unsure he became about what he was doing.''

"So he's supposed to get off scot-free?''

"Certainly not. You punished him pretty well this morning, child, and he's going to suffer a good deal more until he decides what to do with what he knows.''

"So what do *I* do?''

"Far be it from me to tell you what to do.''

Ann laughed for the first time since she'd driven in the driveway. "Come on, Gram. Tell me, please. If I don't agree, I won't do it.''

"Help him uncover the truth, if you can. Then step back and see what he does with what he knows. My bet is, he'll try to find some way to stay in Rossiter. Then he'll ask you to marry him.''

"Got the old crystal ball out, have you?''

"You know I have the sight,'' Gram said huffily.

"Okay, suppose I believe you. How can I possibly help him learn the truth?''

"Try to find out what actually happened to his mother. If she was killed, figure out who did it, because I will guaran-damn-tee you David Delaney didn't. He was far too gentle a man.''

"I hope you're right, Gram.''

"Now, would you like a ham sandwich and a slice of my Lady Baltimore cake? I suspect you could use some sugar in your blood.''

"I sure could.'' Ann hugged her grandmother hard. "Keep your mouth shut, okay? Don't tell Mom and Buddy, whatever you do.''

"I promise.'' She opened the screen door and went into the house.

"Gram?'' Ann said as she followed with Dante practically attached to her hip. "How can I possibly find out who killed his mother? Much less where her remains are.''

''I suggest you start by finding Addy's journal. She was a much worse gossip than I am, and a whole lot meaner, to boot. If she knew, it's in that journal.''

ANN CHECKED for Paul's car before she went into his house, but it wasn't in the parking area. He must still be at the airfield. For a moment she had the terrible thought that he might have flown away, never to return. Then she remembered he couldn't, not in his own plane, at any rate. It was in pieces.

She wanted to finish this job. Buddy had given her a punch list. Now was as good a time as any to tackle a few of the final tasks.

She made her way through the garden to the summer-house. Buddy said it would have to come down. They might save the summer kitchen where Paul's studio had been, but this little pergola was infested with termites. Ann had drawn up a plan to rebuild it with new wood. Now she needed to save one of the Victorian sconces that held up the posts. If Paul wanted to duplicate them to use on his garage or another summerhouse, he'd have a model to copy.

The wooden seat that ran around all eight sides of the little building seemed solid enough when she tested it with her weight. She climbed onto it, took her cat's paw and carefully pried loose the nails that held the sconce to the roof.

Every time she shifted her weight she heard an ominous creak from the wood beneath her feet. She worked quickly, removed the sconce and stepped down from the seat just as the wood gave way.

She caught herself before she fell, but managed to

scrape her elbow. It hurt like the dickens, but didn't bleed. She'd have to clean it up before it got infected.

Could Aunt Addy have left her journal somewhere outside the house? The seats in the pergola opened to provide space to store pillows and linen for picnics. She checked all the openings, but found nothing except a couple of tattered pillows that had not seen service for many years.

Ann only knew Aunt Addy as her piano teacher and had no idea where the old lady would have hidden a journal.

Still, she was certainly familiar with all the hiding spots Victorians built into their houses. They adored nooks and crannies. She'd come across several obvious places in the course of her restoration. That left the ones that were truly hidden. Great.

Aunt Addy had been small and thin. She wouldn't have had the strength to saw pieces out of the floor or cut away part of a baseboard. From the garden, Ann looked up toward the big bay window behind which the piano was silhouetted.

Could there be a hiding place somewhere in the piano itself? It would have to be somewhere that wouldn't interfere with the tone or action of the keys.

In the library Ann got down on the floor and began her search. She started with the piano legs and progressed methodically to the lid and finally to the back. She did the same thing with the padded piano bench. No sign that anything had ever been disturbed. She pulled at a couple of tacks on the seat of the bench, and succeeded only in breaking a fingernail and raising a cloud of dust.

Then she sat on the floor with Dante's head in her lap and cursed.

This was the first time she'd allowed herself to think about this morning. She found she was shivering. Her teeth were chattering as though she was coming down with a chill.

Suddenly she wanted to see the photograph of Paul's mother once more—the woman she'd become when the laughing girl in Uncle David's sketches had been broken by sorrow.

She told Dante to stay and went upstairs, past a couple of painters who were finishing the front bedroom. There was no need to sneak around. She had a good excuse to go anywhere in this house she chose.

Where she chose to go was Paul's bedroom.

Her heart lurched when she closed the door behind her. That dumb mattress! She ought to stick a knife into the thing. She brushed away angry tears and turned her head firmly away.

His suitcase was open on the floor in the corner. Despite his weeks of camping out, everything was in military order. She removed a dozen pairs of socks, picked up the framed picture of Michelle Bouvet with her young son, sat down on the mattress and stared at it.

The shot had been taken in front of some building that looked official. A library, maybe, or a bank.

She wore her hair in a severe style, pulled back in a bun, Ann guessed.

She had on short white gloves, which definitely dated the photo.

Her dress looked as though it had cost some money. It was a plain princess-cut coatdress with three-quarter-length sleeves. Something about the perfect fit, the drape of the cloth—some sort of cotton faille, Ann would guess—said that it had been created for her. French-women always dressed with such flair.

The fabric itself was a black-and-white geometric pattern that looked almost cubist. Her shoes had very high heels and very pointed toes, and appeared to be patent leather. The outfit contrasted sharply with the expression of the woman herself. Had she owned it when she'd known Uncle David?

Ann wondered if Michelle had sewn the dress herself. Surely she couldn't afford a dress that looked like a designer creation. Having a baby had not thickened her waist or swollen her breasts much, either. As a matter of fact, she was almost painfully thin.

Ann looked down at her own full bosom. Clothes never did hang right on her, but this woman could have been a runway model.

She put the picture carefully back into Paul's suitcase. He'd never know she'd looked at it. She slipped out of his room and back downstairs in time to encounter her father coming up.

"I got that sconce from the summerhouse," she said.

"What's with you? You been crying? Your nose is all red. What'd you do to your arm?"

"Just a scratch. I'll clean it up when I get home."

"Where's Paul?"

"Still out at the airfield, I guess."

Buddy looked at her curiously, but she slipped by him and ran out the front door with Dante close on her heels.

She let herself into her loft and laid the sconce carefully on one of her cabinets. Cleaning her scraped skin hurt, but she refused to cry about it or anything else. Crying was counterproductive. She would not speak to Paul until she could be certain she wouldn't break down in front of him.

She checked her answering machine to find a dozen calls. She listened to the first few. All Paul, all apologizing, all wanting to make everything between them right.

"Nuts," she said to the answering machine. Then she sat on her bed and let Dante crawl up beside her.

If she hadn't played right into Paul's hands, maybe she wouldn't feel like such an idiot. "Just want to find out about the family who built my house," he'd said. Right.

He'd had the perfect opportunity to tell her about his mother when they'd found the sketches. But he hadn't trusted her. The Delaneys had always considered themselves a class above the Pulliams and the Jenkinses, but they were still family. Ann had betrayed them with every nugget of gossip out of her noisy little mouth.

But none of her information would do him a whipstitch of good. Uncle David hadn't killed Paul's mother. Maybe he had run away from her, but men ran away from women all the time, and from everything Ann had heard about him, Uncle David hadn't been the staunchest vessel on the ocean.

Possibly *nobody* had killed his mother. Maybe she'd had a heart attack, been sent to a morgue somewhere and was buried as a Jane Doe. Or met a real badass on the road. Heck, maybe Ted Bundy killed her. She certainly fit his profile. Maybe she'd accepted a ride with some trucker who'd gotten too friendly and had lost his temper when she wouldn't put out in return for the ride.

There was not one smidgen of evidence she had ever gotten closer to Rossiter than the bus station in Memphis.

Ann leaned back against the pillows and pulled her knees up to her chest. If Michelle had made it to Rossiter, how had she traveled? She didn't have a car, probably didn't have a driver's license and certainly didn't have money to rent a car.

Ann called her grandmother. "Gram, can you get to Rossiter from Memphis by bus?"

"Not a city bus, but the local bus to Nashville goes

right by on the highway. You can tell the driver you want
to stop. There used to be a bus stop where you could wait
to be picked up to go to Memphis, but I think they took
it down long ago.''

"You have any idea what time of day it used to run?"

"Early morning and mid-afternoon, I think. But it's
been so long, child. I'm sure bus companies have records
of their old runs. You could find out."

"Thanks, Gram."

So it was possible that Michelle could have caught a
local bus and stopped at Rossiter.

Then it was possible she *hadn't* arranged to meet Uncle
David. Maybe she simply dropped in unexpectedly. Boy,
would that be a kick in the teeth. Of course, even if she'd
come to Rossiter on the bus, she'd still have needed a ride
out to Uncle David's house. Must have taken some nerve
to walk up the front drive.

There was one obvious place Ann hadn't looked for
Aunt Addy's journal. She found the button box and
dumped its contents unceremoniously on her worktable in
a jumble of yarn and buttons.

She caught the edge of the leather lining and pried it
up. The glue was old, but it came up in one piece. Nothing. She did the same thing with the top. Again nothing.

She replaced the yarn and buttons neatly. Suddenly she
stopped and her breath caught. This couldn't be.

She had to see that photo of Michelle again. She
grabbed the magnifying glass from her stripping kit and
stuck it and the small envelope from the box into the
pocket of her jeans. Then she and Dante raced back across
the street.

Nobody was in the upstairs hall. Buddy had left for his
shift with the Rossiter police. She could hear voices from

the front bathroom, where the men were installing the new toilet and sink.

She slipped back into Paul's room and picked up the photo of Michelle again. This time she used her magnifying glass.

She took out the small packet of buttons she'd picked up from the box. They were perhaps three-quarters of an inch across. Black enamel painted with delicate white patterns. Here was a bird, there a frog, a rose, a butterfly—there couldn't possibly be two sets of buttons exactly like this in the entire world, and definitely not in Rossiter, Tennessee.

There was only one way they could have found their way into Aunt Addy's button box. Somebody had cut them off Michelle's dress and saved them.

Since Michelle had left her suitcase at the bus station, she wouldn't have had another dress with her.

She wouldn't have taken it off for anybody but Uncle David.

Unless she wasn't the one who took it off. And unless she was past resisting when she was stripped.

Ann couldn't move, couldn't think.

She could not visualize tiny Aunt Addy killing anybody.

But there were two women in the Delaney family who were capable of murder. Karen Delaney Lowrance and Maribelle Norwood Delaney.

Maribelle was long dead. Karen, however, was very much alive.

The new phone lines had still not been installed in the house, and Ann didn't carry a cell phone. She never remembered to charge it, so the battery was always flat.

She had to tell Paul.

She had to tell Buddy. It was time to bring the police in on this.

By now the men were finished for the day. The upstairs was silent when she left Paul's room again. Downstairs in the kitchen she could hear a couple of men arguing about the new countertops. On impulse she opened the door to the dumbwaiter and yelled, "Hey, you guys down there. Anybody got a cell phone?"

"What the…Ann? Is that you up there?"

"Yeah, Cal, you have a cell phone?"

"Sure."

"Stay where you are. I'm coming down to borrow it."

Buddy was out on patrol. The station would give him her message and ask him to swing by the house.

Hack said Paul had left the airfield to get something in town. He'd be back shortly.

Ann didn't know his cell number so she handed the phone back to Cal.

"You want us to stick around?"

"No, go on. I'll wait for Buddy, then I'm out of here, too."

They nodded and left.

She perched on top of the newly mounted slate countertop and worried the cuticle of her thumbnail.

That damn journal! It must have been thrown away. She'd looked every place she could think of.

Across the kitchen, the door to the dumbwaiter stood open. Half-a-dozen gallons of paint sat on the platform inside ready for the ride upstairs tomorrow morning.

"I'm crazy to think this is even possible," she said. She removed the cans of paint and set them on the floor. Would Aunt Addy have gone to these lengths to conceal her journal? She was certainly small and limber enough.

Ann raised the platform so that she could check under it. Nothing.

She took a flashlight off the kitchen counter and shone it down the shaft. No motor. Strictly hand-operated. She shone the light up the shaft, but the light petered out before it reached the top.

Okay, nothing for it but to climb aboard and haul.

"Dante, go lie down and wait for me."

The dog obediently padded off into the dining room and lay down.

She had a problem fitting herself into the dumbwaiter, but she managed it in the end. As she pulled, she checked for any signs of a niche in the walls. Nothing was immediately apparent.

Before she slid out into the second-floor hallway, she shone her light up. The shaft went all the way into the attic. She hadn't seen another door up there.

She took a deep breath and began to pull. It wasn't easy lifting her own weight, even with the counterweights that had been set up to make the platform run smoothly. As the light from the hall faded below her, she held the flashlight between her teeth and used both hands to haul herself up.

She'd almost reached the pulleys at the top of the shaft before she saw it. Someone—Aunt Addy—had fitted a bracket against the side of the shaft. The platform wouldn't have been able to pass it, but then, the dumbwaiter was never used above the second floor. The pulleys cleared it easily.

Ann slipped the brake onto the dumbwaiter and twisted so that she could reach the package.

It came into her hand as though it had been waiting for her.

It was heavier and bulkier than she would have guessed,

and the shape was much more irregular than a single book.

She lowered herself to the second-floor opening and worked herself out without dropping her parcel.

She didn't want to get caught in Paul's room again, but she was impatient to see what she'd found. She slipped into Paul's bathroom, closed the shutters on the window, turned on the light and sat down on the closed toilet to investigate her prize.

She undid the twine with shaking fingers and began to unwrap the parcel. There was no journal inside, merely a sheaf of handwritten yellowing pages that bore the Delaney name and address across the top.

Another parcel had been wrapped separately, then included with this one and wrapped again. She put the pages on the sink and unwrapped the second one carefully.

When she saw what was inside, she nearly threw up.

"CALL FOR YOU in the office," Hack told Paul. It was nearly dark. Both men were exhausted. Paul had worked like a demon all afternoon. He wanted the plane airworthy and he wanted it now.

"Can I call back?"

"Says it's urgent."

"Ann?" he asked, unable to hide the hope in his voice.

"A woman, but not Ann."

"Oh, hell, all right."

He picked up the telephone. He recognized Karen Lowrance's upper-class drawl instantly.

"Mr. Bouvet? Paul, I wonder if you'd do me a really big favor and drive by my house on your way home?"

Her house was in the opposite direction from his home and he told her so.

"It's truly important, Mr. Bouvet."

"I don't think that's such a good idea."

"Marshall, my husband, is here." She gave a husky laugh. "In case you don't want to be alone with me."

He'd rather be alone with Jack the Ripper, but he didn't say that. He tried several more times to get out of seeing her, but she was so persistent that he finally agreed. After he hung up, he turned to Hank.

"I brought some clean clothes. Can I shower in your trailer?"

"Sure. Clean towels on the right as you enter."

When Paul left ten minutes later he looked presentable.

At the Lowrance house the front door was opened by a tubby man with gray hair, bright blue eyes and a puzzled expression. "Mr. Bouvet?" He stuck out his hand. "I'm Marshall Lowrance. I don't believe we've met, sir."

Paul completed the formalities.

"Karen's waiting for you in the library." He led Paul toward the room he'd been in before. As he held the door for Paul, he called out, "Honey, I'll just be across the hall if you need me."

Or if I do, Paul thought.

Karen had on black slacks and a black sweater. "Do sit down. Thank you so much for coming like this. May I get you something to drink?"

He shook his head and took the wing chair across from her. The Manhattan glass on the side table contained only melting ice cubes. He hoped that meant Karen was relatively sober.

She took a deep breath and said in the same easy way, "I know who you are." Her red-tipped fingers gripped the leather armrest hard enough to make dents. Her voice, however, remained calm.

He was not surprised. Nothing about this family surprised him anymore. He'd felt the tightening of her fingers, seen her startled expression the first time she'd shaken his hand. He'd wondered at the time whether she'd seen a resemblance between him and his father.

She'd been so charming afterward, however, that he'd dismissed the idea.

"Really," he said, trying to keep his body and face relaxed. "Who am I?"

She took another deep breath and hugged herself as though she needed to protect her body from him. He could see the muscles along her jaw tighten.

"You're my husband's bastard son by the French whore he had an affair with in Paris."

She spat the words at him, then her eyes opened wide as though the viciousness of her words startled her.

Paul had never raised a finger against a woman, but in that moment he had to clench his fists to keep from leaning across the ottoman between them and slapping her. Not for himself, but for his mother. His face flamed.

He sucked in a breath and tried with only moderate success to stay calm and relaxed. He did manage to force a smile, but from the way Karen recoiled, he must have looked pretty scary. She got up to go to the bar.

He stood when she did. "I'm much more than that," he said. "I am Paul David Delaney's one and only legitimate son. He *married* my mother in France. *Your* son is the bastard."

"Liar!" she screeched, and flew at him.

Her fingers reached out to claw his face.

He caught her wrists and held her at arm's length. "Stop that!"

"Liar, liar, liar!"

She had the strength of a tiger defending her cub.

She kicked at his shins, tried to bring a knee up into

his groin, twisted and squirmed to break his hold on her arms, all the while screaming, "Liar!"

He felt his right arm begin to tremble. She'd be able to break his hold as soon as his strength gave out.

"Honey?" came a plaintive voice from the hall.

"I'm fine, Marshall. We'll be out in a minute."

"It's the truth," Paul hissed through gritted teeth. "Calm down, for God's sake. I don't want to hurt you."

She stared at him openmouthed.

"Hurt me?" She began to shake. "You don't want to hurt me?" Suddenly she was laughing hysterically with her head thrown back so that he could see the sinews in her aging throat.

She went limp. He slid his left arm around her waist and led her to the couch.

When he let her go, she collapsed with her face buried in her lap. The sobs that were half laughter continued to rack her.

Paul poured two fingers of bourbon into a crystal glass, dropped in a couple of pieces of ice and took it to her. "Here."

For a moment he thought she'd slap the glass out of his hand.

Instead, she reached out with shaking fingers, took the glass and brought it to her mouth using both hands.

She drained the bourbon in one gulp. "Another," she said, and held the glass out to him.

"I don't think so. Can I get you some water?"

"Said the executioner as he lifted the ax."

That sent her into another fit of laughing and crying. He stood and watched her. If she'd calm down, he could talk to her, but not like this.

"All right. Water. Lots of it."

He brought her a tumbler filled with ice and water.

Again she took it and drank it so greedily that water ran down both sides of her open mouth and dripped off her chin to form dark circles on her sweater.

She handed the empty glass back to him, but didn't ask for more. When he turned back to her after putting the glass on the bar, she was watching him warily.

He sat down across from her on the ottoman.

"Can you prove it?" she said quietly.

He nodded. "I have the papers. I have affidavits from the *mairie* in which they were married and from the witnesses. I even have the seal from the American Embassy that my...that he had to get in order to be legally married in France."

She closed her eyes. "I don't understand. How could he be married and marry me?"

"He couldn't. Not legally."

She shivered. Her eyes were now very frightened. "We were never married?"

"You lived with him until he died. Even if you were never legally married, you would be considered a common-law wife."

She laughed, but there was no humor in it. "A common-law wife? My God, that's what trailer trash say when they've been shacking up for years without ever getting around to making it legal." She looked at him calmly for the first time. "How much?"

"I beg your pardon."

"How much do you want to go away and leave us in peace?"

"Mrs. Lowrance, I have plenty of money."

"Then what? Do you want it all? What do you know about cattle or soybeans or cotton? Trey has...my God, he has a home, a family, a place in this community. To tell him he's the bastard son of a bigamist, that he's going to lose everything he owns, everything he loves, to some French interloper who literally dropped out of the sky..." She leaned back against the couch. "I'll kill you first." The words were as matter-of-fact as a comment about the weather.

"You haven't been successful so far." He thrust his hands into the pockets of his slacks and walked away from her. After a moment he turned back. "I came here to do precisely what you surmised. Take everything. Own it, make it mine the way I'm making that house mine. I planned to reveal the secret of my birth in a way that would most damage the Delaneys."

"What have we ever done to you?"

It was his turn to laugh. "What have you ever done to me? Let's see. David Delaney convinced my eighteen-year-old virgin mother to marry him secretly. Believe me, in France marrying in secret is extremely difficult. He worked it out carefully. He didn't give her the right information about his family, who he was, where he lived. All because she wouldn't go to bed with him or pose nude for him without a marriage certificate."

"So she forced him to marry her." Karen gave a little nod of satisfaction.

"She loved him, but she didn't believe in sex before marriage. Old-fashioned idea, but then, she was an old-fashioned girl. She also didn't believe in divorce. I have seen some of her letters to my aunt. She didn't give a damn if the two of them starved in a garret while he studied art and she worked in her father's coffee shop. She wanted to spend the rest of her life making him happy."

He sighed. "Funny thing is, she did make him happy. For three whole months. Until the powerful Delaney clan decided it was time to reel him in, bring him home, put him to work at a real job, marry him off to the girl next door. When he left for America my mother truly believed he meant to come back to Paris. How long did it take you all to convince him to stay? That he'd be happier as a planter married to you?''

She stuck out her chin. "Not long."

"He never knew she was pregnant with me. Maybe if he'd known—''

"He would have gone back to France? I seriously doubt it. After all, he must have known he might want to disappear, otherwise why give your mother false information?''

"I can't deny that. But we were talking about what the Delaneys did to me. Marrying my mother, getting her pregnant and then abandoning her was only the first step. She spent the next six years and every dime she could save trying to find him. She finally did. And when she confronted him, he killed her."

"What?" Karen surged to her feet. "Now that *is* a lie. My husband would never harm a gnat, much less a woman he'd supposedly loved."

"Killed her," Paul kept on as though she hadn't spoken. "And buried her body so that it's never been found. So while your Trey was being raised by doting parents and grandparents who surrounded him with luxury, my uncle Charlie and my *tante* Helaine struggled to support two of their own children and me on a plumber's salary."

"You don't seem to have been hurt by the process."

"I was hurt in ways you could never know. But I survived, I made a little money and then, lo and behold, just when I'd completely given up hope of ever finding and punishing my father, I found him, never mind how."

"And you're so certain he is the man who fathered you?''

"Aren't you? You're the one who had Trey steal my toothbrush."

Her gasp told him he'd guessed correctly. He risked a smile. "Took me a while to tumble to that one. How closely does our DNA match? We're only half brothers, after all. I assume you didn't secretly exhume my father just to get some hair follicles."

"I had to know for certain. DNA is the only sure way."

"If you had asked me to provide you with blood for a DNA test, I'd gladly have given it to you. But that would have meant telling me you suspected who I was. Then you'd have had to tell Trey. You didn't want to do that, did you."

"Of course not."

"You recognized me that first day, didn't you. I assume I'm enough like my father to trigger some memory in you. What I don't know is why you didn't simply think I resembled your dead husband without making the connection that I might be his son."

"Because I've been expecting you for over thirty years."

"You knew about me?"

"I was positive he'd had an affair with someone in Paris. I knew he loved her, or thought he did. I didn't know she'd had a baby, but I worried about it. The last few years I pushed it to the back of my mind. I thought we were safe. The nightmares haven't been so frequent."

"I'm sorry."

"You said you intend to take everything."

He shook his head. "No, I said that's what I'd intended to do when I first drove through Rossiter and saw the mansion was half-derelict and up for sale."

He shrugged. "I wanted to take it all, make the remaining Delaneys admit their sins and grovel in the dirt.

I wanted you all brought low.'' He looked up at her. ''But I never intended to keep any of it. I wanted to hand it back to you like a lord conferring a fiefdom on a serf. To have to thank me for giving you your lives back. And then I planned to put the house on the market and leave town.''

''And now?''

''Now you have faces.''

''So what do you plan now that we have faces?''

''I don't know. I still want to find my mother's grave and give her a decent burial if possible. And I want the Delaney family, if not the law, to acknowledge privately not only what my father did to her, but that I am his legitimate son.''

''I see. So I suppose I won't have to kill you, after all.''

''Not if you help me find my mother.''

''I can't. I don't know what happened to your mother, but I do know my husband didn't kill her.''

''You can't know for certain.''

''How do you know she didn't disappear voluntarily? That's she's not living in Phoenix or Los Angeles with a whole new family?''

''There's evidence she came here to meet my father. Then she disappeared before she could tell her family she'd found him. She's not living some other life somewhere else.''

''Then someone she met on the road killed her.''

''Too big a coincidence.''

''Coincidences happen.''

''Not that conveniently, they don't.''

''You have evidence?'' she asked.

''Let's say I have knowledge.''

''But why are you so certain David killed her?''

"Nobody else knew about her, so nobody else had a motive to kill her."

"The whole Delaney clan had reason to kill her," Karen said softly. "I might have if I'd met her and known who she was."

"Did you?"

Karen shook her head. "No." For the first time she looked at him with real compassion. "There is another theory. She had been abandoned with a child. You said she was struggling financially. If she found out that David was married with another child, maybe she couldn't take it."

"You're saying she might have committed suicide."

"Isn't it a possibility?"

"Never. First, she was a devout Roman Catholic. Suicide is a mortal sin. She would never have endangered her soul, no matter how unhappy she was. Second, because of me. She would never have abandoned me without a word. She loved her sister, too. They were on excellent terms when she left. Then there's the problem of her body. She didn't know this part of the country at all. If she'd walked off into the woods and hanged herself from the nearest tree, somebody would have found her. The same with stabbing. She didn't own a gun or know how to use one, and she had no access to poison. If she had killed herself, she would have wanted her body to be found. She would never have left me in limbo all these years."

"This is obviously not the first time you've thought this through," Karen said.

"I've thought of very little else for thirty years."

"And yet you must have been a good student with a good record to get into the Air Force Academy."

"You're saying I should have become a drug addict or a juvenile delinquent?"

"It wouldn't have been outside the realm of possibility."

"It was for me. No matter how much I believed she was dead, for a child, that's merely another form of abandonment. My father had already abandoned me. I decided there were two ways to go. To hell—to show them how badly they'd messed me up. Or to the top—to show them I didn't need them."

"When is she supposed to have died?"

"The last day we know she was alive was the twenty-first of August, 1974."

Karen sat up. "The twenty-first of August. Thank God." She clasped her hands in front of her and closed her eyes. "Then David didn't kill her."

"How can you know that?"

"I not only know it, I can prove it." She surged to her feet and began to walk around the room. "It may take some time to get you the proof, but I swear I can get it."

"What proof?"

"His alibi." She turned to him, her face now radiant. "Every year from the time Trey was born until David died in 1977, we rented a condo down at Destin, Florida, for the last three weeks in August. He couldn't have killed your mother. He was in Florida with me."

"Even if you were registered for the whole time, he could have caught a plane back, killed her..."

"You were against coincidences before, now suddenly you're willing to consider this nonsense."

"And I suppose you have the same alibi?"

"Yes. Neither of us slipped back into town to commit a murder."

"She might have found out he was in Florida and kept on going until she got there. I may have been looking for her in the wrong place."

"She didn't. No one would have told her where we were." She frowned at him. "Condos keep records, and even if they don't, Marshall is a bear about tax records and bank receipts. It may take a week or two, but we will come up with the proof that we were in Florida."

"Can you fly a plane?"

"Good grief, no. Neither could David."

"Did you tell Trey your suspicions?"

"Certainly not. He still doesn't know. He thinks you're exactly who you say you are."

"Then who did you get to screw up my plane?"

"I beg your pardon?"

"The person who punctured my oil line so the engine would quit thirty minutes into my flight."

For a moment she simply gaped at him. Then her eyes shifted to her right. He saw her chest heave. "I hired no one."

"And the stirrup leather? Did you pay one of Trey's grooms to cut it?"

"What are you talking about?"

"Somebody has been making inept attempts to kill me, or at least hurt me. Any idea who?"

She refused to look at him.

"If you didn't tell Trey who I am, what did you tell him exactly? Can he fly a plane?"

She stammered. "He...he took a few lessons, but the ground school bored him. Trey's a good boy. He'd never do anything like that." She looked into Paul's eyes. "He likes you, God help him. He told me so. I warned him how dangerous you were to us, but..." Her face blanched.

"But not why."

Karen shook her head. "Only that you could cause terrible trouble for the family." She covered her mouth with her hand. "I told him that somehow you had to be forced to go away and leave us alone.'' She closed her eyes, ''Dear God, he said not to worry, he'd take care of it.''

Paul handed her the telephone. His face was grim. ''Call him. Get him over here. Now.''

''Please, if you bring in the police—''

''Call him.''

She called. Trey wasn't home. Paul hit the button for the speakerphone. Karen saw what he was doing, but didn't stop him.

''Mother Karen,'' Sue-sue said, ''I thought he was with you. He said you called him and asked him to come over.''

''How long ago did he leave?''

''An hour or so. I tried to stop him. He'd been drinking. Lord, I hope he hasn't had an accident with the car.''

''I'm sure he's fine. Don't worry.'' Karen let the phone drop into its cradle. ''Trey never drives drunk, and I most certainly did not call him to come over.'' She looked up at Paul. ''I'm frightened. We've got to find him before he does something that can't be fixed.''

''I'm not certain any of this can be fixed.''

''Please, nobody's been hurt. We'll pay for your airplane. You know now that David didn't kill your mother and neither did I. Just go away and leave us alone.''

''I can't. Not yet.'' He picked up the telephone, dialed Buddy Jenkins's office, identified himself and asked the dispatcher if there had been any automobile accidents reported that evening. He glanced at Karen. ''None that you know of. Okay. I'll explain later, but at the moment I need you to tell Buddy to locate Trey Delaney. His wife says he's been drinking and he's out in his truck.'' He listened and turned to Karen. ''The dispatcher says a few minutes ago his truck was in front of his office in Rossiter.''

''He's probably inside getting even drunker.''

"Nerving himself up for another little accident?"

Karen grabbed his arm. "I told him that if you hadn't bought that damned mansion, you'd never have come to town."

"You think he'd try to destroy the *house?* That's nuts."

"I don't know."

Paul spoke into the phone. "Look, would you get Buddy on his radio and tell him to check my house?" He hung up. "Come on, Karen, it's time to end this thing."

CHAPTER SIXTEEN

"TREY DELANEY, what are you doing here?" Ann asked.

Trey was kneeling between Paul's newly installed kitchen cabinets when Ann walked in on him. He jumped to his feet and dropped the pipe wrench he'd had in his hand. "You're not supposed to be here."

"Neither are you, so I guess that makes us even."

"There weren't any lights on. I made sure before I came in." His eyes darted around the room. "Go away."

"I was in the upstairs bathroom reading with the shutters closed. And I will not go away. I'm *supposed* to be here. Why are you?"

He made a sound that was half groan and half whimper.

"What are you hiding behind your back? Show me." She reached for his arm playfully, but he shoved her away with more force than was necessary. "Ow! Stop that!"

"I'm sorry, Ann," he said. "I don't want to hurt you. God, I never wanted to hurt anybody."

She felt the hairs on her neck prickle. Nonsense. This was Trey, her dim-witted cousin, a sweet guy she'd known all her life. There was not a mean bone in his body. She didn't need to feel frightened around Trey, did she?

She kept her voice calm. Trey had always responded well to authority. So she'd exert it. "Trey Delaney, you show me what you have in your hand right this minute. I mean it."

"It's just an old candle." Now, he sounded sulky.

"A candle? Why were you putting it on the floor?" She looked past him. "Good grief, some nitwit left the cap off the gas valve to the stove. That could be danger…" Suddenly her eyes widened. "Oh, my God."

Trey threw the candle across the room. "Why'd you have to show up? The house was supposed to be empty."

"I didn't just show up. I've been here waiting for Paul."

"He's at Mama's. She called him. He's not supposed to be back until…until…"

Anger drove out any fear she felt. "You're the one who's been pulling those stupid stunts, aren't you? What'd you do—buy *The Idiot's Guide to Assassination*? You could have *killed* somebody. Dammit, you could have killed *me!*"

He dropped his eyes. "I'm sorry about that. You weren't supposed to get in the way." He opened his hands and reached out to her. "I didn't want to *kill* him, maybe hurt him a little, make him go away."

"Why on earth would you want to make him go away? My Lord, Trey, those weren't high-school pranks. They were dangerous and stupid."

"Mama told me he was dangerous to the family." He drew himself up. "Nobody threatens my family."

"He's not threatening your family. He's a perfectly nice man…"

"No, he's not." Suddenly Trey's face went hard. His hands twisted into fists.

Until this moment she'd never realized how big he was. She felt her pulse race in her throat. She forced her voice to remain calm. "Did she happen to mention *why* he's dangerous to your family?"

"She said she couldn't tell me for a few days, but I know it's about Daddy or Granddaddy. Maybe a vendetta—the son of somebody one of them screwed in a business deal. Something like that, at any rate. Retaliation. Revenge. Mama swore she'd tell me when I stole his toothbrush, but she didn't.''

Ann stared at him in amazement. ''*You* stole Paul's toothbrush?''

''Mama told me to. I gave her the glass he used in my office, too. She wanted his fingerprints.''

''Trey, don't you watch any of those forensic shows on TV? Don't you know about DNA?''

''Sure I know. What's DNA got to do with anything?''

''You can get DNA off a toothbrush.''

''Why would Mama want his DNA?''

''I don't know.'' She closed her eyes and ran her hand over her face. ''Trey, I cannot believe you went out on nothing more than your mama's say-so and tried to kill a total stranger. Don't you understand you could go to jail?''

Now he was back to sulky. ''I didn't really try to kill him. I figured he might land in the hospital for a while, long enough to be convinced to go back where he came from. The Delaneys can make Rossiter damn uncomfortable for anybody they don't want here. We're still powerful. And I wouldn't go to jail. Not in *this* county.''

''You would if Buddy had anything to say about it. You may be rich, but you're no different from anybody else under the law.''

''I'm still a Delaney.''

''Don't be an idiot, Trey. What do you think Buddy would have done if you'd killed me?''

''I'm so sorry about that, Ann. After you fell off Liege I realized I couldn't take a chance on hurting somebody else.'' He took a deep breath. ''The only way to make him leave town is to make doggoned certain he doesn't have a house to live in.''

Suddenly he didn't seem quite sane. His eyes glittered with excitement.

Ann felt her stomach churn. She mustn't throw up.

She had to keep him talking, try to bring him back to the real world where he would never consider arson and murder. She had to stay calm. If she broke, if she turned and ran, he'd catch her. She held his eyes. She must not break the spell between them until she could figure out what to do next.

"Okay," she said, "let me see if I can figure this out. First you take the cap off the gas line inside. Then you light your candle and set it on the counter. Then you go outside and turn on the gas main—that's what the pipe wrench is for, am I right? The house fills with gas, the candle ignites it, and goodbye house.''

"Right.''

"That won't work. You may set off a minor explosion and cause a fire, but you won't blow the house up. It would take a month to fill the house with gas from that tiny pipe. Besides, the minute the first fumes reach your precious lighted candle, you'd get a nice little boom that would blow the flame out. There are smoke detectors all over this place. Buddy insisted on them. The fire department will be here within five minutes, Trey. They're only two blocks away.''

His eyes had turned sly. The smile she had always thought charming now seemed ugly and twisted. He was going to do this horrible thing. There was nothing she could do to stop him.

And she was a witness. He didn't seem to have realized that.

Yet.

"Don't try to kid a kidder, Ann. There's a bunch of cans of varnish and oil-based paint on the floor over there. They'll blow the minute the gas touches this candle." He bit his lip. "That's why I had to do it when I was sure nobody was here. I don't want to burn anybody alive."

"What about the café? You want to burn that to the ground, too?"

"The fire department can keep that from happening."

"Listen to me. So far you haven't caused any real damage. You've got to stop this right now before you do. If you burn this house down, Daddy will make sure you go to jail."

Trey shoved his fingers through his unruly hair. "Everybody'll think it's an accident. I can't go to jail. I've got a family to support. Buddy won't find out."

"He will. Now, for heaven's sake put the cap back on that gas line, and let's go next door for a cup of coffee."

"No. I've come too far. Buddy won't find out if you don't tell him." He stared at her sadly. "But you will, won't you?"

He knew she would. She had to try and convince him she'd keep her mouth shut. She was truly frightened of him now. "I promise I won't tell Buddy."

He sighed deeply and shook his head. "You will, too. It's not my fault you showed up. I got to protect my family."

"Are you threatening me?"

He stood very tall. "I guess I am."

"Trey, you don't want to do this."

"I have to. I'm so sorry." He started toward her with the wrench in his raised fist. "I promise I won't let you burn to death."

She was gearing up to run when she heard a deep rumble from the doorway.

Both she and Trey turned to see Dante. His teeth were bared and every hair on his back was standing on end.

Trey froze.

Dante jumped.

Trey screamed, dropped the wrench and fell with Dante on his chest. There was a sickening thud as Trey's head struck the floor.

"Dante!" Ann yelled. "Dante, no!" She grabbed his collar and yanked.

He didn't move. Only the chokehold Ann had on his collar kept him from tearing out Trey's throat.

Trey screamed. "Get him off me!"

The back door burst open, and Buddy rushed in with his gun drawn. "What the..."

The dog turned his massive head, saw Buddy and immediately relaxed into his slobbering happy self. Ann pulled him away.

Trey sat up, blinking hard. "My head hurts," he said.

"You're lucky that's all that hurts," Buddy said. "Dante could have ripped you to pieces. Now get up from there before I blow your stupid brains out."

"I wasn't really going to do anything." Trey's eyes pleaded with Ann.

"He hadn't done anything *yet*, Daddy." She glared at Trey. "He planned to burn this house down." She didn't mention that the house would have burned with her inside. She was afraid of what Buddy might do.

Brakes squealed.

A moment later Paul rushed in with Karen on his heels.

"Mama?" Trey said. He still sat on the floor with Buddy's gun in his face.

"Don't you say one word until Marshall gets here," Karen said. She turned to Buddy. "He wants a lawyer."

"I was just trying to do what you wanted."

"Shut *up*."

Paul swept Ann into his arms. "Are you all right?"

She held him tight for a long moment until fear gave way to anger. She pushed away from him to glare at Trey. "I'm fine. My idiot cousin was going to blow up the house just to get you to leave town."

He put his hands on her shoulders. "Did he hurt you? If he did, I swear…"

"I'm okay." She looked at her dog. "Dante protected me. I think if I hadn't grabbed him, Trey wouldn't have much of a head left."

"Good boy," Paul said.

Dante sat up and wagged his stump tail.

Ann dropped to the floor and wrapped her arms around him. She began to cry. "Good old dog," she said, and buried her face in his neck.

Trey stood up carefully. He didn't take his eye off Buddy's gun.

"If that's all, Buddy, this has been an exhausting night. I'm going to take Trey home," Karen said. She slipped her arm protectively around her son's shoulders.

"The hell you are," Buddy said. "We're all going over to my office, and we're going to stay there until we sort this thing out."

"But—"

"Karen, I said git. Now git."

"I DON'T INTEND to press charges," Paul said once they were settled in Buddy's office. "Thankfully nobody was hurt and Karen's agreed to pay for the repair to the Cessna and the Stearman. Charges wouldn't serve any purpose."

"I don't give a damn whether you press charges or not. I seem to recall that sabotaging an aircraft is a federal offense."

"You can't prove I did that," Trey said.

"Trey, I told you to shut up. If you want to blame anybody," Karen said, "blame me. He thought he was doing what I told him to do to protect his family."

"I don't intend to press charges, either," Ann said. "I'm the one who got dumped off Liege. Remember, Trey? Me, not Paul. And I'm the one you were threatening to bash with that wrench."

Trey hunkered down and averted his gaze.

"Family be damned," Buddy said. "What is this mess all about? Nobody's leaving here until I know."

Karen took a deep gulp of air. "There's no good way to do this. Trey, meet your half brother, Paul Delaney. Your older half brother."

Trey and Buddy both gaped.

BY MIDNIGHT Buddy swore he was going to lock the entire passel of them up and sort them out in the morning.

Marshall Lowrance managed to calm him down long enough to get him to release Trey and Karen into his custody.

"Sue-sue is frantic," Marshall told his stepson as he led him out. "You call her from my car."

"What about my truck?"

"You are not touching your truck until I know you can pass a breathalyzer. Now come on. You, too, Karen. Sometime I wish I'd never met any of you."

Buddy watched them leave, then turned to Ann and Paul.

"I've about had it. Will somebody please start at the beginning and tell me what's happening here?"

Ann turned to Paul. "I know who killed your mother."

Paul turned to her. "So do I. Took me long enough to

figure it out. The only person who could have killed her was Maribelle.''

Ann gaped at him. ''You knew?''

''I figured it out on the drive over here. Karen and Paul were in Florida when Michelle was last seen. Then I realized, Paul and Karen had just moved into their new house in the country—the house that Trey and Sue-sue live in now. That address wouldn't have been listed in the old phonebook. The only address my mother would have had for Paul Delaney was the mansion in town.''

''That's right. So...''

''So she showed up unannounced at Maribelle's front door looking for my father. I don't know what happened then, but I do know Maribelle must have killed her.''

''You bet she did.'' Ann handed him the brown-paper-wrapped parcel.

''Addy's journal?''

Ann shook her head. ''I suspect that's gone for good. Probably went into the trash a long time ago. This is more like Addy's blackmail material. She wanted to make certain Maribelle didn't kill *her* to shut her mouth. So she wrote a detailed account of what happened. Apparently, she left three copies—one with her lawyer to be opened in the event of her death, one in her lockbox, which she knew would have to be cataloged by a bank officer after she died, and one hidden in the top of the dumbwaiter,'' Ann said.

''Why didn't they come to light after Miss Addy's death?'' Buddy asked.

''Addy writes that if Maribelle dies first and leaves her the house and the trust fund the way she promised, she'll destroy all three. According to Miss Esther, she forgot where she put the one in the house and never did find it.''

"When was all this supposed to have happened?" Buddy asked.

Paul told him.

"You got a picture?"

"In my suitcase."

Buddy motioned to the patrolman manning the front desk. "Pete, run over to Mr. Bouvet's house and bring that picture back. Okay with you, Paul?"

He nodded.

While they waited, Ann continued, "It happened pretty much the way Paul thought." She handed him the sheets of paper. She kept the more bulky parcel in her lap.

Reading Addy's words, Paul could almost feel himself back in the house on that hot August afternoon. The day his mother died.

ADDY AND MARIBELLE weren't expecting company. When the doorbell rang, Maribelle had just come in from digging crabgrass out of her impatiens. She was wearing one of her dead husband's old shirts and a pair of threadbare pedal pushers. She tossed her straw hat on the hat rack, pulled off her gardening gloves and answered the door.

"Yes?"

The woman—girl, rather—at the door was a stranger. Pretty thing, but tired to the point of exhaustion. Too skinny, dark. She wore a black-and-white printed dress much too hot for August and black patent-leather pumps that must have been hell to walk in. She carried a cheap patent-leather handbag and wore short white cotton gloves.

"Sorry, no solicitors." Maribelle was about to close the door when the young woman put out her hand. "No, please, wait. I am not a solicitor. I wish to see Mr. Delaney.''

The sweat running down her face had streaked her makeup. She looked desperately hot.

Addy had come up behind her sister and peered over her shoulder.

The girl had a definite accent. French, Addy thought.

"I'm afraid Mr. Delaney is…not home at the moment," Maribelle said.

Addy glanced at the back of her sister's neck. Why not tell this child he was in Florida?

The girl looked about ready to faint.

"Perhaps I can help you?" Maribelle asked.

"*Non*, madame, it is only Monsieur Delaney who can help me."

"You're French, aren't you."

As if her accent didn't proclaim it like a trumpet. "Yes."

Addy shoved past her sister. "Did you know Mr. Delaney when he lived in France?"

"Yes, I did." The girl swayed. "Madame, please, if I may trouble you? A glass of water? The heat—I am not used to it."

"Of course," Maribelle said. "Any friend of David's is welcome. Please come in."

The girl looked from Maribelle to Addy and apparently decided Maribelle must be some kind of gardener. She smiled at Addy as though she was the hostess. "Thank you."

"Have a seat in the living room, my dear," Maribelle said.

The girl looked from one sister to the other in confusion.

The heavy cream silk drapes in the living room had

been closed against the afternoon sun, so the room lay in shadow. Maribelle motioned the girl to an ornate beige sofa that faced the fireplace.

She sank onto the cushions gratefully, her handbag still over her wrist. Suddenly she stood up, moved quickly to a side table and picked up a photo in a silver frame. Her face broke into a smile. "Yes," she whispered. "This is my David."

"We've never had any of David's acquaintances from France visit before. Was he expecting you?" Addy asked.

"*Non,* madame. I wished to surprise him." She held the picture frame against her thin chest. "I shall be glad to see him. When will he return?"

Addy started to tell her a week, but a shake of Maribelle's head stopped her.

"He'll be along shortly," Maribelle said. "Did you know him well, Miss...?"

The girl sat down on the sofa again, but this time she sat up straight. "My name is Michelle, madame, and it is Mrs.," she said. "Mrs. Paul David Delaney."

"I beg your pardon?" Addy said. She heard Maribelle's sharp intake of breath.

"I said I am Mrs. Delaney." The girl smiled at Addy. "He and I were married in France just before he was called to home to see his father."

"Oh, dear," Addy said.

Maribelle collapsed into the armchair behind her. "Nonsense," she said.

"No, madame, I assure you it is not nonsense." Her hands twisted on the clasp of her handbag. "I have the *livret de famille.*"

"What's that?" Addy asked.

"The certificate of marriage, except that it is a small red book."

"You have it with you?"

"*Non,* madame. It is put away, although it is quite simple to send for it." She smiled at Addy. "I have told you who I am, madame. May I ask who you are?"

"I'm Addy Norwood." Addy leaned across the coffee table and offered the girl her hand.

"And I," said Maribelle, making no move to extend her hand in turn, "am Maribelle Delaney. I am David's mother."

Michelle sat back in embarrassment at choosing the wrong woman. "Oh. Then you are my *belle-mere*—my mother-in-law."

"If what you say is true."

"I assure you it is. When he comes home he will tell you."

"David is—" Addy began.

Maribelle Delaney cut her off. "My son is working in the fields this time in August. He may be quite late. Perhaps you would prefer to go to your hotel and let me have him call you when he comes in."

"I have no hotel, madame. I have just arrived."

"Why on earth did you take so long?" Addy asked, despite a withering glance from Maribelle. "He's been home more than five years."

"It is complicated, madame. David will explain it all when I see him."

"Well," Maribelle said, "it's a shock. I can't deny that." Suddenly she smiled. "To have a French daughter-in-law is certainly unusual around here." She patted Michelle's hand. "Quite a treat, in fact. You've made me forget my manners. You wanted a glass of water. We can do better than that. Addy, is that pitcher of lemonade still in the refrigerator?"

"Yes, Maribelle. Shall I get it?"

Maribelle stood. "No, I'll get it. I admit I need a little time by myself to take all this in. Excuse me, my dear."

Addy didn't know what Maribelle was up to, but this sudden display of charm meant she was planning some devilment.

Purely to make conversation, Addy said, "Michelle, is it? That is a lovely dress. Is it French?"

The girl had a sweet smile. If she married David just before he came home from Paris, she couldn't have been more than seventeen or eighteen at the time.

"My mother worked as a seamstress when I was little. She taught me to sew. I make all my own clothes and some for my...friends."

Addy was certain she hadn't meant to say friends. "You made that lovely dress?"

"Dresses are too expensive to buy."

"And you did all those bound buttonholes by hand? And the buttons! How lovely and unusual. Are they antique?"

"Not quite, but they are old. They are handmade. See, each is different." She proudly showed the tiny creatures on the buttons.

Maribelle came back into the room carrying a tray on which an enormous cut-glass pitcher sat among three equally elegant glasses filled with ice. The girl waited politely until she was handed a glass and a lace doily on which to set it, then waited to drink until both the older women had taken sips.

Maribelle leaned forward chummily. "How did you and David meet? Surely you can't be old enough to have been married long."

"I was barely eighteen when we married, madame."

"Please, call me Maribelle. Madame sounds so formal from the newest member of the family."

Addy stared at her sister. This girl, a member of the family? Just like that? Addy didn't think so for a minute.

"He lived in a small studio in our neighborhood," Michelle said. "I worked for my father. He owns a shop that makes confections and has a small café. David came in from time to time to eat and to buy *marrons glacés*—candied chestnuts."

"Oh, yes, he adores *marrons.*"

"I posed for him."

"Ah." Maribelle nodded as though everything had just been explained to her satisfaction. "You're an artist's model."

"Oh, no, madame. *Pas du tout.* Not at all. I posed for him—with all my clothes on. He wanted more, of course, but my father would have been scandalized. We fell in love."

"I see. Of course he would be enchanted by such a lovely creature."

Somehow Maribelle made the word *creature* sound ugly.

"He wanted me to…" Michelle was blushing. "But I believe that a woman should go to her marriage bed a virgin."

"Admirable. So he married you. How on earth did you manage it?"

"He had his *carte d'identité* with his Paris address. The banns were posted in his *arondissement* where my parents would be unlikely to see them."

"Your English is very good."

"Thank you, madame. If I had not married David, I would have gone to the Sorbonne. I wished to be a simultaneous translator."

"So you were married without telling your parents?"

"We were both over eighteen. We did not need permission."

Was there a slight jut to that pretty jaw? Was she reminding Maribelle that her husband didn't need his parents' permission to marry, either?

"We agreed to keep the marriage a secret so that I could continue to live at home. David's studio was not acceptable for two."

"Secret from us, as well, it would seem."

"He said he must break it to his parents gently. So when he was called home, he said he would tell them—you—and return to Paris as soon as he could."

"To stay?"

"Oh, yes. He didn't want to live in America. He wanted to paint and to make statues. He had already painted several of the people in the neighborhood for small commissions. He would have progressed quickly. He is a wonderful portraitist. Then when he didn't come back, I tried to get in touch with him, but I could not. There was something not right about the address he gave me for his home here."

"I'll bet there was," Maribelle whispered.

From the way the girl stiffened, Addy thought she'd both heard and understood the comment.

"So I assume you got a divorce?" Maribelle asked.

"Oh, no, madame. I do not believe in divorce, and I would never divorce David. I love him. And I know he loves me."

"If he loved you, my dear, he would have given you his correct address, surely. And he would have come back for you," Addy said. She felt genuinely sorry for this child. "Instead, he disappeared and I'm sure hurt you terribly."

"I know that when I see David he will explain." It was obvious she was trying not to cry.

"No doubt he will. To both of us." Maribelle said dryly. "I don't know about you, but I definitely need some more lemonade." She drained her glass, picked up the pitcher and went toward the kitchen. As she reached the hall doorway she turned. "I suspect a French divorce is extremely expensive, isn't it?" Then she walked out.

The girl whispered to Addy, "She thinks I came for money, but I did not. I know David still loves me, and I have one weapon he cannot resist. One look into my eyes, one touch, one kiss, and he will be mine again, whatever has happened between." The chin definitely jutted now. So she planned to defy Maribelle? A dangerous game for one so unsophisticated.

"Can you call him on the telephone?" the girl asked. "And give him some reason to come home?"

"He's out in the fields, dear," Addy said, taking her cue from Maribelle. "He can't be reached by phone."

Maribelle came back through the front hall carrying the pitcher by its heavy handle. "You deserve to be paid for your pain and suffering. And of course to live in Paris in comfort. No doubt we can come to some arrangement so that you can go back to Paris and arrange a quiet divorce like your quiet marriage."

Now there was no mistaking the steel in the girl's dark eyes. She would be a formidable opponent for Maribelle. She had the strength of her love to rely on. Poor romantic little thing. She had no idea how much heartbreak she was in for. Sooner or later they'd have to tell her that David had married again and had a son.

The girl half turned on the sofa to look back at Maribelle. "I know that you mean well, madame," she said. "But I did not come for money. I came for my husband."

"I see," Maribelle said. "Of course I understand precisely how you feel."

Maribelle took one step toward the girl, raised the pitcher and brought it down on the girl's skull. The jug exploded in her hand. She stood there clutching the handle while glass and lemonade cascaded around her.

For a moment the girl was motionless, then she crumpled forward from the waist and slid in a heap between the sofa and the coffee table.

"What have you done?" Addy screamed and dropped to her knees beside the girl. "My God, the poor child! Call an ambulance!"

"Sit down and shut up, Addy." Maribelle kicked aside the shards of glass at her feet. "She fell on the Oriental rug, thank God. We'd never be able to get blood out of that yellow silk upholstery."

Addy reached for the girl's wrist. Her eyes were open, her mouth slack. A thin trickle of blood oozed onto her forehead from under the dark hair. "Belle, I don't think she's breathing. Why on earth did you hit her?"

"Seemed the best thing to do," Maribelle said evenly, and came around to kneel on Michelle's other side. She stuck her fingers expertly beneath the girl's chin. "No pulse. Not much blood. Must have died almost instantly, otherwise you know how scalp wounds bleed—the rug would be soaked."

"Dead? Maribelle, what on earth have you done?" Addy pulled herself to her feet but dropped immediately into her chair. "We have to call the police. You didn't mean to do it—"

"Of course I meant to do it, you idiot."

"What if somebody knows she's here?"

"If somebody comes looking for her, we'll say we never saw her."

"And if somebody in town saw her come into the house?"

"Four o'clock on a hot August afternoon? Don't be ridiculous. They're all on their back porches trying to keep cool. She never came to our door. We never saw her. Period. Never heard of her."

"And what about David?"

"He won't be back in Rossiter for another two weeks. He'll never know she came."

"And Esther? What about Esther? She'll see the mess."

"She won't be back until tomorrow morning. Thank God it was her afternoon off. By the time she gets here the place will be spotless and the girl will be gone."

"Where?"

"I don't know. If we put her into the trunk of my car and dump her out in the woods, some hunter could come across her. They can identify people's remains these days even from skeletons. I suppose we'll just have to bury her."

"Bury her? Maribelle Norwood Delaney, do you have any idea how hard the ground is in August? You may be strong, but Hercules couldn't drive a spade into that dirt."

"He could into the flower beds."

"And have the gardener unearth her? I don't think so."

"How about the basement?"

"That's harder than concrete."

"Then it's going to have to be the garden, Addy. Back behind the old summerhouse. Those rosebushes haven't been dug up in years, and I can keep Vern from turning them again. If we dig a deep enough hole, he can plant rosebushes over her until he's blue in the face without finding her."

"It's got to be deep enough so the coyotes and raccoons

don't get at her, either. Do we have to sit here and look at her like that? She makes me nervous.''

"Go get some of those big plastic leaf bags out of the pantry. Four or five, anyway. We'll roll her up and put her in the window seat until it gets dark and the café closes.''

"What about fingerprints?''

"What about 'em? Oh, very well, put on your dish-washing gloves and bring me my gardening gloves, though how they're going to find fingerprints if they don't find *her* is more than I can see.''

"What about the pitcher?''

"We'll put the pieces in the garbage and tell Esther I broke it.''

"What about her purse? Her clothes? She can't have come with nothing but that dress.''

"She said she didn't have a hotel. Let's hope she put everything in a locker somewhere. When she doesn't pay the fee, they'll open the locker, toss her suitcase into the lost luggage, and after a while they'll throw it away.''

"You hope.''

"Open her purse.''

"You open her purse, Maribelle. You killed her.''

Together they removed the contents of Michelle's small purse. They found fifty dollars and some change, the stub of a bus ticket from Memphis to Rossiter, a powder compact, a lipstick and a lace-edged handkerchief.

"We'd better strip her," Maribelle said.

"What? That's obscene.''

"Get a grip, Addy. We don't want them to be able to identify her by the labels in her clothes, do we?''

"There aren't any. She made her dress.''

"She's wearing undergarments, isn't she? Before we bury her, we'll strip her and burn her clothes.''

"In August?"

"We've got the charcoal grill outside. No reason we couldn't do a little late-night barbecue, is there?"

"You have an answer for everything."

"I have to, since you have all these silly questions. Get the damn trash bags."

"Esther will notice if we use that many bags at one time. She watches those things like a hawk."

"Damnation, Addy, sometimes you drive me to distraction." Maribelle stood up. "All right. I'll drive into town and buy a shower curtain liner. That's plenty big enough to wrap her in. In the meantime, you clean up the mess. Be sure you pick up every piece of that pitcher. One or two of them might have blood on them."

Addy knew it would take Maribelle at least an hour to drive to Collierville, buy the shower-curtain liner and drive back. More than enough time to pick up the pieces of the pitcher and clean up the lemonade.

She realized with a start that she'd become an accessory to murder.

She'd also become a real threat to Maribelle. Maribelle had learned to ignore Addy's long affair with her husband, but now Conrad was dead and unable to protect her.

She'd best protect herself.

She sat down at the desk in the library, took out a sheaf of stationery and some carbon paper, and began to write. She'd make certain Maribelle knew that if anything happened to her, Addy, before Maribelle died, the story of Michelle Delaney's death would be revealed.

She'd assure Maribelle that if her sister predeceased her, she'd destroy all three copies. She wasn't any more interested in being brought up on charges than Maribelle was. The secret must die with the two sisters.

In the meantime Maribelle would finally have to change

her will so that Addy could live in the house for the rest of her life and have enough money to travel.

Maribelle would be furious, but if the confession was finished and in the mail before Maribelle got back, there was little she could do about it.

She gathered up all the shards of crystal, put them into a paper grocery bag, bundled them with the original copy of her confession, taped the entire thing together and hid it in the dumbwaiter. She'd hidden her journal there for years successfully, but it had become too much trouble to climb in and out of the thing now that she was getting so arthritic. Maribelle had only discovered the diary after Addy moved it to the top of her chifferobe.

She had no intention of writing a single word about this incident in her journal, so she didn't care that Maribelle stole it periodically to read what she'd written. She wouldn't have to take the package out of the dumbwaiter again unless she wanted to destroy it after Maribelle's death.

When Maribelle returned with the liner, Addy was innocently scrubbing blood and lemonade out of the rug. She'd wrapped the poor girl's head in a tea towel so she wouldn't have to look at her face.

Burying her took most of the night and all of both women's strength.

They stripped Michelle's body and wrapped it in the liner before they lowered it into the grave.

Filling in the grave was easier than digging it, but still took a couple of hours. Both women had to rest frequently and were bedeviled by mosquitoes.

By the time they finished covering their tracks and cleaning up after themselves, they were much too tired to deal with Michelle's clothes, so Addy took them to her room and hid them in the back of her closet in a shoe box.

Later the next day after Esther had gone home, she cut all those marvelous buttons off Michelle's dress. They were too beautiful to burn. Perhaps one day she'd feel safe enough to use them on one of her own dresses.

They burned the clothes that evening.

All they could do now was wait to see if they'd gotten away with it. It was hell, especially for Addy.

"No one will ever know," Maribelle said to Addy after a lovely welcome-home dinner with David, Karen and Paul Edward, already known as Trey. "No one's looking for her. It's obvious David has forgotten all about her. We're home free."

Not quite, although Maribelle didn't know that yet.

When Addy finally told her about the three confessions, she thought Maribelle would kill her at once. After she calmed down, she agreed to Addy's terms. Addy didn't tell her about the pieces of the pitcher she'd saved with the confession.

Both women tried to get on with their lives, but their relationship—always rocky—was soured for good. Maribelle worried that Addy would get an attack of conscience and confess. Addy worried that they'd get caught.

When her son David broke his neck in the hunt field, Maribelle grew old overnight. She padlocked his studio in the back garden after covering the two canvases he was working on with white sizing paint. She didn't want anyone ever to see the girl's shadowy face painted behind her son's.

She and Karen kept Delaney Farms healthy so that Trey would inherit even more than David had from Conrad, but Maribelle was functioning like a robot. Addy didn't think she ever felt any remorse over Michelle's death.

After Maribelle died, Addy planned to travel.

But when it actually happened, when she was finally free with a little money of her own, she didn't dare leave her house and the rose garden. She burned the two carbons of her confession, but her mind had begun to fail. She couldn't remember what she'd done with the original. She worried about it until the day she died.

"HERE'S THAT PICTURE you wanted, Chief," the patrolman said. He handed the silver frame to Buddy.

He stared down at it for a long time. "A man never forgets a woman this good-looking."

"What?" Ann asked.

"Don't get me wrong, I was already in love with your mother. I hadn't been on the Rossiter police force long. Didn't know everybody in town the way I do now. I just figured she was visiting somebody on Main Street."

"You saw her?" Paul asked. "You remember her after more than thirty years?"

"It was hotter than the hinges of hell. I do remember that. She was tottering down Main Street on those high heels, wearing some kind of black-and-white dress. I remember because she looked so miserable and hot. I think it was this one in the picture. Never saw her again."

"My God," Paul fell back in his chair.

"We never got a missing persons report or anything about her. I haven't thought about that girl from that day to this." He shook his head.

"You couldn't know, Daddy," Ann said.

"Doesn't stop me feeling guilty." He pulled himself to his feet and called to the patrolman, "Ray, get some tape, some shovels and some floodlights. I think we got us a crime scene."

BUDDY REFUSED to allow Paul to work beside the men as they dug up the rose garden. Paul stood as close to the dig as he could.

Ann huddled on the back steps of the mansion and watched him.

She was glad Paul would have his mother's remains after all this time. He'd be able to give her the burial she deserved. He would probably bury her close to her sister. He might even take her remains back to France.

He'd be relieved that his search was finally over, but he'd also be grieving. No matter how long he had known in his heart she was dead, the final confirmation must be terribly painful.

Ann longed to be with him, support him through his grief. But his body language said he needed to go through this alone. She had to respect that. Not once had he looked around to find her.

Of course he was focused on what was happening in the back garden.

But he seemed to have forgotten she existed.

He'd accomplished everything he'd come to Rossiter to do. No matter how hard the Delaneys tried to hush things up, the story would be all over the county within twenty-four hours. They might never officially acknowledge Paul, but everyone would know he was David Delaney's son.

He had his revenge.

There was nothing—and nobody—to keep him in Rossiter.

If Ann ever intended to hold her head up in this town again, she had to act as though none of it mattered to her. They'd had a fling. Period.

She could sob to Dante in private.

Paul would no doubt protest that he truly loved her. Maybe he even believed it. He'd swear that they'd stay in touch, that he'd come back for her. But once he was back in that other world, he'd forget Ann, forget Rossiter. Neither of them was of any use to him any longer.

She would allow herself anger. She had every right to be angry. He'd used her.

The only way to avoid throwing herself into his arms and begging him to stay was to remind herself of how he'd conned her. She had to stay angry. She had to avoid him.

She stood up. She might be able to manage that. She'd have to run home before she started crying.

"CHIEF, I THINK we got it." Ray said from the hole in the rose garden.

"Stop right there. I'll go call the ME." He touched Paul's shoulder on his way by. "Sorry."

"It's all right. I can't take it in. To find her body after all this time. I never truly believed it would happen. What now?"

"Everybody connected with this crime is long dead. Nobody to charge. The ME will have to identify the remains officially. We'll need a sample of your DNA."

Paul laughed bitterly. "Ask Karen Lowrance. She has a brand-new report."

"Yeah. Okay. After she's identified, I guess we release the…remains to you for burial."

"Thanks, Buddy." Paul's arm and shoulder ached. He felt drained. For the first time since his mother disappeared, he didn't have his quest to drive him. He felt numb.

"Go home, Ann," Buddy said. "You look like hell."

PAUL STARTED TOWARD HER, but she glanced quickly at him, shook her head and walked away.

"Look, Buddy," Paul said, "this place is going to be crazy. Is it all right if I pack up and go to a motel?"

"Sure. Leave word with the office where you'll be. I'll call you later."

"Thanks. Could I…see her?"

"Don't advise it. Nothing but bones."

"Sure. Right." He walked upstairs. He longed to call Ann, bang on her door, break through this barrier she'd erected, but he didn't know how. He wasn't thinking clearly, anyway. He shoved his few belongings into his suitcase and carried it downstairs to his car. Beyond the floodlights that surrounded Buddy's crime scene he could see the first lightening that signaled dawn.

The dawn was red. "Sailor, take warning," the old saw said. A red sky usually meant a storm before nightfall. At least it did in the north. Down here it frequently only signaled a dry day with dust swirling in front of the sun.

He closed his trunk and started toward the driver's door. Buddy came up behind him and said softly, "Paul, you given any thought to how all this is going to affect your…well, your position in Rossiter?"

Paul leaned on the side of his car. "I've thought of little else."

"I know you revealed a crime that should have been solved thirty years ago, and I know you and your mother are actually the injured parties here, but folks around here may not see it that way."

"I'm a stranger. The Delaneys are not."

"That's what I mean. Some folks may not take kindly to your coming down here under false pretenses, picking everybody's brain, causing a bunch of scandal to one of Rossiter's oldest families…"

"Seducing one of its prettiest girls."

Buddy looked away. "That, too."

"How do *you* feel?"

"I'm an officer of the law. I'm glad the crime is solved no matter how and when it happened."

"And about Ann?"

"Haven't figured out how I feel about that yet."

"When I started this benighted enterprise, I hadn't met Ann, didn't know any of the people who live in Rossiter, didn't even know my half brother. I was operating strictly on theory. By the time I wanted to back out, it was too late. Too many things had happened."

"Like Ann."

"Like Ann. I hurt her badly. I don't know how to make it right."

"Don't know as you can, at least right now. Tell her what you've told me. Maybe that'll help."

"Thanks."

Later as he lay in the comfortable king-size bed at his motel, he ached to have Ann beside him. He felt as though he might never sleep again. He'd really screwed up. He reached for the telephone and called her. When she answered, he said, "Please, don't hang up."

"I won't hang up." She sounded cool and detached. Much worse than if she'd been angry or in tears.

"I never meant to hurt you."

"You didn't hurt me. You used me."

"It wasn't like that."

"It was precisely like that. Tell me, Mr. Bouvet-Delaney, now that you've gotten exactly what you wanted, when does your house go on the market?"

"What?"

"I assume you'll be leaving as soon as you can."

Then she hung up on him.

ABOUT TWO in the afternoon, in a uniform that looked as though it had been slept in, an unshaven Buddy knocked on Ann's door.

When she opened it, he saw that she had on her safety goggles and a piece of plywood in her hand. "Come in, Dad," she said. "I'm trying to cut a template for those sconces at the summerhouse."

"You sound like nothin's happened." He scratched Dante's ears.

"I'll get around to thinking about it when I can stand to. At the moment I'm trying not to think about anything except this stupid piece of plywood that refuses to do what it's supposed to." She hurled it across the workroom. It cracked against the wall and split down the middle. She took a deep breath. "You have to admit I've still got my pitching arm."

"Sit down, Ann, and stop acting like a drama queen."

"Why not? Want some iced tea?"

"Ann."

"Okay."

"Paul came back to the house a few minutes ago. He gave me this to give you."

"What is it?"

"It's an envelope. How do I know what's in it? Open it and find out."

She pulled a legal-size document out of the envelope with a note attached to it. She said without looking up at her father, "Daddy, this is the deed to the Delaney mansion. It's been signed over to me." She gaped at him. "What does he think he's doing? I can't accept a *house!*"

"Read the note."

She ran her eye down the page. "Oh, Lord. Read that." She tossed the note to her father, dove through her bedroom curtains and began rummaging on the floor for her shoes.

"'Dearest Ann,'" Buddy read aloud. "'You said if you owned the house you'd never leave it, so I want you to have it. I know you'll cherish it the way it should be cherished. Please believe that I never saw the consequences of my actions until too late to avoid hurting you. You're wrong if you think what I feel for you is casual. I love you. I'd like to spend the rest of my life with you. I'd hoped to give you the house when you became my wife, but I guess that's not possible any longer. I'll spend the rest of my life in much more pain than I've ever caused you. Goodbye, Paul.'" Buddy looked up. "What's he mean, goodbye? I haven't given him permission to go anywhere but a motel room."

Ann shoved her feet into her sneakers and grabbed her purse. "He and Hack finished putting his plane back together. Don't you see? He's flying back to New Jersey. Come on."

"Where we going?"

"To stop him, of course." She grabbed her father's arm and pulled him off the couch. "And use the siren."

AS SOON AS Buddy slammed on his brakes at the edge of the airfield, Ann was out of the car and running toward the hangar where Paul's plane had been.

"Oh, no," she said when she saw the empty space. "We're too late."

"Hey, Ann," Hack said over her shoulder.

"How long ago did he take off?"

"Paul? I don't know. Ten minutes maybe."

"Can you communicate with him?"

"Sure." Hack looked at her with curiosity.

"You have to talk him back down here."

A couple of minutes later Hack called the tail numbers of Paul's plane and asked him to come in.

Paul responded at once.

"Need you to turn around and come on back," Hack said. "Over."

"Why?" Paul asked.

Buddy yanked the microphone out of Hack's hand and yelled into it, "Because if you don't, I'll trump up a charge that'll get you extradited from New Jersey before you step foot on the tarmac."

"Buddy?"

"Yeah. Right beside me stands my little girl, and I can sure borrow Hack's shotgun if I have to. You don't walk out on a Rossiter girl you been playing house with and not expect to get a shotgun up your backside."

"Oh, Daddy," Ann whispered. She was crying so hard, she could barely breathe.

"Is that Ann?"

Ann took the microphone. "Buddy's right. You've toyed with my affections, Paul Bouvet or Delaney or whatever your name is. Giving me a house is not going to make up for that. It's marriage or nothing."

She heard Paul laugh.

"Sounds like relief to me," Hack murmured.

"Even if I get run out of town on a rail?" Paul asked.

"When I get through telling people what happened, they'll forgive you for my sake. I live here, remember. I'm not some damn-Yankee newcomer."

"Does that mean I can live there, too?"

"Not as a bachelor, you can't."

"Ann, I'm sorry—"

"We'll talk about that later. Do whatever you have to do to that plane to turn it around."

"Yes, ma'am."

The three, Hack, Ann and Buddy, waited at the edge of the grass strip as Paul's silver Cessna glided to a landing. Ann was running toward him before the plane had stopped rolling.

Paul climbed out and jumped down. "You're not still mad at me?" he said.

"I am," she said, reaching up to kiss him. "But I'll get over it."

EPILOGUE

December 22

THE HOUSE SEEMED to realize that tonight was its official coming-out party. It was no longer the sad harlot, but a shining, vibrant, great lady.

The columns on the front porch and the balcony were wound with garlands of fresh pine. Fairy lights shimmered in the trees. The wreath on the front door was heavy with holly, and the magnolia fan above glittered in the porch light.

In the front hall, the pine Christmas tree rose from the curve of the staircase and reached to the ceiling.

Candles and greenery decorated every table. Paul had been cooking for two weeks with Ann as sous-chef. Then he'd swung into high gear when Giselle arrived with Jerry and her two sons to spend Christmas with Paul and her new sister-in-law.

Melding the two families had been less painful than either Ann or Paul had feared. Jerry and the boys had never been on a duck hunt, so Buddy arranged one for them.

Giselle had been wary of meeting the family of Paul's new wife. They were all, of course, at least marginally kin to the Delaneys.

"But we're not Delaneys," Gram had said. "Not really."

"You're aunts or cousins or something," Giselle said.

Gram patted her hand. "Sometime when you come down for a nice long visit, I'll show you the family genealogy and explain the relationships."

Ann and Giselle had liked each other immediately and spent hours talking about their families.

Tonight Paul ladled champagne punch at one end of the dining-room table and watched his wife circulate, kissing a cheek here, squeezing a hand there. She wore a dark-green velvet empire dress that revealed a great deal of creamy bosom, but didn't quite conceal the small bulge beneath her waist. The baby wouldn't really start to show for another month, although Ann swore she no longer had a discernible waistline.

Paul thought she was the most beautiful woman he'd ever seen.

The fireplaces crackled cheerfully. The house was alive with warmth and gaiety and joy.

"It would seem Rossiter has forgiven your wayward husband. I think you've broken the curse," Gram said to Ann.

"What?"

"The curse on this house. I said once that everyone who had ever lived here had been unhappy and the house knew it. Now I think it finally knows that love has moved in to stay."

"Let's hope so. We've a long way to go before we finish it."

"You won't ever finish. It's an old house. Old houses are always needy."

The doorbell rang. Ann started toward it, but Paul was there ahead of her.

She came up behind him as the door swung wide. On the step stood Karen and Marshall Lowrance with Trey and Sue-sue.

For a moment nobody spoke, then Paul said, "Welcome, and merry Christmas," and held out his hand.

Later Karen sought Paul out in the kitchen. "Could I speak to you alone?"

"Certainly," he said. "I don't think there's anybody in the conservatory."

She followed him across the hall, through the music-room door and into the conservatory.

"I didn't think you'd come."

"I very nearly didn't, but Trey wanted to, and there's something I must tell you. I owe you."

"You don't owe me anything."

"Please, let me finish. You and I may never be friends, but you are my son's half brother and you protected him from his own foolishness."

"Fortunately no one was hurt. I know how sorry he is."

"It could have been so much worse if you hadn't acted like a gentleman. That's why I owe it to you to tell you this." She turned away from him and clasped her hands in front of her.

He waited while she assembled her thoughts.

"When my...when David had his accident, when his horse fell with him, I was the first to get to him, even before Maribelle." She seemed to struggle with the words. "He looked up at me with the sweetest smile and whispered, 'Michelle.' An instant later he was dead." She turned to face him then. "Can you imagine how much I hated that Michelle? How I feared her?"

He nodded.

"Strange, we all tried to do the right thing, and it all turned out wrong."

"How do you mean?"

"David thought he was right to marry your mother. She thought she was right to get pregnant. We all thought we were right to bring him home and keep him here. I thought I was right to make him marry me, although I knew he didn't want to. Even Maribelle must have felt she was right when she struck your mother down, just as Addy thought she was right when she helped cover up the crime."

"I thought I was right to come down here and destroy you all," Paul said quietly.

"But you chose not to. Thank you for that. I hope you and Ann will be very happy. Trey wants to try to make up not only for what *he* did but for what the whole family did to you and your mother. I don't know if you can accept him, but I hope you do."

She smiled and looked back at the carolers singing around the piano. "Since the first Paul Delaney, there's only been one son per generation. You and Trey broke that tradition, as well. I don't begrudge my son his half brother nor you yours. Maybe someday you and I can be friends."

Without another word she walked past him into the salon and back to the party.

Paul stood looking out onto the winter garden until Ann found him. She slipped her arm through his. "Are you okay?"

"Karen said we'd broken the chain of bad choices."

"Gram said we'd broken the curse on the house, too. Now it's happy for the first time since the first Paul Delaney built it."

"It's scary to be so content. I keep waking up in the

middle of the night afraid I'll find you've disappeared, too.''

''No way. You're stuck with me for the foreseeable future.'' She kissed him gently on the cheek.

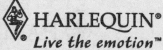

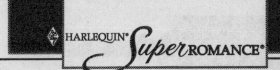

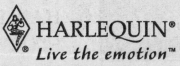

Is your man too good to be true?

Hot, gorgeous AND romantic?
If so, he could be a Harlequin® Blaze™ series cover modell

Our grand-prize winners will receive a trip for two to New York City to
shoot the cover of a Blaze novel, and will stay at the luxurious Plaza Hotel.
Plus, they'll receive $500 U.S. spending money!
The runner-up winners will receive $200 U.S.
to spend on a romantic dinner for two.

It's easy to enter!

In 100 words or less, tell us what makes your boyfriend or spouse a true romantic
and the perfect candidate for the cover of a Blaze novel, and include in your submission
two photos of this potential cover model.

All entries must include the written submission of the contest entrant, two photographs of the model
candidate and the Official Entry Form and Publicity Release forms completed in full and signed by
both the model candidate and the contest entrant. Harlequin, along with the experts at
Elite Model Management, will select a winner.

For photo and complete Contest details, please refer to the Official Rules on the next page. All entries
will become the property of Harlequin Enterprises Ltd. and are not returnable.

**Please visit www.blazecovermodel.com to download a copy of the Official Entry Form and
Publicity Release Form or send a request to one of the addresses below.**

Please mail your entry to: **Harlequin Blaze Cover Model Search**

In U.S.A.	In Canada
P.O. Box 9069	P.O. Box 637
Buffalo, NY	Fort Erie, ON
14269-9069	L2A 5X3

No purchase necessary. Contest open to Canadian and U.S. residents who are 18 and over.
Void where prohibited. Contest closes September 30, 2003.

HBCVRMODEL1

HARLEQUIN BLAZE COVER MODEL SEARCH CONTEST 3569 OFFICIAL RULES
NO PURCHASE NECESSARY TO ENTER

1. To enter, submit two (2) 4" x 6" photographs of a boyfriend or spouse (who must be 18 years of age or older) taken no later than three (3) months from the time of entry: a close-up, waist up, shirtless photograph; and a fully clothed, full-length photograph, then, tell us, in 100 words or fewer, why he should be a Harlequin Blaze cover model and how he is romantic. Your complete "entry" must include: (i) your essay, (ii) the Official Entry Form and Publicity Release Form printed below completed and signed by you (as "Entrant"), (iii) the photographs (with your hand-written name, address and phone number, and your model's name, address and phone number on the back of each photograph), and (iv) the Publicity Release Form and Photograph Representation Form printed below completed and signed by your model (as "Model"), and should be sent via first-class mail to either: Harlequin Blaze Cover Model Search Contest 3569, P.O. Box 9069, Buffalo, NY, 14269-9069, or Harlequin Blaze Cover Model Search Contest 3569, P.O. Box 637, Fort Erie, Ontario L2A 5X3. All submissions must be in English and be received no later than September 30, 2003. Limit: one entry per person, household or organization. **Purchase or acceptance of a product does not improve your chances of winning.** All entry requirements must be strictly adhered to for eligibility and to ensure fairness among entries.

2. Ten (10) Finalist submissions (photographs and essays) will be selected by a panel of judges consisting of members of the Harlequin editorial, marketing and public relations staff, as well as a representative from Elite Model Management (Toronto) Inc., based on the following criteria:

Aptness/Appropriateness of submitted photographs for a Harlequin Blaze cover—70%
Originality of Essay—20%
Sincerity of Essay—10%

In the event of a tie, duplicate finalists will be selected. The photographs submitted by finalists will be posted on the Harlequin website no later than November 15, 2003 (at www.blazecovermodel.com), and viewers may vote, in rank order, on their favorite(s) to assist in the panel of judges' final determination of the Grand Prize and Runner-up winning entries based on the above judging criteria. All decisions of the judges are final.

3. All entries become the property of Harlequin Enterprises Ltd. and none will be returned. Any entry may be used for future promotional purposes. Elite Model Management (Toronto) Inc. and/or its partners, subsidiaries and affiliates operating as "Elite Model Management" will have access to all entries including all personal information, and may contact any Entrant and/or Model in its sole discretion for their own business purposes. Harlequin and Elite Model Management (Toronto) Inc. are separate entities with no legal association or partnership whatsoever having no power to bind or obligate the other or create any expressed or implied obligation or responsibility on behalf of the other, such that Harlequin shall not be responsible in any way for any acts or omissions of Elite Model Management (Toronto) Inc. or its partners, subsidiaries and affiliates in connection with the Contest or otherwise and Elite Model Management shall not be responsible in any way for any acts or omissions of Harlequin or its partners, subsidiaries and affiliates in connection with the contest or otherwise.

4. All Entrants and Models must be residents of the U.S. or Canada, be 18 years of age or older, and have no prior criminal convictions. The contest is not open to any Model that is a professional model and/or actor in any capacity at the time of the entry. Contest void wherever prohibited by law; all applicable laws and regulations apply. Any litigation within the Province of Quebec regarding the conduct or organization of a publicity contest may be submitted to the Régie des alcools, des courses et des jeux for a ruling, and any litigation regarding the awarding of a prize may be submitted to the Régie only for the purpose of helping the parties reach a settlement. Employees and immediate family members of Harlequin Enterprises Ltd., D.L. Blair, Inc., Elite Model Management (Toronto) Inc. and their parents, affiliates, subsidiaries and all other agencies, entities and persons connected with the use, marketing or conduct of this Contest are not eligible to enter. Acceptance of any prize offered constitutes permission to use Entrants' and Models' names, essay submissions, photographs or other likenesses for the purposes of advertising, trade, publication and promotion on behalf of Harlequin Enterprises Ltd., its parent, affiliates, subsidiaries, assigns and other authorized entities involved in the judging and promotion of the contest without further compensation to any Entrant or Model, unless prohibited by law.

5. Finalists will be determined no later than October 30, 2003. Prize Winners will be determined no later than January 31, 2004. Grand Prize Winners (consisting of winning Entrant and Model) will be required to sign and return Affidavit of Eligibility/Release of Liability and Model Release forms within thirty (30) days of notification. Non-compliance with this requirement and within the specified time period will result in disqualification and an alternate will be selected. Any prize notification returned as undeliverable will result in the awarding of the prize to an alternate set of winners. All travelers (or parent/legal guardian of a minor) must execute the Affidavit of Eligibility/Release of Liability prior to ticketing and must possess required travel documents (e.g. valid photo ID) where applicable. Travel dates specified by Sponsor but no later than May 30, 2004.

6. Prizes: One (1) Grand Prize—the opportunity for the Model to appear on the cover of a paperback book from the Harlequin Blaze series, and a 3 day/2 night trip for two (Entrant and Model) to New York, NY for the photo shoot of Model which includes round-trip coach air transportation from the commercial airport nearest the winning Entrant's home to New York, NY, (or, in lieu of air transportation, $100 cash payable to Entrant and Model, if the winning Entrant's home is within 250 miles of New York, NY), hotel accommodations (double occupancy) at the Plaza Hotel and $500 cash spending money payable to Entrant and Model, (approximate prize value: $8,000), and one (1) Runner-up Prize of $200 cash payable to Entrant and Model for a romantic dinner for two (approximate prize value: $200). Prizes are valued in U.S. currency. Prizes consist of only those items listed as part of the prize. No substitution of prize(s) permitted by winners. All prizes are awarded jointly to the Entrant and Model of the winning entries, and are not severable - prizes and obligations may not be assigned or transferred. Any change to the Entrant or Model of the winning entries will result in disqualification and an alternate will be selected. Taxes on prize are the sole responsibility of winners. Any and all expenses and/or items not specifically described as part of the prize are the sole responsibility of winners. Harlequin Enterprises Ltd. and D.L. Blair, Inc., their parents, affiliates, and subsidiaries are not responsible for errors in printing of Contest entries and/or game pieces. No responsibility is assumed for lost, stolen, late, illegible, incomplete, inaccurate, non-delivered, postage due or misdirected mail or entries. In the event of printing or other errors which may result in unintended prize values or duplication of prizes, all affected game pieces or entries shall be null and void.

7. Winners will be notified by mail. For winners' list (available after March 31, 2004), send a self-addressed, stamped envelope to: Harlequin Blaze Cover Model Search Contest 3569 Winners, P.O. Box 4200, Blair, NE 68009-4200, or refer to the Harlequin website (at www.blazecovermodel.com).

Contest sponsored by Harlequin Enterprises Ltd., P.O. Box 9042, Buffalo, NY 14269-9042.

HBCVRMODEL2

HARLEQUIN *Super* ROMANCE®

Twins

A fascinating glimpse into the world of twins.
They're not always two of a kind,
but even when they're apart, they're
never far from each other's thoughts.

**The Replacement
by Anne Marie Duquette.
Available July 2003.**

A child is missing in the winter
snows of Yosemite. Ranger
Lindsey Nelson must join the
search team. Trouble is, her
boss is the man she'd planned
to marry four years ago...until
his twin sister made sure the
wedding never took place.

**Suspicion
by Janice Macdonald.
Available September 2003.**

Ada Lynsky is falling in love with
journalist Scott Campbell. But
her twin sister, Ingrid, is sure
that Scott is interested only in
digging up family skeletons.
For the first time, the twins are
finding reasons to stay apart.

Available wherever Harlequin books are sold.

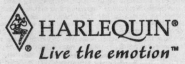

HARLEQUIN®
® *Live the emotion*™

Visit us at www.eHarlequin.com

HSRTWINSJ